JOHN EVERSON

THE DEVIL'S EQUINOX

This is a **FLAME TREE PRESS** book

FLAME TREE PRESS
6 Melbray Mews, London, SW6 3NS, UK
flametreepress.com

Distribution and warehouse:
Marston Book Services Ltd
160 Eastern Avenue, Milton Park, Abingdon, Oxon, OX14 4SB
www.marston.co.uk

Thanks to the Flame Tree Press team, including:
Taylor Bentley, Frances Bodiam, Federica Ciaravella, Don D'Auria,
Chris Herbert, Matteo Middlemiss, Josie Mitchell, Mike Spender,
Cat Taylor, Maria Tissot, Nick Wells, Gillian Whitaker.

The cover is created by Flame Tree Studio with
thanks to Nik Keevil and Shutterstock.com.
The font families in this book are Avenir and Bembo.

Flame Tree Press is an imprint of Flame Tree Publishing Ltd
flametreepublishing.com

A copy of the CIP data for this book is available from the British Library.

HB ISBN: 978-1-78758-222-4
PB ISBN: 978-1-78758-221-7
ebook ISBN: 978-1-78758-223-1
Also available in FLAME TREE AUDIO

Printed in the UK at Clays, Suffolk

JOHN EVERSON

THE DEVIL'S EQUINOX

FLAME TREE PRESS
London & New York

For Geri,
who keeps
the devil at bay.

PART ONE
BESPELLED

PROLOGUE

The space had once served as a suburban bedroom, but this was clearly no longer a place where anyone slept. It was now a place of worship. Or blasphemy. Dark ceremony. The air hung thick with the commingled scents of singed bitter herbs and melting wax. Candles flickered in triad clusters from every corner. The walls were lit in their warm shadows. Thirteen small flames provided the only source of light in the room. The sole window served not as a view to the outside, but rather as a mirror to the candles, the black of night reflecting the events going on within.

A woman walked back and forth there, preparing. She was thin and pretty, with long black hair that fell in waves across a dark silken robe. She set a wooden box before a single candle on the small table near the far wall that served as an altar. It was covered in assorted jars and stone figures. She touched the lit candle to something inside the box. A wisp of aromatic smoke curled in a silent whisper from within.

A golden crucifix hung upside down on a wire above the homemade altar. The Jesus figure was blackened from the residue of the smoke that rose from below.

The woman undid the sash and dropped her robe to the floor. She was naked beneath, her skin covered only by tattoos of a witch's star on her breast and the curve of a snake fashioned from the number six on her arm. She knelt upon a black sheet that covered the floor.

A witch's star was sewn in white in the centre of the sheet, and the woman's knees touched the inside points of one arm of the star. She reached into a large jar placed on the floor beside her and came back with a handful of something dark. Closing her eyes, she pressed the substance to her chest, and began to massage it across her torso and thighs as she whispered strange, ancient words that sounded dark. Words of power.

In moments, she shone like a dark angel in the centre of the candlelight.

When all of her limbs were slick with the balm, she stood, approached the altar and lifted a small blackened clay figure lying there.

"Tonight," she whispered.

She held the figure at arm's length, and a grin slid across her face. She lifted a small dagger from the altar with her free hand and touched the tip to her nipple. When a red bead of blood appeared, she pressed the face of the doll to her naked breast, as if to let it suckle her life.

"Tonight, you will be mine," she whispered. "One taste and you will know only what I say."

She looked up at the blasphemous cross and showed her teeth. "He will be mine as I am yours," she said. Then she lay down with the doll in the centre of the star, spreading her legs and arms wide, offering her body to the Lord of Night.

Offering her soul to the darkness.

CHAPTER ONE

The Secret Room was quiet tonight. There were only three cars parked on the street out front, but the warm neon light of a Revolution Brewing sign beckoned him through the window. A sign of home.

As he stepped in, Austin held his hand out behind him to stop the screened wooden door from slamming him in the ass. A forgotten rockabilly band set an instantly retro mood from small speakers tucked on corner shelves to the right and left of the bar. A familiar strand of Christmas lights twinkled across the shelf of liquor above the bar, and may have provided the brightest light in the place. It wasn't Christmastime, but the bar was 'festive' all year round.

Austin crossed the old plank floor and took an empty seat at the far right of the bar.

The nice thing about having a neighbourhood bar was that if you warmed a stool with any frequency, you were like family. He was barely settled when an amber IPA slid across the polished wood to touch his fingers.

"You want a sidecar too?" Brandon asked, as he wiped down the bar with an old Lagunitas towel. The brewery's logo mascot was just barely recognisable through the brown stains.

Austin nodded. "Maker's, thanks."

"You're starting pretty late," Brandon observed.

"Or I could be starting really early," he said.

"Touché."

Brandon moved down the bar and retrieved an empty pint from a heavyset guy in a Bears T-shirt and a backward baseball cap with the unmistakable blue hue used by the Cubs.

Austin took a deep sip of the Anti-Hero IPA that Brandon had poured without asking (because Austin had to admit, he was nothing if not predictable) and stared at the clock. It was just past eleven-thirty on a Sunday night. Honestly, it was surprising that anyone was in here.

Parkville, Illinois, was typically pretty quiet on a school night. The carpets started rolling up by eight or nine p.m.

"So did she kick you out, or are you on the lam?" Brandon said, carefully setting down a shot glass full to the brim.

Austin grinned. "I told her she could think about what life would be like without me to carry her shit," he said. "And then I walked out."

Brandon nodded. "So, what you're really saying is, you beat your chest pathetically and she told you to get the fuck out and you slunk out of the place with your tail between your legs?"

Austin picked up the shot. "Something like that."

The bartender nodded. "Love and marriage," he said. "So, what's the problem this week?"

"The problem is we got *married*," Austin grumbled, and then shrugged and rolled his eyes. "Seriously? I have no idea. It doesn't matter what I say, Angie goes off on it."

"Sounds like you need an exit plan," a voice offered. A woman in shorts and sandals was sitting two seats down. When she saw she had his attention, she slipped a small journal she'd been writing in back into a purple paisley handbag and met his gaze with hazel eyes that glinted with wry humour. She looked young, thirty-ish, with long black hair that hung in waves down her bare shoulders. "Sorry," she said, grinning sheepishly. "I couldn't help diving in."

"No worries," Austin said. "My life is a pretty open book. Here at the Secret Room anyway."

"I think this *place* is a secret," she said, gesturing behind them at the dark shadows and empty tables.

Austin shrugged. "It's a school night. Come back on Friday after eight o'clock and you'll find the secret's out."

She smiled and took a sip of her drink. It was something that swirled slowly, smoky and red in a wide-rimmed glass on a stem. Austin was surprised Brandon even knew how to mix a froufrou martini.

"What are you drinking?" he asked.

"Witches' brew," she said, and flashed him an evil grin. She pushed the glass toward him. "One sip and you lose your soul."

"Thanks, but I'll pass," Austin said. "My soul belongs to bourbon." He held up his sidecar shot (which was really about three shots, since Brandon poured it in a tumbler, not a shot glass) and took a sip.

"Suit yourself," she said, before taking a long sip of her own poison.

The silence between them grew as the band on the sound system overhead chugged through a standard blues progression. Brandon was on the other side of the bar, talking animatedly with Gail Renfisher, who seemed to have a reserved stool on the north corner of the old bar. Did she ever go home?

"Do you live around here?" Austin asked finally. "I haven't seen you here before."

"I think the line is, 'Do you come here often?'" she answered with a smirk.

Austin couldn't help but grin. "That wasn't a line," he said. "You come in this place much and pretty soon you know just about everyone who ever comes in, do you know what I mean? It's a small circle."

"Fair enough," she said, peering at him over the rim of the martini glass. "I just moved here, actually, so you caught me. But...maybe you'll get used to seeing me here. We'll see."

He nodded and took a deep swig of his beer. The IPA cooled his throat and warmed his chest at the same time. The bitter tingle of hops brightened the night at the same time as it obscured his heartache. He'd barely set the empty pint down when Brandon was there to fill it up.

"You working tomorrow?" the bartender asked. "Or is it going to be a sick day?"

Austin snorted. "That depends on how many you can serve me before last call."

Brandon looked at the old cuckoo clock on the wall behind him. It was an odd addition for a bar, but everyone at the Secret Room had grown used to the call of its mechanical bird. The hands were ominously close to twelve.

"You've got about an hour," he said.

Austin nodded and picked up the glass. "I'll use the time wisely," he said, tilting the IPA back.

"Pretty bad fight, huh?" the woman next to him asked.

He shrugged. "One is much like another," he said.

"Maybe you need to make some changes," she offered.

He made a face. "That's just life," he said. "Same shit, different day."

She shook her head, refusing to accept his complacency. "If you're living like life is over than you might as well be six feet underground, eh?"

The tiny creak and comforting 'cuckoo' of the wooden bird poking through the clock's door interrupted his thought.

"Cuckoo," the bird called.

The woman smiled, and her eyes suddenly lit up.

Cuckoo.

"Quick," she said. "It's the witching hour. The time for wishes."

Cuckoo.

"If you could have anything in the world, what would you want? Answer fast, before the clock strikes twelve!"

Cuckoo.

Austin laughed sadly.

Cuckoo.

"I wish my wife would just go away and die and stop giving me grief."

Cuckoo.

He rolled his eyes. "I wish my wife was dead. How's that for romantic?"

Cuckoo.

She laughed, and flipped her hair back with one hand. It cascaded across her shoulder.

Cuckoo.

Austin caught a glimpse of a blue tattoo mostly hidden by her shirt and bra, but then the shirt and hair shifted back.

Cuckoo.

"Every married guy wants that sometimes, don't they?" she said.

Cuckoo.

"You married?" he asked.

Cuckoo.

She shook her head. "Not anymore."

Cuckoo.

The clock silenced then, the bird retreating back inside its hidden room inside the clockface.

The woman retrieved the small book from her handbag, and wrote something inside it. Then she put it back and took another long pull from her martini.

"Drink," she whispered with a mischievous grin. "For tomorrow we die!"

CHAPTER TWO

Monday wasn't a sick day, though it should have been the way his head felt. But Austin wasn't going to admit that to Angie, so he'd stumbled out of the house, through the day, and back to the couch twelve hours later. It didn't matter in the end. She wasn't speaking to him.

He didn't care about the silence on Monday, but it did start to get annoying on Tuesday. When Ceili cried and he got up from the couch to go check on her, Angie would leap up to push past him and take care of diaper duty. She wouldn't answer when he spoke; it was as if he wasn't even there at all.

The worst part about it was, Austin knew how pigheaded she could be. The silent treatment could easily go on for a week. Nothing he would do or say would change it. And the maddening part was, he truly couldn't even recall what the genesis for the fight was, or what particular things he might have said that had stuck in her craw that she wouldn't let go of. In her head, he knew she had memorised whatever he'd said and was repeating the words of their fight over and over again.

In his head, he heard only silence.

So Austin wasn't looking forward to the night ahead as he pulled into the white concrete driveway on Wednesday. The sun was bright and the sky was a lush deep blue, without a cloud in the sky – a perfect summer evening. But he knew when he walked inside, it would be like stepping into the grey gloom of bitter winter.

He turned off the ignition and leaned back in the driver's seat inside the garage for a moment. Then he took a deep breath and opened the door. You couldn't avoid the inevitable by sitting in a parked car.

Austin opened the house door and stepped into the mudroom outside the kitchen.

And paused.

There were voices on the other side of the door. Which was odd. Angie never had people over. He frowned and opened the internal door from the mudroom to the kitchen.

Angie was laughing as he entered.

"Oh, here he is," his wife said, turning to look at him with a smile. It was the first thing she'd said to him in two days.

"Austin, this is our new neighbour, Regina. She just started renting the house next door. Regina, this is my husband."

He looked past her to see the woman and his jaw fell. The woman wore a purple and blue paisley wrap around her waist and a lavender tank top above. The hint of a tattoo teased from the low *V* of her shirt. Black hair pooled around her shoulders, and her eyes shot sparks when he made contact with them. He recognised her instantly.

It was the woman from the Secret Room. The woman who had smiled when he'd said, "I wish my wife was dead." And now here she was, standing in his house. Laughing with his wife.

Angie mistook the surprised look on his face. "I know, it's weird, right? That house has been vacant for years. But now we'll finally have a neighbour."

"Good to meet you," Regina said, and stepped forward with her hand outstretched.

Austin took it and gave a perfunctory squeeze. She squeezed back and held his hand in her grip for an uncomfortable few seconds. As if she was sending him a secret message through her fingers. He wished he knew what it was.

"Yeah, same," he stammered, and drew his hand back.

"Regina just stopped over to meet us," Angie explained. "I told her that if she needs anything…I'm here all the time."

"I really appreciate it," Regina said, looking away from Austin. "It's hard to start in a new place and not know anybody."

"You'll adjust fast," Angie promised. "Parkville is a good place. People are pretty friendly, even if the place turns into a ghost town after dark. Not that it matters to me anymore. Since we had Ceili, I never get out of this house except to go grocery shopping."

"Well, maybe I can help there," Regina said. "I'm sure you and your husband would love a little time alone again. If you need someone to sit for you once in a while, I love babies."

Angie smiled. "I would love that," she said.

Regina looked pointedly at Austin. "You wouldn't mind a romantic evening out with your wife, would you?"

Austin felt Angie's eyes on him, but he didn't look at her. He didn't break Regina's gaze for a second.

"No," he said. "That would be unbelievable."

Regina grinned and turned to Angie. "Great," she said. "For now, I'd better be going. Lots of unpacking to do. Maybe I'll see you tomorrow?"

"Sure," Angie agreed and the two women both started out of the kitchen toward the front door.

"Nice meeting you, Austin," Regina's voice called from the foyer.

"Yeah," he answered, adding under his breath, "just like déjà vu."

Austin went to the bedroom to change into sweatpants and a T-shirt. When he came back down, Angie was moving around in the kitchen.

"So that's weird, huh," he said as he walked into the room. "Someone actually living next door? That house has got to be a pit after all these years empty."

Angie nodded and pulled a frozen dinner out of the freezer. "Yeah," she answered simply.

She turned her back to him and set the temperature on the oven to 350.

"So, what did she have to say?" he asked.

Angie shrugged. "Pretty much what you heard."

At that moment, the baby began to cry in the other room. Angie immediately turned and walked past him. "I'm just having a TV dinner," she said. "You can throw one in for yourself if you're hungry."

And then she was gone, down the hall to retrieve the baby from her bouncy chair in the front room.

"Gee…thanks so much," he murmured.

He thought of the conversation he'd had a couple nights ago with Regina at the bar, and shook his head.

"I wasn't joking," he said after a minute.

Then he began rummaging in the freezer for a TV dinner.

CHAPTER THREE

It took a few days, but eventually Angie thawed. She needed someone to help with Ceili, and he was the nearest possible candidate…so, like it or not, she had to talk to him.

Although…he might be getting some competition in that regard. Apparently, Regina had been stopping by every day while Austin was at work.

"Want to go out to dinner tonight?" Angie asked him on Saturday.

Austin frowned and looked at her, wondering where this was going.

"Regina offered to watch Ceili tonight if we wanted to go out," she said. "And it has been a long time since I've been out of this house."

"Where did you want to go?" he asked. But in his head he was thinking, *You don't want to go out with me, you just want to go out.*

"Wherever you want," she said. The translation was, *Take me someplace where I'll have a good time, and if I don't…you'll be sorry.*

Great, Austin said to himself. *No pressure.*

★   ★   ★

Regina showed up that night in a long, ruffled sundress swirled in grey and purple and indigo. Austin answered the door but tried not to look at her face, because he really didn't want to talk to her. But staring at her dress wasn't that much better.

She was weirdly provocative no matter where your eyes landed.

"So, you don't mind sitting for the night, really?" Angie asked, breezing into the foyer just as Regina stepped inside.

"Who wouldn't want to watch a baby?" she answered.

"That's what I used to say," Angie said. "It's great until it's twenty-four seven." She grinned and then moved to the stairway. "I'll be right down," she said.

When Angie disappeared, Regina leaned in and whispered, "You know, if you get home early and want to have a nightcap at the Secret Room, I might be interested in hearing about whether you still think your wife should die or not...."

Austin's eyes flared. Regina only smiled. Silently.

"I was upset that night," he whispered.

"I understand." She shrugged. "Everyone's entitled. Do you feel differently now?"

He didn't answer immediately. "It's complicated," he said.

Footsteps thumped behind them, and Angie reappeared, holding a small purse. "Now I'm ready," she said. "Come on, I'll show you where Ceili's bottles and things are."

The two women moved down the hall and Austin took a deep breath and shook his head. Why couldn't he have kept his mouth shut? That's all he needed, for Angie to get pally with Regina and for Regina to start shooting her mouth off about what he'd said. Then the silent war would go on for a month. That said...having the two women become friends could be the best thing that had happened to Austin in months. Angie had only gotten more and more depressive and withdrawn since having Ceili. Sitting in the house all day with nobody to talk to but a screaming infant was enough to drive anyone a little nuts. And if Angie was going nuts... Austin was going to pay the toll. He wandered down into the kitchen and leaned against the table to wait.

When the two women returned, Angie was grinning. She took Austin's arm and pulled him toward the garage door.

"Thanks again, Regina," she said. "You've got my number – call if you have any problems. But like I said, I just fed her and hopefully she'll sleep for a couple hours. We won't be late!"

A moment later, they were in the garage and Austin stepped around the car with her to open the passenger door.

"Such a gentleman," Angie said with a hint of sarcasm.

Austin restrained the sudden urge to backhand her. They hadn't had a night out together in weeks, but he wasn't looking forward to the next few hours. What did *that* say about the state of their relationship?

He slid into the driver's seat and backed the car out. As the garage door went down, Angie asked, "So, where are you taking me, darling?"

She drew out the word *darling*, so that it wasn't a term of endearment at all.

"I thought we could have dinner at Esteban's," he said. The Spanish tapas house was one of her favourite places, so it seemed a sure bet.

"Mmmm, garlic mashed potatoes," she said with a smile. Then her attention shifted away from him as she pulled out her cell phone and started scrolling through Facebook.

Austin considered saying something but decided that the silence was preferable to an argument. He didn't speak again until they pulled into the restaurant parking lot.

"It you want, we can head over to the Secret Room after dinner for a martini or something?"

She shrugged and thumbed off her phone. "We'll see."

★   ★   ★

Things did get better after the first glass of wine. Angie started talking about a mutual friend from college, and the time they had gotten so drunk that all three of them together walked arm in arm down the middle of a street to navigate the three blocks back to their dorm.

He grinned and laughed with her.

"I didn't even remember how we got back to the dorm," he said. "You told me about that walk the next day."

She nodded. "You tried to get us to climb the alma mater statue," she said. "You were going to pee off the top."

He laughed. "All I remember is the headache the next day. I think it was the worst hangover ever."

He could smile at the memory now. It had been a good time in their lives, when they had everything in front of them. Maybe it had been the best time for them. But the reality of the moment soon chased the smile away. That was then, this was now. And now was *not* a carefree time for them.

After Angie downed her third glass of wine, the tenor of the night out grew darker. Instead of happy memories, she started dredging up complaints. Bitterness.

"Here's a thought," she said, after draining the glass and licking her lips. "Maybe tonight, you could get up when she cries and change Ceili's diaper instead of me. I'm not the nanny service, you know. She's your kid too."

"That's not fair," he complained. "I do change her. But you're home all day while I've got to be 'on' at work."

She held her fingers to her thumb and mimicked a duck's bill in silence as he talked. When the waiter asked her if they wanted another drink, Angie said "yes" as he was saying "no."

"Don't you think we should head home soon?" he asked.

She shook her head. "Regina has it covered. I texted her a little while ago and everything's fine. Tonight?" She took a deep breath before completing the thought. "I'm enjoying myself for once."

Enjoyment to Angie seemed to be critiquing every action and opinion of her husband. When they finally pulled up in the garage at just after eleven p.m., Austin turned the car off and got out of the driver's seat as soon as humanly possible, leaving Angie fumbling drunkenly with her seatbelt in the car.

I'm done, he said over and over again in his head, though he somehow refrained from saying it out loud.

When he walked into the kitchen, he found Regina sitting there, alert and waiting for them. While she had internet access and had her laptop sitting open on the table, she didn't appear to be typing anything. She smiled as he walked into the room.

"So, are the lovebirds rekindled?" she asked quietly

Austin shook his head.

She frowned. "That's a shame," she said. "I know Angie was really looking forward to a night on the town with you."

"Yeah, apparently so she could rip me a new one," he said as the door behind them creaked open.

"Tell me more later," Regina whispered, and then looked over his shoulder.

"Angie, how was your night?"

His wife sighed as she walked up behind him.

"It was so good to be out of this house," she said. "I love her, but this place has felt like a prison for the past few weeks. Thanks for watching her. Did you have any problems? Did she take the bottle okay?"

Regina stood up and flipped her laptop lid closed. "No problem," she said. "Ceili was an angel. Took the bottle fine and went to sleep about an hour ago. Feel free to ask me to watch her anytime. I'm happy to do it."

As she moved around the table and passed him, Austin was sure he felt her fingers trail across his thigh. But she and Angie talked and walked to the door together, leaving him behind, and he shook off the odd thought. There was no way she'd felt him up on the way out. It was his imagination.

Angie returned to the kitchen a few minutes later. She weaved slightly as she went to the refrigerator for a bottled water.

"Did you have a good time?" he asked.

She looked at him and shrugged before taking a deep gulp of water.

"Good as can be," she said, and abruptly walked past him to ascend the stairway to the bedroom.

Austin decided he'd be better off not following swiftly. Instead, he pulled a beer from the fridge and sat down on the couch to nurse it. He thought of life before Ceili, when Angie had actually wanted to be with him. Time had moved so fast back then, and the time they were alone together was never enough. He watched the second hand moving in slow, deliberate circles around the clock above the mantel.

Time had never seemed to move so slow.

CHAPTER FOUR

"You didn't turn up last night at the Secret Room. How does it feel the morning after?"

The voice came from the other side of the bush that separated Austin's driveway from the previously abandoned house, that was now Regina's.

Her face appeared a second later, wearing a knowing smile. She also wore another paisley purple and blue dress. Or wrap. He wasn't really sure what it was, the way it creased and fluttered around her. It was a lot like the one she'd worn the night before, but somehow, more lived-in. There was a swirl of pattern around her, but her ankles and feet were bare as she stepped across the dew-laden lawn to reach the sidewalk. She almost floated.

Austin picked up the newspaper. He was only wearing shorts and a stained grey T-shirt. He suddenly felt exposed. These weren't the clothes he wanted to talk to the neighbours in. But nobody was ever outside at six in the morning. It was one of his favourite parts of the day. The air was crisp, the birds were quietly chirping and there were no cars on the street.

"Just like any other day," he answered.

Regina clucked and shook her head.

"That's no way to greet a Sunday morning," she said.

"I should be on my knees?" he asked.

"Depends who is standing in front of you, I guess," she said with a smirk.

"That's not what I meant...."

She put her hands up. "Who you get on your knees for is your business."

"Very funny," he said. "So, you went to the Secret Room last night?"

She nodded. "I didn't stay long though. I was hoping I might see you there once Angie went to sleep. I'm afraid the clientele there after midnight aren't exactly…models of intellect and grace."

He snorted. "I don't think the clientele there is ever that, at any time." He looked back toward the house. "I would have loved to have come up, but Angie was out cold in about fifteen minutes flat, and someone had to be sober if Ceili woke up."

She stroked the side of his face with her hand. "You're a saint," she said.

He rolled his eyes. "No, just responsible."

Regina smiled and lifted her leg. The hem of the dress slipped up her thigh to expose her knee and part of her thigh.

"I prefer barefoot and fancy-free," she said with a grin. "You should try it sometime."

"I have," he said. "That's why I'm married with a kid now."

She raised an eyebrow. "There are phases in life for everything. But you should never give up on your dreams. Sometimes wishes do come true."

"I better get back inside," he said, suddenly feeling uncomfortable.

"As you wish," she said. He could hear laughter in the undertone of her words. "Stop by the Secret Room when you've got some time to talk."

"I don't know when you'll be there," he said.

"That's the beauty of fancy-free," she said. "You just don't know."

Austin frowned. "Yeah, I guess," he said.

He could feel her eyes on his back as he turned to walk up the driveway. When he opened the front door to step inside, he glanced behind him. She was still standing at the hedge.

Her lips were smiling.

CHAPTER FIVE

The Secret Room was almost empty on Wednesday night when Austin walked in after work. Things at home had slowly returned to normal; Angie was back to talking to him again as if they'd never had a fight and gone through a week of 'the silent treatment'. But 'normal' wasn't what Austin wanted. The words that Regina had spoken to him on Sunday morning kept replaying in his head. He thought about being responsible and doing what he was supposed to. And he thought about going barefoot and doing whatever the hell he felt like.

He thought about talking more to Regina.

He thought a lot about stopping by the Secret Room on Sunday and Monday and he almost did on Tuesday.

On Wednesday, he texted Angie just before he left work and just said that he'd be late, and not to wait on him for dinner. And then he drove straight from the office to the Secret Room.

He still could take his own path once in a while. And tonight, he felt like having a beer and talking to Regina if she was there before he went home.

He settled at the bar and looked around at the handful of patrons. There was a couple at one of the highboy tables, and another on the other end of the bar, talking animatedly about something related to baseball and apparently a bad umpire call. But Regina was not in evidence.

That's what you get for being 'free', he told himself. But he went ahead and ordered a beer. Then he asked for the menu. He might as well enjoy the peace of his refuge awhile, and maybe Regina would ultimately show up.

But when the grease had congealed around the few crumbs left on his plate, and he pushed back his fourth empty pint, and the cuckoo had called its alarm eight times, Regina had still not appeared.

Stupid, he thought. *It's not like she lives here. And now you get to face the wrath of a woman left home who's going to smell beer on your breath.*

Austin called for a check, and Brandon nodded from across the bar. A minute later he slid a white receipt across the wood and grinned. "Time to face the music, huh?"

"We all have to sooner or later," Austin said, and scrawled his name across the bottom of the receipt. "If I survive, I'll be back in a couple nights."

"You'll survive," Brandon assured him. "You're a survivor."

"Something like that." Austin grinned, and slid off the stool with a groan.

★   ★   ★

The house was dark when he pulled up to the driveway, which was unusual. There didn't seem to be any lights on upstairs or down. It was still light outside, but dusk was moving in. Austin frowned and turned the car off. He took a deep breath, spit the peppermint gum he'd been chewing into a tissue, and got out of the car.

"Angie?" he called when he stepped into the house. And instantly regretted it. She'd yelled at him in the past for doing that because it woke the baby – typically about ten minutes after she'd just gotten Ceili to sleep.

There was no answer this time, however, from his wife or the baby.

Austin walked down the hall and flipped on the light in the kitchen. The breakfast bowls were still in the sink, but there was no evidence that Angie had made dinner.

He went into the front room and bent to turn on the light next to his favourite recliner. It was strange to come home at night and not have the TV on. The quiet made him feel strangely uneasy.

He walked to the foyer to see if Angie was sitting with the baby upstairs, and abruptly stopped short.

Angie wasn't upstairs.

She was lying at the base of them.

Her feet were still on the third step, and her eyes stared with a look of surprise at him from where her head lay twisted oddly on the tile of the foyer. The bad part was...her eyes weren't blinking. And she almost looked as if she were looking at him from over her shoulder. Her neck was turned in a completely wrong angle.

"Angie?" he whispered.

She didn't answer. His stomach turned to ice. He knew that she wouldn't answer. Couldn't answer. But he didn't want to admit it. Couldn't accept it. This was *his* house. This was *Angie*. Death was not part of this place.

Only.

He knew that Angie was dead. Nobody lay on the floor like that and got up to laugh about it. He bent down and put his hand on her cheek. Her skin was cold. He traced his fingers across her cheek and forehead, and she did not respond. He could feel her...but she did not feel anymore.

Austin felt his world suddenly contract. Angie was dead. The words went through his head, and he could see all of the letters in his head. Like a marquee. But they did not make sense.

Angie could not be dead.

The words of Regina came back to haunt him. "If you're living like life is over then you might as well be six feet underground, eh?"

Well, now one of them was ready to be.

As he touched her cheek and thought about what it meant for his wife to be gone, he suddenly had a flash. What about Ceili? If his heart had constricted before, it really did now.

Austin tentatively stepped over Angie's body and then vaulted up the stairs to see if his baby girl was okay. She wasn't crying. The house had been silent since he'd walked in.

The fear ate him alive. He could barely move his legs. While his wife was now gone, it was his daughter that really made his a life to live. And now she would be depending solely on him.

Austin took the stairs two at a time and when he reached the landing dashed down the hallway toward Ceili's room.

The nursery was quiet.

His heart pounded. She had to be okay.

He stepped across the room to the bed to look into the crib at his baby. There was nothing in his world that he cared about more. Her face looked up toward the ceiling, still as a doll.

Austin's chest tightened.

He bent over the crib rail and touched his fingers to her soft cheeks.

Ceili was not cold like her mother. Her skin was warm, and she shifted in her sleep when he put his fingers on her forehead.

"Sleep, little girl," he whispered. "Tomorrow is going to be a long day, I think."

Ceili stirred and shifted her arm across the pillow.

Austin bent down and kissed her. He held his hand on her head until she settled. No reason for her to start crying now.

There'd be plenty of time for that in the morning.

But for him…there was only shock and fear and hurt. He started to leave the room to go back downstairs but realised he couldn't leave her up here alone. Not because she needed him, but because he needed her. He needed to hold her even if it woke her up.

Austin reached down and lifted Ceili from the mattress. Her tiny arms reached out and clutched for him. And as her tiny fingers made him smile, he remembered her mother at the foot of the stairs.

He had to call the police. Life for Ceili and him was about to change.

Drastically.

CHAPTER SIX

The night lasted forever. There were paramedics and policemen and, for some reason he couldn't fathom, the fire department. They didn't move the body, but they moved *around* it for what seemed like forever. Pointing and marking and consulting with each other in half-finished phrases and side-handed whispers.

Those people didn't talk to him. Noise and lights and people filled his house as he tried to keep Ceili calm and answer what he could to the people who did talk to him. He held the baby close, patting her back and stroking her head, trying to keep her quiet as the police asked him questions. At some point, Regina came walking through the front door, and without even asking what was going on, she patted his shoulder and took the baby out of his arms. Moments later, she was sitting across the room with Ceili on the couch. He smiled sadly at her, trying to express his thanks with just a look, and went back to talking. Eventually, he lost track of both of them and walked outside with the officers and paramedics when they finally decided it was time to move the body.

The whole event was surreal. Austin couldn't have described what he said or what was asked but the words went on and on as the people looked at and prodded the body of his dead wife. And then they lifted her on a stretcher and moved outside and the red and blue lights echoed weirdly off his face on his driveway as he watched the men in uniforms load her corpse into the ambulance…without urgency.

There was no urgency anymore…she was dead.

Dead.

The word kept echoing in his head. The girl he'd made out with in a movie theatre once….

Dead.

The girl he'd tried pot with for the first time in a back alley behind Allen Harpstrom's house....
Dead.
The girl who had told him he was going to be a daddy....
Dead.
The girl who had turned into a nagging, carping woman who had ultimately made him wish that she would die.
Dead.

★   ★   ★

At a certain point, nothing really registered anymore. The night became a blur of strange voices and flashing emergency lights. And then the rear doors of the ambulance closed and the engine audibly powered up and it began to creep out of his driveway before turning right to go down the block toward the main road out to town.

And the cop cars along the curb slipped away one by one until the last officer said he was sorry and walked back to his car, leaving Austin alone on the white concrete of his driveway.

Two hands suddenly slipped over his shoulders and squeezed.

"How are you doing?" Regina asked.

"I honestly don't know," he said.

"Come on," she said, and pulled his arm to move him back toward the front door of the house. He followed without thinking. There was no thinking at this point...he was numb.

When they stepped across the threshold, something in him sparked. He saw the empty stairs leading up and the empty couch in his living room. And the empty floor where his wife's body had been.

"Where's Ceili?" he asked.

"I put her to bed," Regina said. "I didn't think you'd mind. She just wanted to sleep."

He nodded. "Okay, good, thank you," he said. "I can't tell you how much I appreciate you helping with her...I don't know what I would have done..."

"You would have done what you had to do," Regina said. "But I'm glad I was able to be here to help you do it."

She reached up and touched his cheek. "I'll be around if you need me," she said.

And before he could answer, she'd turned and started to walk back out of his front door.

Austin followed but stopped at the threshold. When she disappeared around the hedge, he closed the door and turned the lock.

Then he walked like a zombie up the stairs to check on Ceili. She was tiny and peaceful in her crib, blissfully unaware that her mother was gone. What would it be like tomorrow when she looked for Angie and couldn't find her momma? Austin tried to put that from his mind. But Ceili wasn't the only one who would struggle with that painful reality soon.

Moments later, he lay down in his own bed, but unlike the baby, he didn't fall easily asleep. Instead, he stared for hours at the empty pillow where nobody lay next to him.

CHAPTER SEVEN

Life doesn't sit still for death. If anything, it moves faster.

The next few days were a whirlwind of unfamiliar business for Austin – contacting the funeral home, reaching out to the newspaper for the obituary, tearful conversations on the phone and in person with both Angie's family and his own. The hours of every day slipped by quickly. There were moments when the silences in the house reminded him that Angie was gone forever, but most of the time seemed to be taken up with simply taking care of the mundane details that needed to be done.

Whenever it got too much, when Ceili was crying uncontrollably and his cell phone ringing for the fourth time in a half-hour, Regina seemed to turn up. She'd knock three times on the front screen door and then let herself in, usually catching Austin struggling in the kitchen with a bottle, a phone and the baby all at the same time.

She'd raise one eyebrow, hold out her hands, and he'd hand over the baby, who would stop crying almost instantly. Some things just took a woman's touch.

On the morning of Angie's funeral, Regina came to the door, but this time didn't knock; Austin was already standing right there at the foot of the stairs. He'd been straightening his tie in the mirror on the wall in the foyer.

"Looking sharp," she said through the screen.

Austin looked up and stifled a grin.

"Mind if I come in?" she asked.

"Never," he said, turning away from the mirror.

Regina stepped inside, the hem of a now-familiar indigo paisley dress swirling in the breeze of the closing door.

"Are you all ready for this?" she asked.

Austin shrugged. "As ready as I can be, I guess."

She reached up and adjusted the knot of his tie. "I can help with

Ceili today if you want. But I know it's a private thing, if you'd rather I didn't come."

Austin considered for a moment, and then shook his head. "No, it's fine for you to come, if you want. But I don't want you to feel like you have to. You've done so much for me already this week."

"It's fine," she said. "I did know Angie, after all, and I love taking care of Ceili. I always wanted to have a baby of my own but...."

He opened his mouth to ask why she hadn't but then stopped himself. Whether it was because she was sterile or had never found a man to have one with, it probably wouldn't be a 'happy' story. And it was none of his business.

She broke his silence with an unexpected question.

"Listen, I've been thinking," she began. "You're going to need someone to watch Ceili when you go back to work. What if I did that for you, instead of her going into some daycare place?"

Austin shook his head instinctively, though the idea was instantly attractive. It would solve a huge problem for him. "I couldn't ask that of you," he said. "You've been such a big help this week but...."

"Well, I wouldn't do it for free," she said, cocking her head. "You're going to have to pay someone to watch her, and I don't have a job right now. I've had a nice little nest egg saved up, so I was able to pay my rent way in advance, but I'm eventually going to need to get a paycheck. So...why not pay me? I could even come over and do it right here in her own house. How easy is that?"

"I...I guess that could be all right," he said. "I've already called a couple of daycare places but I hadn't settled anything yet. They're all so expensive and some have waiting lists."

"Then it's a deal," she said. "We can figure out what you'll pay me later, but I promise I'll work cheaper than your standard daycare centre."

Austin felt a weight lift off his chest. He knew he had to find at least a temporary situation for Ceili before going back to work next week, and he'd poked at the problem, but getting through the funeral had been his first priority.

"You're a life saver," he said. "Thank you. I...just...thank you."

"You can thank me later," she said. "Right now, we need to get the two of you out of the house. Where is she?"

As if on cue, Ceili began to cry in the nursery. Regina patted Austin's shoulder and moved past him to walk up the stairs.

A few minutes later, she walked into the kitchen with the baby. Ceili was bright-eyed and sucking on a pacifier. Regina had dressed her in a onesie covered in cartoon bees and daisies.

"I hope this is okay," she said. "I found it in her drawer. I didn't think you wanted her to go in a diaper and stained T-shirt."

Austin snorted. "No, but that would be the look Angie's mother probably expects from me. So, thanks." He took Ceili from Regina's arms and held her up to appraise her. "Looking good, kid."

"Do you need me to make up a bottle?" Regina asked, moving toward the fridge.

"Nope," he said. "That's one thing I actually managed to do on my own. But thanks."

"Amazing," she said, pulling the bottle out of the refrigerator. "What about diapers?"

He pointed at the blue canvas bag on the table. "Believe it or not, we're packed and ready to go. I have learned a few things these past few months. Do you want to ride with us or follow? I don't want you to be stuck there if you need to leave."

"No worries," Regina said, taking the baby back from him. "I'm yours for as long as you want me. I've got nothing going on."

"You do now," he said, raising his fist in the air in mock excitement. "We're going to a funeral!" He tried to make his voice sound psyched, but the humour fell flat. He shook his head and scowled, admitting his real sentiment. "I just want this day to be done."

Regina nodded sympathetically and followed him to the car.

*　　*　　*

The funeral was actually a beautiful, moving thing. Angie's two brothers, along with her friends from college, served as pallbearers, and when Linnea, her best friend from high school, talked about the time she had stayed up with her in college until five a.m. after drinking too much and watching a scary movie, even Austin had to laugh. He remembered *that* girl. Angie had been so high-strung and sensitive and easily affected. She had clung to him for strength and love and support in a way he had never experienced before. He had been so happy to be her roots, her rock. And she had given him her heart and soul and body with an energy and desire he couldn't refuse. The girl he'd asked to marry him was so unlike the woman she had eventually become, who seemed to spend half of her waking hours complaining about Austin's inadequacies and the rest of the time simply not speaking to him at all.

He had fallen in love with the girl who Linnea talked about. He didn't really know the woman she'd become...who lay still inside the coffin now.

Which made no sense.

But it was how life was sometimes. People grew and changed in ways you could never foresee. If there was one thing that Austin knew, it was that you could never keep things the way they were.

Certainly, that was more than true now, as he stood in the front pew of a church listening to people tell heartbreakingly warm stories about his wife, as they prepared to put her wooden-shrouded body in the ground.

Austin cried during the service, and his dad put a strong hand on his shoulder when he did. The strength of his father was palpable in that touch, and it truly helped him make it through the rest of the day. His dad never said much, but in his father's silent, solid grip, he knew he wasn't alone.

And when he looked to his right, he found Regina at his side, holding Ceili in her arms. Angie's child. His child. The baby stayed strangely quiet through the service, which was a blessing.

There were people around him who cared for and supported him. If Angie's life had ended, during the priest's homily and the remembrances that people told, he realised somehow that his had not.

At one point, he had to go to the pulpit and say a few words of his own about his wife. He had written some things down and pledged that he wouldn't cry in front of the whole congregation.

His friend Bill had held his arm and led him partly up the aisle. Once at the podium, Austin had said things about meeting Angie at the bookstore in college. And taking her to the student union afterward. And proposing to her in a college bar (he maybe could have improved his romanticism a bit).

"I only know one thing for sure," he'd told the small congregation. "She was the only girl I ever met that I truly wanted to spend my life with. I guess I'm lucky that she let me spend part of it with her."

When he'd returned to his seat, his cheeks were wet. He'd stepped over Regina to reach his seat, and when he did, she held out Ceili for him to hold. The sweet scent of his baby made some of the ache in his heart slip away, and he pulled her cheek close to his.

Regina put a comforting hand on his right shoulder, as his father did the same to his left. With Ceili in his arms, and their support on his arms…Austin felt as if he could actually get through this.

CHAPTER EIGHT

A new rhythm soon began to transform his life.

On Monday, Regina met him at the door in the morning and slipped past him into the house when he opened it, instantly moving toward the kitchen, where Ceili cried.

"Where do you keep the bottles?" she asked before he'd even reached the room. He pointed and she was filling one before he could blink twice.

By the end of the week, she was letting herself into the house in the mornings with the key he'd given her. It had only seemed right that she have a way to get in on her own in case she stepped outside during the day and accidentally locked herself out. He couldn't risk a situation where Ceili got locked inside with no way for anyone to get to her.

And so, on Thursday, he walked down the stairs for the first time in the morning, still buttoning his shirt for work, and there she was, already in his house, barefoot in a knee-length cotton sundress moving about in his kitchen.

"Morning," he said simply, heading toward the coffee maker. Regina turned and smiled, her eyes shining bright as the sun.

"It is," she agreed.

He opened the ceramic coffee-bean container and dropped a handful of scoops into the grinder.

"I wasn't sure how much you used, or I would have started it for you," Regina said.

"Oh geez," he said. "You don't have to do that. But thanks."

"So, five?" she noted.

"You're observant." He grinned and poured the water into the coffee maker.

"I like to know how things work around me," she said. "So I pay attention."

"I'll keep that in mind if I'm ever opening a safe near you," he said.

She smirked but said nothing.

Austin shook his head and poured himself a bowl of cereal. It felt a little strange to be feeding himself while another woman was moving about in his house taking care of his baby, but he couldn't pretend it wasn't a relief. And Regina didn't complain constantly while doing it. He missed Angie, but he did not miss those tense, frustrating mornings in the kitchen before leaving for a nice long tense, frustrating day at work. Regina was so good with Ceili; the baby quieted almost instantly when Regina picked her up and rocked her. And the colic she'd been fighting lately seemed to have stopped over the past couple days. The baby was as happy as she'd ever been, despite the absence of her mother.

He had a hard time not feeling guilty about it, but he couldn't deny that he felt more upbeat than he had in a long while as well.

*　　*　　*

That positive feeling was still with him when he pulled into his driveway on Friday night. Before Angie died, Austin had begun to dread the long weekends at home with a sullen wife and crying baby. He'd buried himself in work from Monday through Friday to avoid it, actually. But tonight, as he put the car in park, he realised he'd been looking forward to getting home for the weekend for hours to see what Regina and Ceili had been up to.

When he walked into the house, there was music playing, something exotic and atmospheric, with a woman singing almost incomprehensible lyrics in a plaintive voice. The music of a dream.

Regina was sitting on the couch with her legs crooked, her feet tucked underneath her butt as she wrote in the same small journal he'd seen her writing in the night he'd met her at the Secret Room.

Ceili lay on her belly on a blanket on the floor, surrounded by small toys. Her eyes were bright and she slapped at a red ball with one chubby, tiny hand.

"Happy Friday," Regina greeted him, looking up from her writing.

"That it is," he agreed. "Especially now that I'm home."

"Ah," Regina smiled. "Did you miss us?"

"Of course I missed you," he said, and then felt a qualm for saying it. He should be saying he missed *Ceili*, not Regina. But there was no room to change his answer. Regina closed her little book and got up off the couch. She ran a light hand over his shoulder as she walked past him.

"Did you eat?" she asked.

He shook his head. "No, I figured I'd finish off the leftover chicken."

Regina's voice lilted from the kitchen. "I hope you don't mind, but I fixed something from what I found in the refrigerator. I just felt like cooking, and some of that stuff was going to go bad."

"Oh my God, you didn't have to do that," he said, following her into the kitchen. She was setting a plate and utensils on the table. A single setting. She pulled a pot out of the oven with two potholders and set it in the centre of the table. Then she motioned for him to sit.

He did, while she got a serving spoon from the utensil drawer and then began to scoop out a big portion of something with noodles and red peppers and green vegetables and chunks of chicken beneath a raincoat of white cheese.

"What is it?" he asked.

Regina shrugged. "Food. I don't name it…I just put stuff together and hope it turns out okay."

"Aren't you having any?" he asked, when she hovered near the table but made no move to make a place for herself.

"I should probably head home," she said with a smile.

Austin shook his head. "Oh no," he said. "You cooked it… you're going to enjoy it with me."

"You're assuming you'll enjoy it," she said.

"I know I will," he said, and stood up. He walked around her and grabbed a plate and utensils. Then he set them on the table and pointed at the chair.

"Sit," he demanded. "I'll get Ceili and we can enjoy a Friday night dinner together."

She nodded meekly and slid into the chair. Austin went to pick Ceili off the floor and returned to put her in the high chair so they could keep an eye on her during dinner. He went to the refrigerator and pulled out a jar of pureed beef and peas. They made the most disgusting food for babies.

"Oh, I fed her already," Regina said. "Why do you think she's so quiet?"

"A full belly is a great comforter," he laughed, and returned the jar to the shelf. He put some Cheerios on the high chair tray for Ceili to play with, and then sat back down.

"Thanks for cooking this," he said, digging a fork in and enjoying the long strands of cheese that stretched out as he lifted it toward his mouth.

Regina beamed. "I enjoy just making recipes up. Especially when it's someone else's refrigerator. You don't know what you'll find. It's kind of a creative challenge."

Austin chewed, and rolled his eyes in appreciation. When his mouth cleared, he said, "Well, you beat the odds with this one. I don't know what was left in the fridge, but this tastes awesome."

"It's all the secret magic ingredients I put in," she said with a laugh.

He watched her as she took a bite. She didn't say anything, but her face lit up as she chewed. She was obviously proud of the way her concoction had turned out.

"So, are you all moved in at this point?" he asked. "It's been a month or so now, right?"

She nodded. "About that," she said. "I didn't come here with much though, so it was an easy move."

"What brought you here, of all places?" he asked between bites. "Parkville is not exactly a mecca for…anything really. This is more like the place to go just before you die."

"Well, I don't intend on dying anytime soon," she said.

"Did you come here for work, family, a boyfriend…?"

"Yes," she said. She made an amused face but did not elaborate.

"Okay, I won't pry," he said. "But you're renting the house, right? Will you be staying long?"

"As long as it takes," she said. Her eyes sparkled with playful humour. She was baiting him. "But it's a one-year lease, so don't worry. I'll be around awhile no matter what."

Austin shook his head and pushed a Cheerio toward Ceili's pudgy fingers. She was being amazingly quiet, but she had slowly nudged all of the cereal just out of reach.

He ate a couple more bites in silence and then shook his head and moaned in appreciation. "This is so good," he said finally. "I wish I could make it up to you, only I'm not much of a cook. I can char meat on the grill but that's about it." And then he hesitated, but the words came out on their own anyway. "I'd love to take you out to dinner someplace nice."

Regina's eyes widened. "I'd love to go," she said.

"Really?" he said. "I mean…I probably shouldn't even be thinking this but I'd love to have an adult night out again. Angie and I didn't do that much this past year. And the last time didn't really go well."

"Then it's long past time you did," she said. "What kind of clubs do you like to go to?"

Austin laughed. "Clubs? I don't know. I don't think there even are any in this town. The last time I went out to a place with a band or a DJ might have been college. Or maybe my friend Bill's bachelor party. We did hit a blues club in Chicago then."

"There are places we could go," she said. "There are always places."

"Well, the problem is, I don't have a sitter," Austin said with a frown. "Cuz that job's yours."

Regina shook her head. "I know a couple girls in town that would watch her for the night. If you're serious."

Austin's stomach suddenly flipped. It almost sounded like a challenge. Something he couldn't just back out of. Not that he wanted to.

"I am serious," he said. "I'd love to take you out for a night. It's the least I could do to say thanks for all you've done."

"I don't want you to take me out as some kind of misplaced feeling of duty," Regina said. "But if you actually want to go out with me, say the word."

There was an awkward silence for a moment. The air was charged. The gauntlet was down. Was Austin interested in going out with Regina because he was interested in Regina? Yes. But was it appropriate to say that a week after his wife's funeral? No.

"What are you thinking?" she asked after another moment went by.

"I'm wondering if you'd want to go out to dinner with me tomorrow night," he said. "But I don't know if it's really appropriate for me to ask you."

"I think you just did," she said. "And the answer is yes."

"And Ceili?"

"I'll bring one of my friends over tomorrow around seven," she said. "Is that okay?"

Austin could almost feel himself blushing. "Yeah," he said. "That's *very* okay." And then he shovelled another mouthful in, so that he didn't have to speak anymore as he lost himself in the light of her eyes.

CHAPTER NINE

Austin spent Saturday morning and afternoon in a wildly oscillating state: while Ceili napped he paced the kitchen, one minute filled with anticipation and the next considering cancellation. But while his brain vaulted back and forth between *should*s and *should not*s, he luckily had other distractions. This was the first full day he had of watching Ceili completely on his own, without Angie or her mother or Regina in his house helping out. And being with his baby girl – rocking her, feeding her, crawling on the floor next to her in the family room – helped push his silly adult worries of propriety to the back burner over and over again. At the end of the day, whether or not he went out to dinner with his neighbour, his true mission in life was to make sure this little girl was happy.

He held her in his arms and pressed his nose to hers, laughing as her eyes grew wide and her lips crinkled into the kind of unrestrained happiness that only an infant can display. She cooed and lifted her pudgy fingers to grab at his cheeks.

That was all that mattered.

And that was the position he was in when the doorbell rang.

Austin walked to the door and opened it with the baby in his arms.

A young woman with long golden hair and a hot pink T-shirt stood on the other side of the storm door. "Hi, we're here with your Girl Scout Cookies," she said with an exaggerated grin.

Regina was right behind her.

"I didn't order Girl Scout Cookies," Austin said.

"What about Girl Scouts?" Regina asked.

Austin shrugged. "Now those I might be able to use."

He stepped aside as Regina opened the screen door and the two stepped into the foyer.

"Austin, this is Brandy," Regina announced. "She'll be your Girl Scout for the night."

"I thought *you* were my Girl Scout for the night," he said.

Regina shook her head. "Nope, I'm your date. Don't get it confused. You don't date Girl Scouts, do you, because...."

Austin shook his head. With that, Brandy lifted Ceili from his arms and held the baby up to look at her. "Well, aren't you a doll," she said.

"Come on," Regina said, leading the other girl toward the kitchen. "I'll show you where all of her things are."

Austin closed the front door, and then smiled as he listened to the two women laughing and talking in the other room. He had a good feeling about the night.

★   ★   ★

Two hours later, after a heavy dose of pasta and fresh-baked bread at Martinelli's, they walked into the Secret Room and took two seats at the empty half of the bar. After Brandon pushed a pint and a martini glass across the bar at them, Regina held her glass up for a toast. Austin tapped his to hers, and she pronounced, "To déjà vu... and new beginnings."

Austin nodded and took a deep sip of his beer. "I think I might be sitting in the same stool I was when I met you," he said finally. "Things were pretty different the last time we were here though."

"Life is about change," she said.

"I've seen plenty of change over the past two weeks," he said.

"I know," she said. "I hope I've made it easier for you."

"I could never have gotten through it without you."

Regina smiled and looked at him with wide eyes over the rim of her martini.

Across the bar, someone cheered. At the same time, someone else swore. Austin looked up at the baseball game on television and saw the Cubs had just taken the lead in the weekend Cubs vs. Cardinals series. The two teams were huge rivals, hailing from relatively nearby big cities. With Parkville poised halfway between Chicago and St. Louis, there were always an equal number of fans of both teams on hand for any game...which could lead to bar fights from particularly enthusiastic and passionate patrons.

"This game is running way late," he observed.

"I think there was a rain delay in St. Louis," she said.

"That would make sense," he said. "Are you a Cardinals fan?"

"Would it change your mind about me if I was?"

He shook his head. "Not as long as you don't mind going to a Cubs game."

"Oh, are you asking me on a field trip date?"

Austin laughed. "Maybe?"

"Then I can tell you that I think Wrigley Field is one of the most beautiful parks in the world," she said. "But Busch Stadium is really nice too."

"Playing both sides of the field?" he asked.

She shook her head. "Playing both fields. I keep my options open."

"Well played," he said, and raised his pint.

Brandon was there a minute later, asking if he needed a refill. Austin shrugged and got them both another round. When the game ended in Austin's favour an hour later (the Cubs built their lead to a healthy 7-3 after a surprise three-run homer), Austin still couldn't tell for sure which team Regina rooted for…if either. But she did know about baseball and joined him in critiquing umpire calls and defensive strategies employed by both teams.

When it finally ended, and Austin looked at the clock, it was nearly midnight.

"Déjà vu again," he said, pointing at the clock behind the bar.

"The witching hour is nigh," she said. "Do you want to make a wish?"

Austin's chest constricted. The last time he'd been with Regina and made a wish, albeit an offhanded one, very bad things had happened.

"No," he said, shaking his head. "I think I'm good right now."

"Suit yourself," she said with a wink. "But you never know what you could get."

"I hate to say it, but I think what I need to get is home…I should check on Ceili and let Brandy go home."

"She's a big girl," Regina said. "But I'm ready whenever you are."

Austin settled the check and they headed home just after the cuckoo called the hour. Regina followed him in through the garage door. Brandy was sitting on the couch in the family room, reading something on her Kindle. She flashed them a grin and quickly hopped up.

"How was your date?" she asked.

The question made Austin feel a little weird since he really believed he should not be dating anyone this soon after his wife's death. But before he could answer, Regina said, "We had a great time, and Austin discovered I might be a Cardinals fan."

"I did?" he asked, thinking back quickly on all of her baseball comments. In his mind, she had actually never given her allegiance away.

"Or, I might be a Cubs fan," Regina continued, and Austin shook his head.

"Thank you so much for watching her," he told Brandy. "Did you have any problems?"

"She was an angel," the babysitter proclaimed. "I gave her the last bottle about two hours ago, and she's been sleeping ever since."

"She's so good," Regina said.

Austin pulled two twenty-dollar bills from his wallet and offered them to Brandy. The girl slipped them into her front jeans pocket and thanked him before heading to the front door. "Call me whenever you need me," she said, and let herself out.

As the door closed, Regina took his arm and leaned in to give him a peck on the cheek. "Thanks," she said. "I had a really good time."

"Thank *you*," Austin said. "I am so glad we did this."

She didn't say anything, but moved closer to him, as if to give him a hug. But when her hand slipped around his shoulder and drew him closer, she instead leaned up to give him another kiss. On the lips this time.

The heat of her body was palpable, and he let his own arms pull her even closer, enjoying the softness of her body, the silky heat of her lips.

It was instinct and desire and the natural culmination of the evening. He couldn't have pulled away from her if he had wanted to. And while a nagging bite of guilt somehow touched the heat in his chest, it couldn't stop his tongue from answering the tease of her own. She swayed her body slowly as they kissed, her feet edging closer until they touched either side of his. Her hands slid slowly up and down his back, pausing occasionally at the base of his neck to ruffle his hair.

In minutes, they were on the couch, Regina's summer skirt hiked up to expose the soft silken skin of her thighs, and Austin's short-sleeve button-down shirt unbuttoned and hanging loose over her. Regina drew him into her embrace, and they kissed with an increasing fervour that she finally broke when his fingers released the hooks of her bra. He could finally see the full tattoo that had teased him from her cleavage – a five-pointed star inside a circle.

"You haven't shown me your bedroom yet," she whispered.

"It's not that exciting," he said.

"I think it's about to be," she promised.

Austin was off the couch and helping her up in a heartbeat. Regina grabbed her handbag and he took her by the arm to lead her tiptoeing up the stairs. They stopped for a second in front of Ceili's room and peeked in, confirming that the baby was still asleep. And then they were closing the door to Austin's bedroom. He turned up the speaker on the baby monitor, and the static of 'empty' sound warmed the air.

Regina shrugged her shirt to the floor and then she was in his arms, pressing her hands up his ribs and shoulders and working his shirt off as well. Then her hands slipped lower, to unbuckle his belt.

She punctuated her every hand movement with a soft kiss somewhere on his lips or neck or chest. In moments they were nearly naked and beneath the sheets of his bed, grabbing and probing each other with a fever wild and uncontrollable.

Austin gasped for breath at the same time as he pressed his lips to her breasts and belly, needing more of her, his burning need to taste every inch of her overriding his basic need for air.

Regina seemed just as eager. Her mouth covered his skin with kisses as her nails left their marks in his back and butt and thighs. She drew him inside her suddenly and with a desperation that he could not deny.

In the end, when they lay spent and gasping for air next to each other, sweat sticking her hair to his shoulder and the sheets to her breast, Austin whispered one word.

"Wow."

"Yeah," she agreed. "That was pretty all right."

He snorted. "That was the best ever."

"You're easy to please," she said, rolling over to lie atop his chest. She kissed him lightly. "But I think we can do even better."

"We do much better and you'll kill me," he said. "I still can't catch my breath."

She slapped his hip. "You're out of shape. We'll fix that."

Austin grinned. "This is the kind of workout I don't mind at all."

Regina held his face in one palm and stared down into his eyes. "I hope not," she said. "Because I'd like to see what the best ever really *could* be like."

He stifled a yawn. "I can't even imagine," he said.

"You need sleep," Regina said, pushing off of him a little. "Ceili will probably wake up in a couple hours, right?"

"Yeah, probably," he said. "She'll go four or five hours sometimes."

"If you want, I can get up with her later," Regina offered, and then tilted her head quizzically. "That is, if you don't mind me sleeping over?"

Austin's eyes opened in shock. "Well, you're not going home after that!"

"Good," she smiled. "Because I really don't want to."

She sat up in the bed, and the sheets fell away from her. Austin admired her in the moonlight as she slipped her legs onto the floor.

"Let me just take care of one thing and I'll be right back," she promised, and then grabbed her handbag and disappeared into the bathroom. Austin heard the faucet run a moment later. He lay in bed staring at the ceiling, flashes of their lovemaking playing back in his head.

★   ★   ★

In the bathroom, Regina sat down on the toilet and opened her bag. She withdrew a tiny plastic jar and a thin wooden spoon. She set the jar on the countertop next to her and then pressed the wooden spoon between her legs. She closed her eyes and wiggled it deeper between the folds before withdrawing and holding it up to the light. The spoon glimmered with a pale milky white payload. She smiled and fingered the slippery substance into the jar.

Regina repeated the process three more times until she was satisfied, and then she put a lid on the small jar and returned it to her purse before finally urinating and washing off her hands and the small spoon.

She took a long drink of water, and stared into the eyes that looked back at her from the mirror. They were filled with a golden fire, and a thin smile woke the corners of her mouth. Then she nodded with satisfaction at her reflection and turned out the light.

Austin was already almost asleep when she slid back beside him in the bed. She touched his cheek and he moaned softly in appreciation.

"Sweet dreams, my prince," she whispered.

CHAPTER TEN

Austin woke on Sunday morning to the smell of bacon. His stomach instantly rumbled in anticipation. He pulled on his navy-blue University of Illinois shorts and a grey T-shirt and after brushing his teeth, walked down the hallway to check on Ceili.

Her crib was empty, so he continued downstairs to the kitchen.

Ceili was sitting bright-eyed in her high chair. Her hands waved anxiously in the air when he entered the room.

"Hey there, baby girl," he said with a smile.

"I haven't been called that in a while," Regina said from the stove behind him.

He turned and laughed. "I meant Ceili, silly."

She faked a hurt look with downturned lips and eyes, and he shook his head. "But you're a beautiful *big* girl," he said.

She put a hand on her hip. She'd clearly been in his closet this morning – she wore one of his Chicago Cubs World Series T-shirts and from the way it draped her body, she apparently wore nothing else. It hung halfway down her thighs, but somehow looked as sexy as lingerie on her.

"Big? Are you calling me fat?" she asked.

"Not in a million years," he said, and slipped one arm behind her to draw her close for a kiss. She allowed him one quick peck but then pushed him back. "You'll burn the bacon," she complained. "Go sit down."

She had already set the table with plates and glasses of orange juice. After she stirred the frying pan, she walked over to the table with a pot of coffee and poured him some in the black mug near his plate.

"Damn, full service," he said.

"You shouldn't swear in front of the baby," she said.

Next to him, Ceili cooed and slapped her hands against the

high-chair tray, sending a cascade of Cheerios to the floor. It was as if she knew that Regina was talking about her.

"I'll try to behave better," he said, stroking the soft blond curls on Ceili's head. The baby's eyes lit up and she grabbed with tiny fingers at his arm.

A moment later, Regina carried a frying pan to the table and spooned out a pile of scrambled eggs onto both his plate and an empty one next to his. Then she put the pan in the sink and returned with a plate of perfectly crisped bacon strips. He reached out and took two with just a little bit of pink tenderness still left in them and a white ruffle of fat on the ends.

"I could get used to this," he said, shovelling a forkful of eggs into his mouth and then moaning in appreciation. "I love onions and cheese in my eggs," he said a moment later. "I didn't even know we had any cheese left!"

Regina smiled and crunched a strip of bacon.

"So, you didn't mind me sleeping over?" she said finally.

He shook his head. "You can sleep at my house anytime you like."

"I might just take you up on that," she said. "I am going to have to leave you after breakfast though. I've got some things I need to do today."

Austin finished chewing a mouthful of eggs and asked, "Will I see you later?"

"Do you *want* to see me later?"

He nodded eagerly.

Regina smiled, and took a sip of orange juice. Then she suggested, "Since I made breakfast, maybe you can burn us some meat on the grill tonight."

"It's a deal," he said.

After breakfast, Regina disappeared upstairs and returned a few minutes later wearing the dress she'd had on the night before and carrying her thin leather sandals. She kissed the top of Ceili's head and then did the same to Austin's. She pulled away before he could draw her into a real kiss.

"I'll be back to check on my babies later," she said. "Be good."

Austin walked her to the door. He was still standing there when she reached the porch of the house next door. She waved, and then disappeared inside.

*   *   *

Regina crossed the dusty family room of the house next door and walked straight to the kitchen. The room was bare; the counter tops were empty of dishes or clutter, and there was a breakfast nook that was meant to hold a small table, with a bay window facing the back yard. However, the nook was empty of anything but dust.

She opened the white-painted cabinet doors above the sink. That space was *not* empty. Regina shuffled some things around until she found the bottle she wanted. She set it to one side and then brought down a small satchel and another jar filled with brown leaves. She jammed it all in her handbag and walked through the kitchen to another room down the hall. When the house had been built, the room had been intended to serve as a bedroom.

But now....

The room was empty but for one thing on the far wall. An altar. The one window to the outside was shuttered, and so the altar hid in grey twilight. Regina quickly resolved that. She picked up a pack of matches and walked about the room lighting the three candles in each corner – black tapered stalks that rose from candelabras set on the bare wooden floor.

At last, she lit the thick blood-red candle in the centre of the small wooden altar. The guttering flame reflected on the golden crucifix suspended upside down from a wire tacked in the ceiling.

Regina reached into her bag and retrieved three bottles, the satchel and the jar with the semen she'd rescued the night before. Then she walked back to the kitchen. In the bay window, there was a small terrarium with several plants growing inside. She reached in and pinched off a leaf of *Atropa belladonna*, better known as deadly nightshade. Then she picked up a small pot that held a Venus flytrap and returned to her special room. She set the plant on the altar and withdrew the wooden spoon from her handbag. Carefully, she unscrewed the top of the jar, and withdrew a small string of semen. She held it over the open mouth of the flytrap plant, and the mucous-y strand soon elongated until a large drop released from the spoon and fell into the mouth of the plant.

The flytrap snapped shut, its green 'fingers' gripping and hiding the residue of Austin's lovemaking like a prisoner.

"Only in the darkness can we see the light," she whispered. With her fingernails, she severed the closed leaves of the trap. She placed the severed pod in the small brown satchel, and then dropped in the nightshade leaves along with a pinch from a jar of white bone powder. The label on the jar read *Carolyn*. She crumbled a brown stem and leaf on top of that, and then walked to the side of the altar where she retrieved a tall thin plastic cup, the kind joggers and bicyclists carry to stay hydrated. Only this one wasn't filled with water. The plastic inside was beaded with moisture at the top from condensation and a long thin red thing smeared against the plastic. Regina didn't hesitate, but retrieved the used tampon, and held it over the satchel, squeezing at the bottom of the tube until two crimson drops from her last period fell into the bag to coat the leaves.

She wrinkled her nose at the odour, and then returned the tampon to the jar, screwing the lid back on tight.

"Only mine," she spoke softly, and then said several words that sounded ancient and filled with arcane meaning. Then she held the satchel up to the feet of the figure on the upside-down cross above the altar.

"Mine for eternity," she said.

CHAPTER ELEVEN

"How would you like to go out to a *real* club tonight?" Regina asked.

It was Friday night, just three weeks since Angie's death, but his past life already seemed like another life.

"I guess I would," Austin said, unbuttoning the first and second buttons of his blue dress shirt. He had just walked in from the garage and couldn't wait to get out of his work clothes and start the weekend. "But I didn't think Parkville had a real club. And...I didn't set up a babysitter."

"It does, and I did." Regina smiled. "I plan ahead, you know?"

Austin laughed. "You're amazing. Let's do it. I am so glad this week is over. I want to celebrate."

"Perfect. I already asked Brandy if she could come by around seven. She loves Ceili. We could grab something for dinner and then head out from there."

"I'm in," Austin said. "Out on the town twice in one week? That's crazy talk!"

"Let me go home and change," Regina said. "I'll be back in a few."

*   *   *

The doorbell rang a half-hour later, and Austin answered the door with Ceili in 'burp position' on his shoulder. Brandy stood outside, wearing black lounge pants and a Taylor Swift concert T-shirt.

"Hey," she said. "Regina said you needed me."

He nodded. "Yes. Come on in. I guess we're going out."

"You *guess*?" a voice came from just beyond the hedge. "I thought you wanted to go out. Cuz, if not, I suppose...."

Austin shook his head anxiously as Regina stepped into view. "I do, I do," he insisted. "And, by the way, you look amazing."

"Flattery will get you everywhere," she said, stepping onto the stoop.

Regina wore one of her trademark blue and purple paisley dresses with intricately strapped brown sandals and silver earrings in the shape of the moon. Her hair was pulled back and twisted into a bun, making her cheeks look thinner than usual. There was a hint of rouge on her face too, and maybe mascara; her eyes looked sleeker than he was used to seeing when he walked in after a long day at work.

"You clean up good," he pronounced.

Regina stepped past him and into the house. "You sure know how to make a girl feel special," she said.

Austin followed her back into the family room, where, when he entered, Regina was already giving Brandy instructions for the night. He suddenly felt like the 'extra' instead of the 'head' of this house. And yet…it was comfortable to have Regina taking control. It took some of the pressure off.

She turned and took the baby from him, kissing Ceili on the head as she did.

"We should be home by two," she promised. "Text me if you have any questions, okay?"

"Wow," Austin said. "We're staying out until two?"

Regina shrugged. "Keeping our options open!"

She started walking toward the door and Austin said, "Hang on, let me grab my keys."

She shook her head. "I'll drive this time," she said. "Beats giving you directions."

He raised his eyebrows. He hadn't even realised that she had a car. Stupid, but he'd never seen her drive one.

"Just call me a kept man," he laughed.

Regina only nodded. "I'll take care of you."

Regina drove them to a part of town that Austin had never explored, which was weird, because Parkville really wasn't that big. But once they crossed over the freight train tracks and weaved through a few twists into an old brick-housed subdivision he'd never turned into, Austin found that he really didn't quite know where he was.

"There's a little Asian place here that is really amazing," Regina said. And a moment later, they pulled into a strip-mall parking lot near a sign that promised a *Joyful Plate*.

"Sounds happy," he observed.

"Joyful Plate is not a joking matter," she warned. "This is seriously good food. And if you don't think so…we might have to reevaluate our relationship."

"Wait," he said. "We have a relationship?"

She slapped him.

*   *   *

The food was as good as she had suggested. Austin ordered the Pad Kee Mao (Drunken Noodles), which came beautifully colourful with yellow baby corns, white onions, red peppers and fresh green basil mixed throughout wide rice noodles. The flavour was intense and amazing, and he moaned in pleasure at the first bite.

Regina had a yellow curry with chicken, which he also tried. His eyes widened at the flavour, and he shook his head.

"How have I lived here for over a year and never found this place?"

"Look around," Regina said quietly.

He did and grinned in acknowledgement.

There were six tables and an equal number of booths in the restaurant, and four of them were empty. The rest were filled with Asian customers. They were the only white people there.

"Point taken," he said. "It's apparently a family secret."

"You can thank me later," Regina said.

He drank the last sip of his Thai iced tea and said, "I'm ready to thank you now."

She shook her head. "Our night is only just beginning. Are you ready for the main event?"

"After that meal, I'm probably ready for a nap," he said.

She pursed her lips and gave him a bitter raspberry. "It's the weekend," she said. "Try to keep up."

A quiet, thin Asian girl arrived at just that moment with the check and bowed slightly as she set it on the table in front of him.

Austin nodded in answer without thinking and dropped his credit card on the black vinyl check holder. It disappeared a moment later, as he was busy tearing the wrapper off his fortune cookie.

"You will see things you have never thought to see," he read. "Magic numbers 6, 13, 52, 15."

Regina smiled. "Mine says, 'There are those who would say stop. But you must always go.'"

"I like that," he said.

"I suspect a guy wrote it," she said. "What do you think, are you ready?"

He signed the receipt and nodded. "Take me to the party," he said.

★   ★   ★

It had not quite been sunset when they'd walked into the Joyful Plate, but it was nearly dark when they walked out. They'd parked just around the block on the street, and Austin slipped into the passenger's seat of her Civic and groaned as the meal shifted.

"Oh my God, I am full," he complained.

"We need to get you a drink or two," she said. "Ease the digestion."

He smiled. "You just want to get me drunk."

She shrugged. "Whatever works." She reached into her handbag and pulled out a long black silk scarf. "In the meantime, I need you to humour me."

"How do you mean?"

"Well, there's a reason that you've never heard of the club we're about to go to," she said. "It's a private club, and if you don't know about it, you don't know where it is. And until you're a member, you *can't* know where it is. So...."

She held the scarf up in the air in front of his face. He got the drift quickly.

"You want to blindfold me?" he said, aghast.

"Do you mind?" she asked with a hint of pleading in her voice. "I promise it will be worth it. But...I can't bring a neophyte there without having his eyes covered. It's the rules."

"Huh," he said. "I seriously didn't think there were places like that left in the world, let alone here in Parkville."

He shrugged and bent forward, extending his face toward her. "Have at it," he said. "I'm yours."

Regina's face was impassive. "I am glad you said that," she said, and brought the silk close to his eyes. "It will make things a lot more enjoyable."

"What things?" Austin asked. It seemed an odd turn of phrase.

"You'll see," she promised, and with that, the car jolted away from the curb. Austin settled back in the seat for the ride, not knowing how long he'd have to stay in the dark. As it turned out, it wasn't long. He felt the car turn to the right twice and bounced in his seat a bit when one of the roads they drove down was clearly in need of repair. The potholes were palpable…against his ass. Then the car rolled over a stretch of bumps and gravel to a stop and Regina said, "We're here."

Austin reached to undo his seatbelt, and she put her hand on his arm. "Wait a minute," she said. He sat still and heard her rustling in her bag. Then she pressed a wet finger to his forehead, drawing it down toward his nose, then crossing it horizontally.

"What's that?" he asked.

"Call it…the Mark of Cain," she said.

"Um, okay…." he said. "But I didn't kill anyone."

"Not yet," she said.

He snorted. "What kind of club is this?"

"Don't worry," she laughed. "You're going to love it. But we have to do something to make sure the posers don't get in. So… we have our ways. You need a blindfold and a mark to show you're mine…and they'll let you pass."

The blindfold had seemed a little freaky, and he had to admit for a few moments he'd wondered if Regina was actually going to kidnap him for some reason. Then he'd thought of the past couple of nights with her in his bed and he'd shrugged the worry away. But to be anointed before walking blind into some exclusive club? His stomach suddenly felt cold and nervous, instead of hot and full.

"This all seems…really weird, I have to tell you," he said.

"I know," she said, and kissed him on the cheek. Her lips were soft and lingered there a moment. "But it'll be worth it, you'll see. This place is amazing. That's why it's a secret. Now, stay there a second and let me come get you so you don't trip and knock yourself out."

She pushed away from him and got out of the car. The door slammed, and for a second, his nerves began to knot and bind. He almost tore the blindfold off, but then his door was opening and Regina was there, putting her hand on his arm and guiding him out onto the sidewalk.

"You're not going to strip me naked and then take my blindfold off and I realise I'm standing on the stage of the Pickwick Theatre in front of a big crowd or something, are you?"

She laughed. "Not even close."

She guided him along a sidewalk. The neighbourhood, wherever they were, seemed ultra-quiet. He didn't hear kids or dogs barking. Just the hum of generators and distant traffic noise. It was silent enough that he could almost hear the breeze as it blew past his face, rippling the ends of the blindfold.

"Here we are," she said presently, and guided him down a sidewalk and up a step.

Something buzzed, and he heard her say her name. And then a door clicked open and she pulled him inside a building.

As soon as they stepped across the threshold, Austin could hear that they were near a club. Suddenly the pounding of a techno beat reverberated against his feet. The floor vibrated and as Regina walked him down a hallway, it grew deeper and more intense. He could hear the oscillating hooks of a synthesiser and the throbbing dark electronics of a dance bass as they opened another door and suddenly his ears were awash in the sound.

"Dying in the moment I feel/a bullet from your eyes," a seductively low-key male voice crooned from overhead.

A closer male voice addressed Regina. "What have we here?" he said. "Will he be baptised tonight?"

"Soon, I hope," she said. "But not tonight."

"Then you know the rules," he said. "Blind coming and going. He did not see how to come here, did he?"

"I know the rules," she said. "He's been blindfolded since we got in the car. And I'll cover his eyes for the ride home. But now, I think he should be allowed to see."

"That is your choice," the voice said.

Regina's hands slipped up Austin's cheeks, and beneath the silken blindfold. She drew it up and off of his head, and he heaved a sigh of relief as his eyes met hers again. They were sparkling in the low light of the black-walled club they stood within.

"Cell phones, please," the man said. Austin turned and saw a thin man in black eye makeup holding out two tickets.

"Can't have people taking and posting pictures inside the club," Regina explained, and handed her phone to the man, who gave her a ticket in exchange. Austin reached into his pocket and grudgingly turned over his own. Then Regina grabbed his arm and spun him around to face a crowded main dancehall.

"Now, look around," she said. "This is one of my favourite places in the world. Welcome to Club Equinox."

CHAPTER TWELVE

The room was alive in red and blue lights and moving, gyrating people. The music built and peaked, growling voices on top of pounding beats and pulsing electronic noises.

"I hope you like to dance," Regina said, grabbing his hand and pulling him out of the entryway and onto the wooden floor. There were dozens of couples there already, most of them dressed in a mix of black and violet. Some of the guys wore black eye makeup and fishnet sleeves, which made Austin raise an eyebrow. He had never seen a goth in Parkville, but obviously, they were here. Apparently hiding out in Club Equinox.

"Just relax and let the beat move you," Regina instructed. Which he interpreted to mean that she thought he was dancing like he had a stick up his ass. And that appraisal didn't surprise him at all. Austin would much rather *watch* the dance floor than be on it. Nevertheless, he tried to surrender to the throbbing bass lines and follow Regina's fluid arm and hip movements as they moved and shifted deeper into the crowd. He didn't recognise the music, but he appreciated the dark aura of the place. There were pinpoints of light across the ceiling and the walls, and purple, red and blue glows from all corners. But the light didn't truly 'light' the room; it just created a wall of moving shadows. It hid more than it unveiled, and so Austin could feel more secure in letting his body move the way it wanted to with the music. Who could see him in the shifting shadows?

He focused, not on the crowd, but on Regina herself. She danced in front of him like an exotic goddess, her hands and hips moving and gyrating in sensual rounds and rhythms that he could never hope to match. He could only echo her dance and serve as the foil to her beauty. The rich purple paisley dress she'd worn tonight seemed oddly at home here, though most of the women wore more overtly counter-culture extreme garments; black leather and latex were popular, as were outfits of chains and mesh and lace.

The walls of the dance hall were dotted with T-shaped windows that glowed blue and purple; Austin wasn't sure if they were stained glass, or if it was just the lights behind the glass that were tinted. But they gave the whole room an eerie, church-like aura. A stairway curved from the floor up to a darker upper level where more figures shifted.

After a couple of songs, Regina led Austin to a bar on the far side of the lower level. It was almost as crowded as the dance floor, but it was better lit. Two well-tattooed women and a tall, swarthy guy moved up and down the bar. They all wore the same black tank top with a logo and the word *Equinox* in white on their chests – the word glowed purple-hot thanks to black lights above the bar.

"What's your poison?" she asked, as they found a rare empty space at the bar.

"You?" he asked.

"Nice, but you can't drink me in public. Choose again."

"Hmmm, do they have IPAs here, or is this one of those gothy places that just has absinthe?"

"Oh, we like our bitter beer here on the dark side too. I think you'll be surprised."

At that moment, a waitress wearing jeans, belt chains and an old faded black crop top that read *The 13th Floor* across her chest leaned on the wood of the bar and asked, "What are you having?"

Regina ordered a Bombay gin martini with extra olives, and Austin smiled inside. No froufrou flavoured vodka stuff tonight – Regina could order a real martini when she wanted to.

"Do you have Revolution or Lagunitas on tap?" he asked. She nodded.

"I can do both on draught. You want Anti-Hero or Lil' Sumpin' Sumpin'? Or we have Citra Hero in cans."

Tough choice. Both of his two go-to beers on tap?

"I'll take an Anti-Hero," he said after a pause. She nodded and disappeared to fill their order.

"So, what do you think?" Regina asked. "Did I do okay?"

Austin looked around the dark club filled with flashing lights and writhing bodies and nodded.

"I didn't know we had a club in Parkville," he said. "I figured you'd have to go to Chicago to find a place like this."

"Oh, they exist everywhere," she said. "You just need to know the right people to find them. There are some versions that don't even stay in the same building from night to night. They crop up once a month in a new place every time and people only get in by invitation. So, you really have to be part of the in-crowd to go to those. This one isn't that crazy; it's here all the time. But there are a lot of people who wouldn't allow this kind of club to exist if they knew it was here. So...we don't let them know."

"I thought you were new to Parkville," he said. "How do you know about it?"

Regina took a sip of her martini and smiled. "New to Parkville," she said, "but not to the network. I can always find a home, wherever I may roam!"

"Well, I get that there are a lot of goths here," he said. "But what is so special about this place that it needs to be secret? I mean, they're just playing gloomy synth music. And people are wearing a lot of black. Speaking of which, I'm underdressed. You could have warned me." He gestured around the room. "But seriously, what's the big deal? It's a dance club."

"You haven't seen it all," she said. "This is the main floor. It's basically just the entrance. People come here from all over – in fact, most of the people you see probably aren't from Parkville at all. There are rooms in the back where people do a lot more than dance. And the upstairs...you have to know someone to get in there."

"Do way more than dance, huh?" he said. "Sounds...um... interesting. What kind of club did you bring me to exactly?"

Regina winked. "The kind of place your mother would have told you to stay away from."

"That's not saying much," he said. "My mother wasn't happy unless you were on your knees praying for one cause or another."

"They like it if you get on your knees here," she said. "But it rarely has anything to do with praying."

Austin raised an eyebrow. "Wow," he laughed. "Okay then."

"Do you still want to see the upstairs?" she asked.

He hesitated for a moment, but then nodded. "I'm not a prude."

"That's a start," she said. "But Equinox tests more than your crotch."

She rose then and motioned for him to do the same. He picked up his pint glass and followed her as she moved through the middle of the dance floor, avoiding the twirls and arm motions of the throng until they reached the other side. Then she started up a black wrought-iron stairway that curved around as it climbed into the air. Austin held the cold metal rail tighter the higher they got; the loft of the club was high in the air, especially when you looked down from a narrow curving staircase.

Regina reached the top but didn't immediately step out onto the floor. There was a man there, blocking the exit. He was clearly screening people before letting them pass. He was tall and thin, his face long and drawn and pale, especially so in the lights of the club. Austin couldn't help but think that he looked like death warmed over.

Regina extended her arm and pulled up her sleeve. The man looked at a tattoo there, and then motioned for her to pass. She grabbed Austin's hand, and pulled him from the stairway onto the wooden floor of the loft. Before he even looked around, Austin grabbed at Regina's other hand.

"What did you show him?" he asked. "Why did he let us in?"

She smiled and turned slightly to give him a better view of her shoulder. Then she pushed her shirtsleeve up until he could see the blue and grey outline of a tattoo. It resembled the shape of the number six, only the top section ended in the open fangs of a snake, and the bottom loop extended beyond the shape of the number, to display the thin flange of the serpent's tail.

"What does it mean?" he asked.

"Call it the Mark of the Beast," she said. "If you decide you want to come to Equinox on your own without me, you'll need to get one yourself. If you pass the test."

"Test?" he said. "I thought this was a club, not a university."

She grinned. "It is a club…and a way of life. There's no way to keep it under the radar if just anyone can wander in off the street. So…there's a test of sorts. Call it an initiation. It proves you're really one of us, not just a thrill-seeker."

"Interesting," he said. "But what about me? I'm here, and I'm not a member."

"You're here on my honour. And if you say anything about the club that exposes it, I'll be renounced. So…behave."

"Damn," he said. "Exactly what do I have to do to…um… behave?"

"Just follow my lead," she said. "And don't talk about anything you see here when you go to work on Monday."

"Nobody would believe that I went to a goth club anyway," he said.

"Well, it's not really a goth club," she said, and motioned for him to look around the upstairs room.

That's when he noticed the difference between the downstairs and the up. Here, there was no dance floor. There was a metal railing that extended around the edge, with a bar rail and stools, so people could peer over to watch the floor of the club below. And there were a few people doing just that. But behind them, there was no dancing.

There were people hanging from chains.

Austin's eyes bugged a little when he realised what was going on behind the rail.

There were wooden torture racks along the shadowed wall at the far end, and men and women were cuffed or tied to the rails. Behind them, people stood with whips and floggers, and doled out punishment – or pleasure, depending on the perspective – one swing at a time.

The people hanging in chains from the ceiling had a different fate. People walked past them, and reached out to fondle their privates, not seeming to care whether the hangers were male or female. Austin watched aghast as a couple holding martini glasses walked along the line of chained men and women, all naked or nearly so. The two reached up to each and every chained person and fingered thighs and bellies and sex organs alike. The men responded visibly, the women less so, but their moans betrayed them.

"So, it's not a goth club, but a sex and bondage club?" he said.

Regina shrugged. "Yes," she said. "And no. You'll see. Equinox is not a place that is easily defined for most people. It's not just about music…or goths…or BDSM…or pain…or pleasure. It is about all of those things…but it's about so much more. It's really a magical place that I can't begin to explain, but I can try to show you."

"I don't have to get chained up, do I?" he asked. He was starting to feel a little worried.

Regina laughed. "Not unless you want to. Nobody here is doing anything they don't want to do, just remember that."

"Okay," he said, but he knew his voice sounded unsure.

Regina caught the inflection. "Follow me," she said, and began to walk along the rail. They passed a dozen people hung from the ceiling. Some clung to the bars of metal cages, others were wrapped in heavy chains. All looked out at the people milling about below them, and many received their attentions in the form of both slaps and caresses.

"Where are we going?" Austin asked as they wound around the upstairs room.

"One of my favourite places," she said. And just as she said it, she walked away from the railing, and toward a small door that led inward, away from the open expanse of the upstairs club.

When she reached the door, Regina gestured for him to step inside. He hesitated but stepped around her and entered the room.

He was confused at first by the tableau within. There was a mix of tables and beds. And a wide array of people in varying states of undress.

But one thing was in common. All were covered in grease and alcohol and…food.

"This is the tasting room," Regina explained. "Here, people can eat and drink whatever and however much they want. There are no restrictions. If they join Club Equinox for the tasting room, they will eat and drink their fill always."

"Holy shit," Austin whispered. What he saw was like a scene from some bizarre surreal painting.

As he looked around, he saw women with barbecue sauce and chunks of meat sticking to their naked breasts and men with enormous guts sitting with gallon-size glass mugs that looked to be filled with beer in front of them. The one closest to Austin had chest hair as wooly as a sheep, and slivers of meat and chunks of fat stuck to his naked chest. But the man didn't seem to care if he was sloppy…he had also eschewed utensils. He reached out with a fat fist to grab a handful of something that looked like potatoes covered in dark gravy and slopped the mess into his wide, hungry mouth. Bits dripped onto his hairy body, but he didn't react. Instead, with a greasy paw, he reached out to the gallon of beer and upended it into his mouth until suds escaped his lips and leaked into the tufts of hair below on his chest. The beer only served to wash fragments of meat and potatoes lower, and that's where Austin's gaze ended. He did not want to focus on the crusted debris of lost meals that had ended up caked in the dark mess of the man's lap.

A woman stood near him, helping him to reach the smorgasbord of food nearby. She handed him chicken legs and slopped potatoes and pudding and more onto his plate.

But he was just one of dozens of gluttons in the room. Near him, an equally large woman lay naked on a rubber platform table, surrounded by food. Her heavy breasts were slathered in meats and gravies; her middle was nearly obscured by grilled squash and beans and peas and asparagus, and between her thighs there were mounds of potatoes and pasta salads and coleslaw and corn and more. She reached out one by one for all of it, sucking one handful after another into her mouth. Her hips seemed to shake with every bite…it was clearly a sexual experience for her, to wallow in food. To eat. To gorge.

"This is disgusting," Austin said after a minute looking around the room at similar indulgences of excess. At people swimming in food, and clearly – some of them loudly – getting off on it.

"Eye of the beholder," Regina said. "It's not my thing, but here, they can do their thing. Who am I to say no?"

"I thought you said this was one of your favourite places," he said.

Regina shook her head. "No, we're just taking a shortcut through here. Follow me and be careful not to slip. You can pick up some nasty stains in this room. Trust me."

Regina wound carefully around the smorgasbord, stepping over people who had collapsed in an overindulged stupor to the floor amid piles of discarded bones and spilled slop. Austin threaded his way behind her, around two long banquet tables covered in black tablecloths and silver meat serving and carving trays. She nodded at what was apparently one of the room's servers – he was wearing black pants and a black buttoned shirt, with a burgundy vest. In his hand, he held a long carving knife. A huge platter with a pig's head and a pile of thin sliced pork sat on the table before him.

"Hungry?" he asked, and Regina laughed.

"I'm on a diet."

The server shook his head and shooshed her. "Never say that," he said. "Not in here."

Regina's lips creased; she knew very well that what she'd said was off limits in a glutton's paradise. "Oops," she said, "I wasn't thinking." She passed the man with a wink and a secret chuckle that said she'd known exactly what she was doing.

And then they were out of the room, and into a dark corridor beyond. Austin realised how rich the air of the dining room had been. Suddenly all of the thick smells evaporated, and instead of roasting meat and curry and other heady mouthwatering scents, he smelled...mothballs.

There were small silver wall sconces lit with flickering candles. The flames wavered as they stepped past, throwing an eerie undulating light against the avocado-green of the corridor walls. The floor was of some kind of thin tile; Regina's shoes clacked against it with short staccato beats.

"Where are we going?" Austin asked.

They reached a staircase that wound down to a room below. She put one hand on the black wrought-iron rail and turned to smile at him. "I'm taking you to kind of a club within the club. It's called the Cloister."

He followed her down the narrow winding steps until they stepped off onto a beautiful, well-polished oaken floor.

Austin looked around the room and stifled the urge to whistle. They stood in a long ballroom with an arched ceiling. Pillars of marble supported buttresses that held up the tall ceiling. Each pillar was carved with an ornate figurehead; the faces of monks and nuns and other figures peered down upon the room from the bottom of the ceiling arch. They looked down upon the room as if sneering or smirking at the inhabitants.

And there were quite a few people in the room. One dark wood wall hosted the richly polished wood of a bar, and a man dressed in black moved back and forth behind it, juggling martini shakers and pint glasses and a bottle opener with the fluid ease of a longtime professional. Several people sat nodding and gesticulating around the bar, though the room itself seemed strangely quiet outside of the clinks of glasses and ice. There were also low tables with cushioned lounge chairs set at intervals between the pillars. Regina spotted one that was open and beelined toward a small loveseat with a round wagon-wheel table in front of it. Two empty leather chairs faced the small couch on the other side of the low table.

"Do you mind sitting here?" she asked softly. "These are almost never open."

"Sure," he agreed, and a moment later he eased his back into some of the most luxuriously soft leather he had ever felt.

"Oh my God, that's amazing," he breathed, shifting his back and shoulders against the supple leather.

As if on cue, a nun in a long black habit and white guimpe across her shoulders and chest approached them from a nearby pillar.

"Uh-oh," Regina said softly. There was humour in her tone. "You took the name of God in vain. You shouldn't do that in here."

The sister stepped up to the table in front of them with her hands pressed together in front of her chest in the universal sign of prayer. She didn't say a word, but shook her head slowly, and bowed slightly. Then she raised her arms to the air, as if reaching out to God himself.

That was when Austin realised that the black of her habit was actually not the appropriate material of a habit at all. It wasn't the stern cloth of any nun he had ever seen. It was sheer silk that completely showed off the fact that this 'sister' was not wearing any other clothing underneath. When she raised her arms, the white drape of the guimpe shifted up and Austin could see the globes of the woman's breasts pushing through the almost transparent black beneath. Her nipples were obvious against the sheer fabric, as was the dark cleft of her sex.

A moment later she brought her hands back down in a symbol of prayer that once again hid her chest, and she walked away.

"What was *that?*" Austin asked, turning to Regina.

She put a finger to his lips and pulled it down until his lower lip curled over to expose the tender pink skin normally inside his mouth. "Shhh," she said. "In the Cloister the golden rule is silence."

"She was not a nun," he whispered.

"Who are you to say?" Regina said softly. "A sister is simply a member of a religious community who has taken vows. Some of chastity, some of obedience. What do you know of her vows?"

"Nuns don't walk around half-naked," he insisted.

"Maybe not Catholic ones, but I can assure you that Catholicism is not her sect."

"So then what kind of nun is she?" he asked.

Regina put her fingers on his lips once more. "Just watch," she suggested. "Listen. Enjoy."

Austin was perplexed but held his tongue. After the shock of seeing a half-naked nun had worn off, the oddity of being shown this bizarre place by his 'girlfriend' set in. He'd realised from the start that Regina was different to any girl he'd ever known. She was earthy in a hippy-esque way; she wore clothes that reminded him of old sixties movies and always seemed to take things in stride. But she wasn't lackadaisical and slow, like a throwback flower child who smoked pot all the time. She was sharp, keen-witted and he often had a time keeping up with her. She referred to esoteric things in everyday conversation as if they were normal, and sometimes he needed to ask what she was even talking about. Sometimes he was too embarrassed to ask. Regina could run rings around him, and that was not something he was used to at all. She was an exotic mystery that he was enjoying unravelling more with every day.

She'd proven a highly erotic and sensual partner in bed over the past week, which was a welcome surprise. But he hadn't expected her to bring him to a club where people were being whipped, hung from the ceiling in cages and walked around in outfits that would get them arrested on the street. It was a lot to take in.

A moment later the 'nun' came back with two menus that had been hand-drawn on parchment and fastened with corner holders to a darkly stained piece of polished wood. Regina nodded when the menu was presented to her but said nothing. Austin followed her lead and found himself strangely embarrassed to meet the nun's eyes. But if he looked lower, he was staring at her chest. He could feel his face flushing slightly, and quickly bent to stare at the menu.

The drink names read like a list of witch's potions:

Selene's Spell
Lavender-infused Three Women Vodka with seven drops of aged blood orange aired for power beneath the light of the last full moon. *Sensual and serene.*

Arcane Wisdom
Fifteen-year Four Roses Bourbon buried beneath a crypt in Resurrection Cemetery for thirty-one days with a stalk of rare vermillion sage and poured over grave mint leaves and ice. *Sip the promise of transcendence.*

Red Tide
Three Women Vodka aged with Samsara rose petals and shaken with crushed raspberries and three drops of Sister Evangeline Lust Oil and one splash Coitus Burgundy wine. *Prepare to be naked.*

Spirit Unbridled
Three Women Gin poured over midnight-picked rosemary and Mediterranean olives anointed by the flower of a virgin and aged beneath a whore's pillow for three nights. *Open your mind to all.*

Austin read the menu with increasing disbelief. Coitus wine? Bourbon aged in a crypt? Olives slept on by a whore? What the hell was this shit? He had to admit they did keep with the theme, but he didn't buy the exotic ingredients one bit.

He leaned over to Regina and whispered, "No Miller Lite here, huh?"

She snorted and shook her head. But then she pointed to a listing on the right side of the menu that held the beer-related offerings.

Seminal Milk
Cask-conditioned Irish stout brewed with vanilla beans used in the Dark Night Festival and semen spilled on the Venus Altar. *Drink the milk of life.*

Passion Mead
Ancient mead imbued with the harvest of the Secret Procession and blessed by the Bishop and Irreverent Mother. *Your vision may steam.*

Bitter Love
Mosaic Hops steeped in the gold of the Cloister Servants during the Maypole Celebration. Steam brewed for clarity. Earthy, bitter and bright at the same time. *See with the focus of lust.*

Blood Wine
Grapes imported from the secret vineyard of the original Cloister. Crushed by the bodies of the Sisterhood. Sweetened by the innocence of the November Girl. Soured by the sins of the Head Master. *Your heart will pound.*

Austin grimaced as he read the descriptions. "They don't really put cum in the stout, do they?" he whispered. "Or real blood in the wine?"

Regina nodded. "Just a small amount, to bring the magic of the ceremonies into the brewing. The alcohol kills the flavour. The Seminal Milk is really sweet."

"You've tried these?"

She grinned. "I've helped make some of them."

He opened his mouth to say something, but then the nun was back. She said nothing but raised her eyebrows. Regina smiled and pointed at something on the menu and then the nun turned her gaze to him. He was torn between sticking with hard liquor to kill any of the funkiness that they supposedly added to the drinks here and trying a beer. But there was no way he was drinking anything with 'man's milk' in it, so instead of the stout, he pointed to the Bitter Love. He was a hops guy anyway, and bitter was always good.

When the nun walked away, Regina turned toward him and put one hand on his shoulder. "I know it's a lot to take in the first time," she whispered. "But just relax. It's meant to take your mind off the outside. This is a secret place, with secret rituals. When you are here…release yourself and enjoy the freedom of being here. There is no other place right now."

She leaned in to kiss him, and her lips were warm. Wet. Her hand pressed down on the zipper of his jeans and he realised that he had the start of an erection…which she was only making worse.

"Drink and let go," she whispered in his ear before biting at the lobe. "That's all I ask you to do tonight. Don't judge and don't hold back. Just do what you feel."

Their drinks arrived; the nun carried them on a small silver carrier in the shape of an X. Its four short arms each had a round indentation for a glass. Austin couldn't help but think that it would be too easy to overbalance the thing and end up with glass on the floor, but he tried to follow Regina's advice and put his brain on hold.

The beer was cool and cloudy – in the dark shadows of the bar it still seemed bright gold in colour, but like many small-batch beers, it was clouded with sediment.

Regina's drink came in a large snifter. It was almost electric pink, but with a tinge of orange too. She lifted a silver spear out of the glass and opened her mouth to insert the maraschino cherry that was speared at the end of it. She held it between her teeth for a moment, before biting down to chew it with a smile.

When she put the spear back in the glass, he noticed that the top part was shaped like a cross, with the faint outline of a figure on it. The head of the tiny figure faced down, toward the glass.

"What are you drinking?" he asked.

"Globes of Hell," she said. "It's got melon and a special kind of citrus liqueur in it. Want to try it?"

"No bodily fluids?" he asked.

"Actually, it has the milk of a mother and the spunk of a father to represent the circle of life. The fruit of human globes, you know!"

Austin wrinkled his face and shook his head. "I'll stick with beer," he said, and swallowed a mouthful. It was surprisingly good, with the tropical notes of the Mosaic hops layered just right over the malty back base. There was a heaviness about it, and a spike of bitter that sat perfectly in the back of the throat. His mouth buzzed with the tang of the ale as it emptied. He could drink a few of these.

"You like it?" she whispered.

He nodded. "And no blood or semen or anything."

She shook her head. "Just a sprinkle of virgin golden showers."

His eyes shot wide.

"Don't think, just drink," she said. "It will make you horny. Everything in this room is about letting yourself...release."

Austin nodded as if he understood. But then he carefully set the glass down on a black coaster on the low table in front of them.

*　　*　　*

The low chime of a bell made him look up. All of the heads at the bar had turned to stare down the long corridor of arches toward the end of the room. Austin followed their gaze to see a line of nuns gathering to the left of the pinnacle of the arches. To the right, facing the line of nuns, a group of men wearing priest garb gathered. After what he'd seen of the 'nuns', he was sure that they were not ordained in the ministry. The low chime echoed through the room again, but this time, he could see the source.

A small man in a black cowl stood at the centre of the corridor holding a metal tube out before him. He tapped it with a mallet, and again the sound rang out. But this time, the first two members of the lines of nuns and priests answered the call. It looked like a holy wedding procession, Austin thought, as a nun and priest walked slowly to meet in the middle of the aisle. They stood face to face, and then the nun knelt, to press and hold her face to the priest's crotch. When she stood, her partner knelt and returned the votive. Then he rose, they locked arms and walked to the front of an altar.

The chime rang again, and the next two members of the nun and priest line repeated the slightly obscene ritual, before taking their place, arm in arm, at the altar. The ritual repeated five more times, until the lines were empty. Then the bell clanged loud and long, and the heads in the room suddenly all looked backward, away from the altar toward Austin. He followed their lead and looked. A new couple stood waiting at the start of the room. A man clearly garbed to mimic a bishop, draped in stunning white silk with a ruby-studded cassock, a tall pointed white hat, and holding a shepherd's hook that ended in a cross, had begun to walk down the aisle. At his side was a nun in black silk, with a tall, ornate headdress denoting some higher office, perhaps mother superior. She wore hundreds of Rosary beads in loops around her neck, and their crosses dangled before the nearly exposed delta of her sex. The black of her habit was all silk, and all translucent. The shadows of her nipples beneath the beads, and her pubic hair beneath the crosses, were visible as she stepped closer to Austin. He realised, with a shock, that it wasn't simply the nun's garb that was almost transparent.

The bishop's white garb was also made of silk. As the cassock moved, the man's penis and testicles could be seen dangling and shifting between his legs as he walked and the low candles on the adjoining tables flickered and illuminated the couple in passing.

When the head couple passed, the people at the tables nearby stood, and began to follow the obscene bishop and mother superior down the aisle.

Regina gripped Austin's hand and pulled him to his feet. They joined the procession and took up a position standing around the perimeter of the altar with the rest of the patrons of the Cloister.

The bell sounded again, and all of the priests dropped to their knees before their partners. Behind the altar, the bishop lifted the veil and headdress from the mother superior and set it on a table to the side. Then he unbuttoned the back of her habit, and the silk slid to the floor, leaving her naked except for the Rosary beads around her neck.

She undressed him next, setting his bishop's hat next to her own ceremonial headdress on the side table. The naked bishop put his hands around her waist and lifted her so that she could lie back on the altar. With the cross at the end of his staff, he traced a blessing, or a spell, upon her body. He ceremonially touched her head and breasts and sex with the wooden cross, and then set it in a floor holder nearby and before ascending three stone steps positioned beside the altar to join her on the wooden platform. His sex no longer dangled uselessly; he was clearly ready for consummation.

Austin looked away from the altar and realised that the rest of the nuns and priests had also eschewed their clothes. As the bishop lay down upon the mother superior, all of the nuns suddenly dropped to their knees and took their partners by the hips. *Holy shit*, he thought. Regina had brought him to a sacrilegious live sex show?

Around the altar, a group of hooded, monk-like figures suddenly appeared. They walked in from either side of the room and bent down to light small black pots that encircled the altar. In moments, the heavy white smoke of incense rose in a cloud around the sexual exhibitionists. The black hooded figures then formed a line and locked arms, blocking the view of the fellating nuns and copulating bishop. For the first time since Austin had entered the room, there was sound; the monks began to raise their voices in a low, moaning melody. The sound grew in volume as the fleshy sounds from the altar also became more noticeable. The mother superior was now making fast squeaking noises as the bishop drove her to public orgasm, and there were other wet sounds emanating from the couples around the altar.

The erotic whispers and incense and dark-cowled border guard all played together to send Austin's brain into a spin. He felt almost dizzy and leaned in as Regina's hand slipped around his side.

"It can be intense," she whispered in his ear. "Do you like it?"

He nodded just as a bell chimed.

The monks abruptly were silent and turned to file back out of the room the way they'd come.

The mother superior lay still on the altar, but the bishop had somehow disappeared.

Then Austin realised that all of the men around the altar had gone, leaving their robes crumpled on the floor.

The couples from the bar were all turning and starting to return to their seats, and Regina gripped his hand and pulled him to do the same.

When they reached their couch, Austin picked up his beer and drank half of it without thinking. His throat was dry, and his head strangely foggy.

"What is in that incense?" he asked Regina.

She smiled. "It helps everyone relax," she said. "Do you want to go somewhere where we can be alone?"

He nodded, and she took his hand. They walked toward the entrance to the room, but instead of going through that door, Regina turned right and took him to a small corridor where there were a series of dark wood doors. She turned the knob on one, but it was locked. The next one opened easily.

They stepped inside. It was a closet-sized room lit only with two candles on two small tables on either side of a long chaise longue.

"Lie down here," she instructed, and he eased his body back on the dark burgundy velvet of the sofa chair. Before he was settled, Regina had slid her body on top of his. She'd unbuttoned the top of her dress and he found himself kissing her chest and then her lips with a passion he couldn't restrain.

"I feel so—" he began. She pressed her lips against his and stifled his words. Then she whispered, "The Cloister teaches us to act without words. Let your body do what it will."

In moments, he was stripping off her clothes and heeding her words. The chaise became their own private altar of lust.

CHAPTER THIRTEEN

"I hope that wasn't too much for you," Regina said.

They were driving home through dark streets that Austin didn't recognise. She had blindfolded him before they left the club and walked him past the doorman that way. But after a few minutes in the car, she'd reached over and pulled the cloth from his eyes again. It didn't matter; he couldn't read the neighbourhood street signs. Until they crossed a set of railroad tracks, he had no conception of what direction they were going. He knew the tracks cut through town north to south, so that at least told him they were headed east or west. He bet east.

"I have to admit, I didn't think places like that really existed."

She grinned. "Oh, they are there for the finding…if you want them badly enough. People come from a hundred miles away to spend a couple hours in Equinox. Hardly anyone in Parkville even knows it exists. Nobody driving by has any idea that there's a club at all in there. It just looks like an abandoned building from the outside. That's the only way it could ever work."

"I'm reasonably sure the mayor would not like to find out about it," Austin said.

She nodded. "You can see why I had to blindfold you," she said. "I hope I won't have to do that in the future when we go."

"So you're going to take me there again?"

"Do you want me to?" she asked.

"Sure. But what do I have to do so that I don't need the blindfold?"

"You'd have to go through an initiation," she said. "You might have to be one of those druid people for a few ceremonies at the Cloister, or fill a role in one of the other rooms that I didn't show you."

"What else is there?" he asked. "The place didn't look like it was that big from the outside."

"There's a lower level," she said. "You haven't seen half of it yet, I can tell you."

"I can't imagine what else they do there."

She shook her head. "No, I bet you can't."

★　　★　　★

They pulled up in his driveway and Regina parked the car and walked to the front door with him. When they stepped inside, Brandy was on the couch, writing in a leather book. It looked a lot like the journal that Regina kept – he'd found her writing in it several times when he'd gotten home from work.

"How was Ceili?" he asked.

Brandy smiled and shrugged. "Just a doll, like always. How was Equinox?"

Austin was taken aback. "You know about Equinox?"

Brandy nodded. "Sure, how do you think Regina and I met?"

She stepped past him toward the door and for the first time, Austin noticed the tail of a serpent in the shape of a six peeking out from beneath the sleeve on her arm. The same tattoo that Regina had.

For a second, he had a flash of the image of her blond hair trailing over the black see-through silk of a nun's outfit from the Cloister room and had to gulp. *Holy shit, what was Regina getting him into?*

The door closed, and Regina turned toward him. "Do you mind if I stay over?" she asked.

She was already unbuttoning her dress.

Austin shook his head.

She left her dress on the fourth stair. He didn't bother to pick it up.

CHAPTER FOURTEEN

Regina stopped going home.

And Austin was happy with that. In the evenings, he returned from work wiped out from intense days of office politics and too many fast and furious projects. But the sight of Regina there waiting, rocking Ceili on her hip or sitting on the couch writing in her journal while the baby crawled on the floor, washed away all the troubles of his day. Sometimes he'd walk in and they'd both be on the second floor. The house seemed weirdly empty in those moments and he would instantly call out for her and head toward the stairs.

Regina had completely taken over the centre of his life and he found it hard to think of a day without her in it. He'd had some doubts after the bizarre visit to Equinox, but after spending a couple subsequent 'comforting' nights in bed with her, all of those reservations faded away. So she was kinky. He couldn't say that he minded that.

He hadn't mentioned her yet to his parents, but he wanted to soon. He was worried about what they would think; how long did his wife have to be gone before it was 'acceptable' for him to date? He'd almost slipped over the weekend, when he talked to his mom on the phone over coffee and Regina had walked into the kitchen with the baby.

"Hey baby," he'd said, and instantly realised his mistake.

"Who's that?" his mother had asked, and he'd covered quickly, explaining that Ceili had just made a funny face. It was going to be bad enough to admit that he already had a girlfriend, let alone one who was basically living with him.

A week after their first trip to Equinox, Austin came home to find Regina wearing a black robe and cowl. Her eyes beamed at him from beneath the lip of the hood.

"Tonight is your initiation," she said.

He didn't even have to question what she meant. The cowl could only mean one thing. Instead he said, "But we don't have a sitter."

"I've taken care of it," Regina said. "Paulina is with Ceili now."

"Who's Paulina?" he asked.

"A friend," Regina said. "Brandy couldn't come tonight."

"I can trust her?" he asked.

"Do you trust me?"

He nodded.

"Okay then," she said. "Why don't you go change, and then we can grab something to eat on the way."

"What if they don't have an initiation spot for me tonight?" he asked. Regina had not talked about going back to the club since last weekend. This all seemed very sudden.

"Oh, they have a spot," she said. "Trust me, I made sure of it."

"I don't have a cape," he said, thinking of all of the men he'd seen in the Cloister wearing black capes or priest garb.

Regina smiled. "You will earn your cape tonight."

"I don't know if I like the sound of that," he said.

"You're going to enjoy it," she said. "Trust me."

At that moment, a girl with short black hair and a nose ring walked into the room holding Ceili. She wore a black T-shirt with an occult symbol across the chest. A star inside a circle. There were words written on the poles, but Ceili's body obscured what they said.

"Hi there," she said. Her voice was high and musical. "You guys have a good time tonight and don't worry about a thing."

She walked to the fridge and pulled a bottle off the top shelf. Then she walked over to Austin, who took the baby from her arms and gave her a kiss. He held Ceili up in the air, and the baby giggled and drooled; her eyes lit as she recognised her father.

"You be good and I'll be home soon, okay, baby doll?"

He gave her a hug and a pat on the back, and then handed her back to Paulina. The babysitter smiled and walked out of the room. As she turned, Austin saw the now-familiar tattoo of a serpent six on her arm.

Of course, he thought. *All Regina roads lead to Equinox.*

*   *   *

"If I pass the initiation, do I get to stop wearing this stupid blindfold?" he asked when Regina stopped the car an hour later. They'd stopped for a sandwich and then once back in the car, she'd covered his eyes again for the second half of the drive to the club.

"Eventually," she answered. "Once you've earned the trust of the sisters."

"What do I have to do?"

"We'll find out your assignment soon enough," she said. "But first, we have to get inside."

She traced the Mark of Cain symbol on his head once more, and then got out of the car and came around to the passenger's side to help him out and then guide him across the street and through the doorway.

The doorman greeted her by name. "They're waiting for you in the Chalice Hall," he said.

Regina pulled the silken blindfold off of Austin's eyes and leaned up to kiss him. "I am so excited that you're doing this," she said. "I think you'll find everything you've been looking for at Equinox."

"I didn't think I was looking for anything," he said.

Regina laughed. "When I met you, you were not a happy man."

He nodded. "Well, that's true enough. But since I met you, things have been getting better and better."

Regina smiled. "Just wait until you're a full member of Club Equinox. You'll find things here that you didn't even know you dreamed of. But you did."

"I'm looking forward to it."

In truth, Austin was nervous. He had no idea what would be expected of him, and honestly, he had no interest in 'performing' in public for some ritual. He'd joked about not having a cape but... what if they wanted him to wear one of those see-through things?

He felt an increasing burn in his stomach as he considered all of the strange things they might expect him to do tonight. Regina had said the things he had seen last time were only the tip of the iceberg of what went on here. And those had been crazy. But he also knew how important it was to Regina that he be part of this. He wanted to make her happy. He had to admit he'd enjoyed their last visit here, though it had been both shocking and more than a little weird. Something about it had called to him. The eroticism, of course. But also the secret nature of it. The taboo-ness, the dark rituals. The club represented the alternative to everything his milquetoast life had stood for up to this point.

And he had not been happy with his life in a long while.

He was open to the attraction of Equinox. He needed something very different in his life.

And Regina was giving it to him. Both in his home, and by bringing him here.

*   *   *

She led him through the front dance club area, where blue laser lights flickered and spun across the ceiling and the floor. Women in short leather skirts with chains across their chests and men in black shirts and spiked hair danced in jerky spasms that would have looked comic, if they had not been so serious about it.

Austin gave them credit; he would never have danced like that in public, let alone tried to be as expressive.

Luckily, Regina wasn't calling on him to dance. Instead, she walked across the floor to an arched doorway on the far side. The door led to a narrow corridor into the secret places of the club lit only by candles in small cubbyholes in the brick walls. They walked a few steps and then Regina opened an ornate wooden door that led to a stairwell down.

As they descended, the air grew cooler. They were now below ground, and the dampness touched the bones with a chill instantly. The bricks changed to walls of rock slabs and concrete as they reached the bottom and stepped into a chapel.

Well, it was *like* a chapel. But no Christian would have worshipped here. There were candles everywhere – in sconces carved into the walls, in tall metal stands, in candelabras, and on small tables throughout the room; the smell of wax filled and warmed the air as they stepped away from the stairs. The glow of dozens of tiny flames lit the air and the paintings on the walls around them. In a church, these would have been stained-glass depictions of the stations of the cross. But here, they were underground and there was no place for windows.

Nevertheless, the paintings were set up to *look* like windows. They took the same tall arched shape as church windows, and each painting had a cascade of candles beneath it to light the unholy images depicted above.

Austin's eyebrows rose as he realised that this was actually a *Kama Sutra* version of the Christian stations of the cross. To his left, a man in black robes with his hands bound in coils of rope faced a throng of nuns with his head bowed. It might have been a Christian image of some kind, except the nuns were clearly dressed in the translucent habits of the Cloister. In the Bible, Christ had never faced a tribunal of flagrantly erotic sisters.

In another painting, that same nearly naked man, now wearing a crown of thorns, appeared tied to a rack, as three nearly naked women in nun-like headdresses whipped him with long leather straps tipped with hooked barbs. There was nothing religious about the lascivious looks on their faces.

In the next image, the Christ figure dragged a wooden cross past a licentious crowd where women fellated men in the very centre of the street as the men pawed the bared breasts of the women leaning beside them, reaching into their loose-hanging tunics to grope and grin.

In a fourth image, two men held the cross off of the shoulders of the Christ figure, as he knelt to appease with his mouth the erection of a fat man standing along the road.

Austin wasn't religious, but the blasphemy of the images made him uncomfortable regardless. He felt as if he'd seen something forbidden that he shouldn't have witnessed. Something that he would never be able to erase from his mind.

And so he looked away from the rest of the images on the wall to see that there was a group waiting at the head of the room. Presumably, waiting for him. His heart leapt.

"Welcome," a tall woman at the centre of the group said. She stood apart from the rest, with a uniform that looked slightly more… extreme. She wore the black transparent silk of the nun outfit, but beneath the hazy garb, her body was clearly wrapped in a weave of thin straps and chains. Her head, however, was crowned in the black-and-white headdress of an old-school nun. He recognised her as the mother superior he'd seen on the altar before.

"Who is that?" Austin whispered to Regina.

She smiled and said in a low voice, "The Irreverent Mother. She oversees everything that happens here."

The woman at the centre of the circle stepped forward. "We have been waiting for you to pledge your obedience to us. We trust you are ready to become a member of Equinox."

Regina squeezed his hand, and then released it. Austin took that as a cue to step forward.

"I am," he said.

"Regina has spoken well of you and said that you are ready to join our ways. You may not understand them all yet, but with her tutelage, we believe that you will come to the enlightenment that all of us who have gone before you have found here. When you have completed your path, you will find that you will live for Equinox. You will die for Equinox. And you will find your spirit fulfilled in Equinox."

Austin didn't know what to say to that exactly, so he remained silent.

"Your instruction is in the hands of your sponsor," the woman said. "But your first lesson is ours. The lesson of obedience. All in Equinox must learn it. To earn the privilege of domination, you must first understand subjugation."

She motioned for him to approach.

"Come forward," she said.

He stepped toward her, and as he did, he could more clearly see the leather straps that bound her body beneath the black silk that mocked a nun's habit. It served the opposite purpose of a habit, actually. Rather than promote modesty and hiding the enticement of the female form, it displayed all of her curves at their most provocative. Beneath her 'habit', the woman was adorned in barbs and chains. Three small chains led from a leather strap across her hips to disappear between her thighs. They connected to the base of a round tube. Austin realised with a shock that the majority of that tube was buried inside the Reverend Mother. She was pleasuring herself with every movement of her legs or hips.

"Kneel," she commanded.

He dropped to his knees in front of her. His face was level with her hips, and he could see the neatly cropped runway of her pubic thatch just inches from his face. He felt himself blushing. And then she stepped forward, until her crotch was touching his nose. She gripped the back of his head with her hands and pulled him forward, forcing him to breathe in the scent of her sex. He could feel the chains and the base of her dildo toy against his nose.

"You are brought to Equinox by Regina, but you do not belong to Regina. You belong to us. All of us. We will use you as is our wont."

She stepped away from him then, and Austin was embarrassed to realise he had an erection. Luckily, his jeans mostly hid the evidence. At least, that was his thought until the Irreverent Mother's next words.

"Remove his impediments."

At that, three nuns in black hoods and see-through vestments stepped forward from where they had stood silently behind the altar. Two flanked him on either side; the third took a position directly before him. The two grabbed him beneath the arms and drew him up to his feet. The one before him lifted his black T-shirt over his head, as the other two moved his arms to accommodate.

The shirt disappeared, and suddenly cool fingers worked at his belt. Austin didn't know what to do. There was a ring of spectators now gathered around the altar, and he could see Regina standing off to one side watching. Her face betrayed no emotion. What was she thinking as other women disrobed him?

He couldn't imagine. If Angie had been there, she either would have marched up and slapped the nuns out of the way, or strode angrily out of the club alone, cursing all men as pigs. Maybe both. But he had not initiated this strange attention; Regina had. He shrugged mentally. If this was what she wanted....

His jeans fell to the floor, and the nuns ran probing fingers down his bare legs. If he hadn't been aroused before, he couldn't help but be now. And just as he thought that, two fingers slipped between his skin and the waistband on his briefs and yanked them down.

His cock sprung out for all to see, and Austin closed his eyes for a moment, refusing to acknowledge that he stood naked and hard before his girlfriend and a room of voyeurs.

The Irreverent Mother said something. He wasn't sure what

until he opened his eyes and realised the nun before him was now kneeling. And the warmth of her mouth now engulfed him. He understood the syllables suddenly.

"Kneel and eat," had been the words.

"Jesus," he whispered.

"Not here," the Irreverent Mother answered him. With two quick slaps, she hit his face on either side as the nun on her knees continued to give him a blow job.

The shock of the slaps actually made him even harder; he could feel the tip of his cock pressing against the back of the girl's throat and the pleasure as she moved her mouth and tongue around him was more intense than almost any he'd ever known. He was naked and getting head before an audience and it was the strangest, most perverse and intense thing he'd ever experienced. Austin wasn't sure what to do. Did he let go? Did he pull back and run for the doors?

His body answered for him.

As he began to come, his head tilted back and he moaned without thinking. And as he did, the woman behind it all chastised him.

"Did you have permission?" she asked.

He couldn't answer, so intense was his orgasm. He could not even open his eyes.

Again the hands met his cheeks, and then he couldn't help but meet her gaze.

She shook her head in sadness. "You will come only with our permission. Or be punished."

The Irreverent Mother reached down and pulled at the collar of the fellating nun. She rose, and as she did, her cowl fell back, exposing a mess of blond curls.

Austin gasped. The ice-blue eyes of Brandy stared back at him. Her lips were moist, and he saw the glisten of pearl in one corner of her mouth.

His stomach contracted. He'd just gotten head from his babysitter.

She smiled faintly, and stepped back, as the Irreverent Mother stepped forward in her place. "With every pleasure, comes pain," she announced, as much to the group as to him. "Take him to the Hall of Suffering," she said. And at that, hands gripped his arms and the two nuns who had flanked him before pulled him forward, past the altar, and down a small stairwell on its side. They pressed him forward until he reached the last stair, and then walked into a hidden room at the bottom. Hands on his waist propelled him forward until he stood in the centre of a space no larger than his bedroom. The wall before him held a giant mounted sculptured head. It was a man's face, with pointed beard and heavy eyebrows. And protruding from its thick dark curls of hair were two ram's horns.

He understood what the figure represented instantly. It was a giant bust of Lucifer.

"Kneel," a voice from behind him commanded.

Someone kicked at the back of his knees, and he couldn't help but comply.

CHAPTER FIFTEEN

"Will you accept the pleasures of Equinox?" the Irreverent Mother asked. "Say 'I will.'"

"I will," Austin said. His eyes could not leave the detailed carving of the Devil's horns. How had he come to be in a situation like this? His mind reeled.

"Will you accept the punishments of Equinox?" the Irreverent Mother asked.

Austin hesitated, and a hand clenched harder on his arm.

"I will," he said finally.

"Then your initiation begins now," she said. The head nun stepped around those who held him to block his view of the statue. She was nearly nude now, her habit gone, leaving only chains, a shimmering black veil that hung over her shoulder to cross her hip and a headdress of black and white.

At her words, the two nuns who had held him for Brandy's attentions gripped his shoulders and pushed him forward to a wooden cross to the left of the Devil. They made him face the cross, pressing his cheek to the centre and lifting his arms until his fingers touched the wood. Then they fastened leather straps around his wrists before stepping back.

"There is only one way to understand pleasure," the Irreverent Mother said. "And that is to feel pain."

Something snapped behind him, and Austin struggled to turn his head to see what. But all he could see was the crowd. A mob of people had gathered behind him, forming a semicircle of bodies anxious to view whatever punishment he was about to undergo. He struggled to find Regina's legs amid the crowd, but to no avail.

A face appeared on the other side of the cross from him. A blond girl with big blue eyes and full lips. Brandy leaned over the bar his arms were fastened to, and pressed his lips with a soft, warm, wet kiss.

She was naked, her breasts smashing against the cross, and the honey-coloured hair of her crotch shifting just inches away from his own.

Austin had to admit that he wanted to fuck his sometime babysitter in that moment.

That's when the pain began.

The crack of a whip echoed through the air as a white-hot strip of pain suddenly shot down his back.

"Give…and take," Brandy whispered on the other side of the cross, and puckered her lips into the semblance of a kiss as she stepped back. A moment later, another snap, and the whip racked his back again.

And again.

Austin jumped as it hit a fourth time. It felt as if his skin was splitting.

The whip snapped again, and he shifted, trying to avoid it, but that only meant that the leather hit his shoulder blade instead of the middle of his back. Teeth bit into the top of his ass as the leather pulled away.

"That's enough," he cried.

But he was instantly answered by the Irreverent Mother.

"Enough is when *we* say so," she said. "How much is the ecstasy of a blow job worth in pain?"

The whip cracked again on his back. He could feel his skin burning.

"It's a price that's hard to quantify," she continued. "But you will learn that even the pain can bring pleasure."

A hand reached between his legs from behind as she said it, and fingernails trailed along the underside of his cock. He realised that even though he was being whipped, he was still half-erect. And the hand toyed with him, urging him on to more.

"Is it good?" the nun asked from somewhere behind.

The hand slipped away, as he gasped and nodded yes.

And then the whip cracked again and drove away the pleasure of her touch with fire.

"There is not one without the other," the Irreverent Mother said. "This is your lesson."

And the whip cracked again, this time catching him more on the ass than the back. He jumped to the side.

"There's no escape, only acceptance and…eventually…enjoyment."

Austin got the kink factor but could not imagine truly enjoying being whipped.

Another crack took him in the lower back and upper thigh. And then suddenly, the two nuns who had held his arms before were there, pressing the warmth of their chests against his ribs, as they reached up to undo his bindings.

He pulled his arms out of the restraints and turned to see Brandy standing there now holding the whip. She moved her hand up and down slightly, as if getting ready for another blow. Then she laughed and leaned forward to kiss him on the lips.

As soon as her heat left his face, she dropped the leather to the floor, and disappeared into the crowd.

Austin saw Regina then, finally, standing just a few feet away next to the head nun.

"Come forward," the nun commanded, and he moved toward Regina.

"You have taken the first step into Equinox," the Irreverent Mother said. "But only the first. Your sponsor will take you to the next. And if you pass, we will see you again. And you will learn more of the mysteries of pleasure and pain. Only on the blade of hell can you find the heaven you seek. Only in the fall from heaven can you find the beauty of hell."

The Irreverent Mother lifted her arms to the sky and the thin black veil slid from her shoulder so that she stood naked in the centre of the mass of watchers. All of them pressed shoulder to shoulder, forming a human wall behind her.

"If you let go, you can find everything you have ever desired. But you must surrender to find the truth in flesh."

She brought her arms down and gripped at the small chains that wreathed her body. When she pulled them, they yanked her skin up in tiny tents. The chains were hooked to her flesh with curved barbs. They cut into the skin of her belly and thighs and even her nipples and breasts, which stretched as she gripped and tortured herself with her own chains.

"We are all prisoners," she said. "And in our chains, we find freedom."

PART TWO
BEWITCHED

CHAPTER SIXTEEN

Austin couldn't sleep. Regina lay next to him, one arm over her head, clutching at the pillow. Her mouth hung half open and let out the faintest snore. The blue LED clock said 1:17 and Austin had looked at it at least five times since they'd gone to bed an hour before.

He carefully slipped his feet out from the sheets and pushed himself out of the bed, trying not to make the mattress creak. Regina's gentle rhythmic breathing caught for a moment and he stopped moving. But then she settled back into whatever dreamscape her mind walked through.

He tiptoed out of the room and down the hall to the stairs. Sometimes when he couldn't sleep, he found a big glass of milk somehow worked to make him drowsy. It was worth trying, because he had to get up for work in five hours, and he really didn't relish going in after a night of no sleep. Work was stressful enough without being wiped out at the start of the day.

Austin pulled a glass from the cabinet and filled it with milk. Then he walked into the family room to sit on the couch. He clicked on the end table lamp and took a couple gulps of the cool liquid before leaning his head back on the couch cushion. There was no reason for him to be awake right now. It had been a decent day. Ceili had gone to bed around nine and hadn't woken up since. And Regina and he had had sex, which usually sent him into a deep sleep pretty quickly. She wore him out with her energy.

Still, his mind wouldn't shut down tonight. He tried to push thoughts of work back with memories of their last trip to Equinox over the weekend. After the shock of his first initiation night, the erotic actions of their next visit had been much easier to absorb... and enjoy. The images in his mind were scandalous, but they weren't relaxing whatever anxiety was keeping his thoughts jumping.

Austin set the milk down after another swig. Regina's journal was on the table next to his coaster. It was a small black book with a silver half moon stamped into the cover. He'd never really looked at it, but he saw her writing in it almost daily. She'd actually written in it tonight after Ceili had gone to bed, while he'd been sitting in the recliner reading the newspaper.

He'd asked about the book a couple weeks ago as she'd been writing and she'd only shrugged.

"I call it my Book of Shadows," she said. "I use it to keep track of my thoughts and wishes and dreams."

"Is there anything about me in there?"

She smiled and raised an eyebrow. "Maybe. I do think about you."

"But do you dream about me?" he countered.

She shut the cover of the book and set it to the side. "You are the answer to my dreams," she pronounced. She'd gotten up then and come over to lean provocatively over his chest. She'd kissed his chin and then his lips before taking his face in her hands. "You should come upstairs," she'd teased, and then slipped away to walk into the kitchen, turning off the lights before walking up the stairs herself.

Austin was left alone with one light on and the faint scent of lavender. He'd grinned and turned off the last light in short order to follow her up to the bedroom.

The memory made him smile, and he reached out to pick up the black book. He didn't intend to snoop, but he did crack the book open to look at the pages. He riffled through them, noting the dense lines of script inside. Regina wrote very neatly, with all of her letters aligned in narrowly slanted loops and hooks. The words all hugged the faint guidelines on the paper, neatly staying just within the lines. Now and then he saw that she'd sketched some kind of diagram or drawing. He didn't mean to read the script, just to leaf through the pages to get a glimpse of the contents. But then he landed on a page right at the end of the used section of the journal and stopped when a word caught his eye.

Ceili.

He didn't want to snoop, he didn't. He'd just wanted to sneak a peek at the pages and how much writing Regina had done, not the actual words. But once he saw his daughter's name, he had to know. Austin held his finger on the page and opened the small book all the way. In the centre of the page, with space above and below, Regina had written:

Ceili = 3 days plus Moon in Hades

There was a half moon drawn at the end of the words, and three underlines beneath his daughter's name.

What the hell?

The text above and below didn't help him understand the meaning any further. Just before Ceili's name, she'd written a paragraph that sounded a lot like nonsense.

Two expand the magnitude. But one will do if needed. The seed could be snuffed by the flower, but that is a lot to hope for. There is precedent – the Sisters of Carrillon were successful with a similar attempt thirty years ago. But was their flower weaker, more easily controlled, or innately evil? The innocence of the mission is also important. We surely have that in our favour. The ceremony must be held on the equinox for complete success.

And then came the equation that included his daughter's name.

The words that followed seemed to have been written on another day. There was a gap and Regina had written about her morning, celebrating the smell of dawn and the heavy light that slipped through the cracks in the hedge at the back of the yard.

He flipped back a page and found a series of odd symbols, and words that might have been Latin. Or Russian for all he knew. All he could confirm was that he couldn't read them. The symbols were interesting, a mix of triangles and what looked like an eyeball shaded in with a blue pen, whereas the writing itself had been done in black. There were small numbers etched to the right of strangely shaped multi-angle boxes so that it almost looked like a high school student's geometry homework. But the insertion of a witch's circle suggested that this was certainly not the kind of homework you could turn in.

He leafed back and forth a few pages and shook his head. The journal was a maze of disconnected thoughts and text. In some places, Regina wrote in a poetic flow about the highlights of her day; he found a reference to him that made him smile – she had had a faint rash from his stubble that she said made her feel warm still after he'd left for work.

But then in other spots she wrote recipes that looked like a magical spell, or scribed a mix of strange words and symbols that he couldn't decipher. On some pages, she'd written all the way around the margins as if it were important to keep all of the triangles and circles and devil's horns and foreign words encased by one page.

He'd known that she considered herself a 'witch' but for the most part, he'd ignored it. He didn't believe in witchcraft, and if she wanted to think that putting leaves and blood and chanting words over a jar accomplished some strange magical feat…let her. He'd stopped arguing with people over their religious beliefs years ago, and this felt no different. It was a little weird; Angie hadn't had any interest in the occult or Wiccan religion. But…Angie hadn't had sex with him every night either. Or taken him to bohemian, gothy BDSM clubs. So… comparing Regina to his late wife was kind of foolish.

He shook his head. If Regina wanted to make potions and spells, he didn't care. Though he'd like to understand why Ceili had something to do with "a moon in Hades."

Austin leafed backward in the journal a few pages. Many, though not all, of the entries were dated. He found one that was longer than the rest; Regina had written several paragraphs that ran over two pages, dated last month. In fact, the date was the week Angie had died.

The place still holds a veil of power. I felt it before I entered. A dark sadness that hangs in every shadow. The stories of this house must be true. Before I looked at any other rooms, I found the door to the basement and went downstairs. Each creak of the steps gave me pause. It felt as if someone was going to step out of nowhere and try to stop me. But nobody did. The basement was cool and slightly damp; it had that smell of an old house that has not been used in a long time.

I pulled on a string that was attached to a bare lightbulb mounted on one of the ceiling beams but nothing happened. Still, there was enough light through the dirty glass of the window wells that I could see. There wasn't a lot left in the basement. A laundry tub stood against one wall, flanked by a washer and dryer set that looked like it was from the fifties. I wondered if they still actually worked. There were a couple of old boxes scattered around and a workbench with a few rusted wrenches and tools hung from the opposite wall.

Something drew me to the wall behind the staircase. It looked as if it had been made out of quarry rock, all uneven with rough edges. There was an old iron grate latched to the wall. I tried to open it, and at first it wouldn't budge. But then it gave when I pulled harder, and a screech echoed through the basement that sounded like a coffin opening in one of those old black-and-white movies. I couldn't help but shiver, but the feeling only lasted a moment. As soon as the door was open, I could feel the mouth of darkness. The centre of the thing that I'd felt upstairs as soon as I'd opened the door was here.

I pulled out my cell phone and turned on the flashlight app to look inside. The walls were blackened with soot, but the base had been cleaned of any debris. I could see faint markings on the walls that made me smile. The sisterhood had been here. Nobody else would have thought anything at the half moons carved in the stone, but I knew what it meant .

The offering symbol.

This had been the secret hearth. The place where offerings were made. And if the stories were true, there was a relic of power buried here.

There was an iron ash shovel propped against the wall nearby and I grabbed it, to see if I could test my theory. The base of the fireplace was laid with unmortared bricks. I pressed the edge of the shovel into the widest crack and tried to pry it up. At first, it wouldn't move and the shovel just popped up with a clang. I kept working at it, until the brick itself began to shift against the others. It lifted about an inch before it got caught, wedged against the brick next to it. I grabbed the edges with my fingers and let it settle back in to be more level, and then lifted again. It came out with a cloud of white dust. And then I could move the ones that had been next to it easily.

I stacked up a handful of them, and then used the shovel to move the pea gravel that sat below. It only took a minute before I found what I was looking for. My fingers grew icy with every shift of the shovel. When I reached down and actually touched the small ivory shards that hid within the blanket of stone, my hand grew almost white-cold.

I was touching the bones of a baby that had been hidden beneath the fireplace. This had been the source of the sister's power who had once lived here. The child's name had been Carolyn. And her bones were the relic I had come here for.

I hoped that they could amplify my own magic as they once had for another coven. I smoothed out the gravel and set the bricks back into place before returning upstairs. There were many preparations to make.

Austin frowned. Regina really did consider herself some kind of witch. And apparently one who was tapped into a much broader network. To Austin, witches were the stuff of Disney movies – old hags who stirred iron cauldrons. He knew that there were modern ones who believed in drawing power from the natural energies of the world, but he'd never paid much attention to that. But the idea of someone burning things on top of the bones of a baby in order to accomplish…what? Cast an actual spell? It sounded ridiculous. But obviously Regina didn't think so.

He considered the erotic rituals at Club Equinox. He'd dismissed them as fake trappings to make the whole sex and bondage thing they had going on there feel more like a dark fairy tale. But maybe it was more than that. Maybe the 'sisterhood' really were modern witches? And the tattoo that Regina and Brandy both had was the symbol of their coven, more than the symbol of a sex club.

It was a lot to take in at one in the morning. And not something he could easily bring up to discuss over coffee tomorrow. He could just imagine saying, 'So, last night I was reading your journal and….' No, that wasn't going to fly.

He set the journal back where he'd found it and finished his glass of milk. Somehow he didn't think it was going to help him get to sleep tonight.

CHAPTER SEVENTEEN

"Wake up, sleepyhead," Regina said. Her voice sounded as if it was coming from far away. Austin groaned and shifted, pulling the covers higher over his shoulders. But Regina wasn't having it. Suddenly all of the covers and sheets slid away, and her hands were on his back, kneading and teasing.

"You've got to go to work," she said. "I let you sleep an extra fifteen minutes, but you're going to be late."

He rolled over and saw the light in her eyes and the playful glint of her smile. She bent down and kissed him, and a feeling washed over him that took away all of the nervousness and uncertainty that her journal had imparted just a few hours before. Whatever weird shit she was into, she was not some evil wicked witch. She was the woman who had saved him.

Austin smiled and tried to roll over again.

"I don't think so," Regina said, pouncing on him to hold his back fast to the bed with her weight. "I've got something that will wake you up."

She shifted her hips against his, with her lips brushing against his neck and ear.

"That'll do the trick," he agreed, reaching around her waist to grab at her rear. But Regina slipped out of his grasp and escaped. She stood by the bed and shook her head. "No time for that. But tonight, if you're good...."

He swiped at her, but she eluded his grasp. "Not fair," he complained. But she disappeared from the room, ending the argument. He reluctantly got out of bed and shambled into the bathroom to get ready to face the day.

The only upside was that it was Friday. In just a few hours, he'd be done with the hourly cavalcade of work emergencies and free to spend two full days with Ceili and Regina. He couldn't wait to get to work because of that – the sooner he got through the day, the sooner he could return home. He looked in the mirror in the bathroom and pressed his fingers to the sides of his eyes, pulling the skin until the small wrinkles went away. He was feeling wiped out at the end of the week. Hell, it wasn't just the week. The past few months had not been kind. It should not be a shock that his eyes were looking tired and saggy.

Austin shook his head. He didn't need to start looking old yet. He was barely thirty years old. He looked down and saw one of the little incense bags that Regina had begun leaving all around the house. There was one tied to the bed behind his pillow, and one at the foot of Ceili's bed. He picked it up and held it to his nose, taking a deep breath. There was a hint of lavender in the fragrance, and something more earthy too. Regina said the bags were there to soak up bad harmonies. Or harmonics. Something like that. He didn't care really. They had a decent scent and she put them in ornate little drawstring bags that reminded him of the kind of things you got expensive but tiny gifts in.

Whatever Regina wanted to put around the house, he was okay with. He breathed it in again, and the scent brought a smile to his face. He had to admit that every time he smelled one, his whole body relaxed. The scent reminded him of the warm smell of Regina's hair when he buried his face in her neck. The thought made him smile, and he set the bag down. He needed to get himself ready and out of here.

* * *

Regina waited until she heard the garage door creak closed and then she went upstairs. There were things she had to do before tonight. Things to prepare.

She went first to the master bathroom, pulled the sundress over her head and dropped it to the floor. Naked, she then knelt down next to the toilet. Anyone watching might have thought she was about to be sick. But a moment later, she lifted a curly black hair from the floor and smiled.

That was step one.

She set the hair on the white counter next to the sink and then went to the closet to retrieve a satchel that she'd left there with the things she'd need. It included a number of items she'd gathered from Austin, as well as other supplies. She reached inside and removed a small box of sculptor's clay. She opened it and cut the square into thirds, before rolling a chunk of the clay between her hands until it warmed. When it was easily pliable, she quickly crafted a crude human figure from it.

She pressed the pubic hair she'd rescued from the floor into the appropriate anatomy of the clay figure. She then pulled a hair from Austin's hairbrush and smooshed it into the clay of the figure's head. Then she opened a small plastic case that once had housed makeup. Now, it held a thin yellow sponge. Austin drooled in his sleep, she'd discovered. Which made it pretty easy to harvest saliva without his knowing. She mopped the damp sponge across the face of the clay figure, and then removed another small case from her bag. This one also held a sponge; however, the yellow was smudged in red.

It was amazing what you could do with a razor when someone was deep asleep. The thinnest slice on the back or arm, and the sleeper didn't feel it, at least not enough to wake up. Maybe their dream suddenly changed and in the dream they got a paper cut to echo what was going on in the real world... but they didn't wake up. The night she'd gotten this harvest, Austin had stirred slightly when the edge of the blade had touched his arm, but then his breathing had grown deep again as she'd held the sponge to the tiny cut.

The next day, he'd probably assumed that he'd scratched himself with a fingernail in his sleep.

Regina rubbed the sponge across the body of the clay figure, anointing it with Austin's blood. As she did, she spoke the words of a joining spell:

"His blood is mine
His kiss is mine
His head is mine
His love is mine."

She held the doll up to her lips and pressed her tongue to it. Then she pulled a needle from her bag, and pricked a finger. She pressed the dot of blood that emerged to the centre of the doll's chest.

"What I say to you, I say to him.
What I tell you to do, he will do.
His heart now bound in blood to my heart.
His will now bound in a kiss to mine."

She whispered the words over and over like the prayers of a Rosary. With each repetition, she held the clay figure to a different part of her body. Her lips. Her breasts. Her sex.

When she was through, she held the doll up to her face, and said softly, "Tonight, you will continue your training. You won't question me. You will enjoy every moment as it comes. And there will be many moments that come...."

*   *   *

The one predictable thing about being in marketing is that there is always an emergency. Something broke on the news that needs to be countered with some well-placed PR. A competitor touts some new feature that must be answered before their spin erodes market share. Someone in the product development team forgot to plan for a convention banner or flyer or postcard or wants to know why the thirteenth email in a series of product promotions hasn't gone out yet. Demanding personalities. Internal politics. External tsunamis. It was an hourly sap on the psyche, but it was his life.

He loved the challenges and thrived on the creativity needed to bull through every tempest in a teacup that someone else's poor planning created. But at the same time, every day he turned on his computer, he wondered why he hadn't followed his dream, packed up his car on the last day of college and driven west. He had always wanted to try his hand at screenplays. If he'd gotten a tiny apartment near L.A., he could have focused his time and energy on one of his own dreams, instead of constantly having to find ways to meet someone else's. His life would have been so different to what it was now.

Whine of the working man, he chastised himself, just as Bernie walked into his office. The head of the finance team reminded him of Drew Carey – he was a burly guy with a balding head and retro glasses with thick black plastic frames. He took a deep breath before almost every sentence he spoke; Bernie always sounded as if he'd just run up the stairs. But Austin knew better. Bernie never ran anywhere.

"I need the Las Vegas conference brochure on the street next week," Bernie said after a moment. "Are you going to hit that?"

Austin nodded. "Already hit. It went to press on Wednesday. The mailing house should have it on their schedule on Monday. This time next week, people will be reading all about how much fun they could have with us in Vegas."

Bernie betrayed a hint of surprise, but then covered it with a smile. He'd clearly hoped to rub Austin's face in a missed deadline, and instead, the marketing manager was ahead of the game for once.

"What are you up to this weekend?" Bernie asked, switching the subject since he couldn't crucify Austin on a missed marketing step

"Just hanging out with Ceili and Regina," he said.

"Regina, huh?" Bernie asked. "Is that the girl you said you met in a bar? Because, well, I know how *those* kinds of things go. But do you really expect me to believe that she didn't wake up the next day, take one look at you and bolt? I can just see her the morning after, slapping her head and asking what the hell they put in her drinks."

"Very nice," Austin said. "But luckily for me, not the way it happened at all. Regina is funny and sexy and amazing and I can't wait until five p.m. today to get back to her."

Bernie shook his head. "I'm not buying it. You're making her up. She's a figment of your imagination. No girl that good could fall for the likes of you."

"Don't you have numbers to crush?" Austin asked. "Quit trying to crush my balls."

The big man snorted and shook his head. "Yeah, I've got forecasts to finish today. Maybe I'll call a budget meeting at four-thirty today once I've gotten through them."

"They don't call you Bernie Buzzkill for nothing," Austin said.

The finance director grinned with shark teeth. He took the nickname as a source of pride. "The summer outing is coming up in a couple weeks. You'd better bring this Regina to it. I want to see what delusional looks like in the flesh."

"Ha ha," Austin said. He resisted saying any more. If Bernie could only have seen them at Club Equinox last week he'd have choked....

* * *

Luckily, Bernie did not call a four-thirty meeting and ruin everyone's weekend, so Austin was happy when he walked into the house from the garage. He had been singing along to a Green Day song in the car, and now the track was stuck in his head.

Regina was on the couch with her journal as Ceili slept in a baby seat perched on a blanket in the middle of the family room floor.

"How was your day?" she asked, looking up from the book.

He shrugged. "The most important thing is that it's over. What would you like to do tonight to celebrate?"

Regina grinned. "I had a feeling you'd want to do something, so I asked Brandy to come over tonight at seven. I hope that's okay."

"Absolutely," he said. "Where are we going?"

"You have to ask?" She shook her head. "It's Friday night; do you know where your sexy, satanic friends are hiding?"

"So, Club Equinox it is," he said with a grin. "Do I have to wear a blindfold still?"

She nodded. "But once we get you fully initiated, we can drop it. So...maybe tonight we can move that process along?"

He shrugged. "Maybe. Depends what they want me to do. And what the membership fee is?"

"Worry not," she said. "If you watch Ceili, I'll go get ready."

Austin looked at the baby, who was strapped into her baby seat and dozing with a pacifier in her mouth.

"I don't think that's going to be much of a problem," he said with a grin.

"Just give me five minutes," she said, and disappeared up the stairs.

Austin sat back on the couch and stretched with an audible yawn. It had been a helluva week, and he was definitely ready for some relaxation. He wasn't sure if a club was really what he needed, but....

He smiled as he watched Ceili breathing slowly. Every now and then one of her eyes would start to open, and then she'd suck harder on the pacifier only to have the eye close again. He wanted to lift her up and hold her, but he didn't want to wake her either. So he stretched and sunk deeper into the couch. As he did, Regina's 'little black book' slid down from where she'd set it on the middle cushion to touch his thigh.

Austin pushed it back up to the centre of the cushion, but after glancing at the stairs to make sure Regina wasn't in sight, he flipped it open.

Her familiar script covered the page he'd flipped to. It was dated quite a while ago. Austin leaned over to read it closer. She was writing about rituals.

I finished reading the Elysian text today, which was enlightening on a lot of levels. I wasn't allowed to remove it from the rare book room at the university library, so I've had to go back and forth for the past few days to go through it. I took a lot of notes. I'll copy them here over the next few days, so that I've documented it all in one place. It's amazing to me that an ancient book of rituals like this is locked up in a library special collection versus being hidden in a secret drawer in some witch's desk. It seems far too precious – and underground – to be in a public collection.

The text was written almost six hundred years ago now, so it was difficult to decipher some of it with the language differences. There was a lot of description of the basics – using candles poured with the blood of an innocent when trying to set a protection ward. Using the hair and fluids of a body to secretly bind it to your will. Or, most powerfully, using the bones of an infant in a circle to establish a ward that can repel almost anything. The power that can be divined from a child's bones is actually an entire chapter of the text, which, naturally, was one of the parts I was most interested in. They used to keep the skulls in their pockets, because if you inserted your fingers in the eyeholes and invoked the child's spirit, you could instantly triple the intensity of any spell you cast. Apparently, the covens of old used to pulverise the rest of the bones of innocents once they were sacrificed, in order to stretch the amount of protection they could glean from the children as far as possible. They'd sell 'baby powder' in small bags in the black market – and it wasn't the kind of powder that you put on diaper rash. I wish I'd been alive back then to visit one of those markets. So many rare and strange things!

The text also goes into a lot of the theory behind blood bonds, and why sharing blood in a ritual with someone you are close to can work as part of a warding spell. Basically, if your blood mingles with the blood of another by choice, you can invoke the power of earth to cement the bond and help preserve your lives inside your circle of blood. It's like a shield. Creating a circle of infant bones is more powerful, but a blood bond can go a long way toward warding off the unwanted…"

There were footsteps on the landing up above, and Austin quickly closed the book and left it on the centre of the cushion on the couch. Regina breezed into the room seconds later, and held out her hand to him.

"My turn?" he asked. "I'm not sure I can compete with that." He nodded at the sheer black silk top that draped perfectly to show cleavage, and the skirt that showed a daring expanse of black hose.

"You don't need to compete," she said. "You just need to keep up! Now, get changed – Brandy will be here any minute."

*   *   *

Regina took the blindfold off as soon as she had guided him over the threshold of the club doorway. "Maybe this will be the last time you have to wear it," she suggested. He blinked as his eyes adjusted, and saw Regina frown.

"Almost forgot," she said, and reached into her purse for a vial of clear liquid. She wet her finger and inscribed his forehead with the Mark of Cain. The mark was invisible on the street, but it shown like a beacon in the blacklight areas of the club.

They handed in their phones to the doorman, who clearly recognised them and thus barely looked at them twice. Then they made their way straight to the bar. The DJ was already filling the room with a pounding beat. It sounded gothy and dark, but with a more manic energy than typical darkwave. Austin had to admit it made him want to dance. And he never danced.

They sat at the bar and watched as the room slowly filled; by nine o'clock, there was a steady stream of people filing through the front door.

Austin was on his third beer when a thin man in a black T-shirt and the club's ubiquitous half-moon symbol emblazoned in red came up to Regina and leaned in to whisper something in her ear. He watched as her face lit up, and then she nodded.

"We'll be there," she said loudly over the music, and the guy faded back instantly into the crowd gyrating on the floor nearby.

"What's up?" Austin asked.

"Something good," she said, leaning in to his ear. "Tonight in the Sacristy, they're holding the Ritual of Letting Go. You'll be able to take Dark Communion and empty your need into the chosen vessel."

"That all sounds pretty…oblique. And possibly obscene," Austin answered, nearly yelling into her left ear to be heard.

"You'll enjoy it," she promised, and lifted her Jack and Coke to toast him. "It's a special night that doesn't happen often."

"So what do we do?"

"We wait until the time is right," she said. "We wait for the signal."

Austin raised one eyebrow at that but said nothing. He lifted his pint and closed his eyes for a second as the cool bitter ale slid down the back of his throat.

A short while later, in the midst of an amped up remix of The Cure's 'Closedown', an ominous bell sounded somewhere in the hall. The music did not stop, but the tolling bell was easily heard.

"That's our cue," Regina said, and emptied the last swig from her glass before setting it back on the counter and pushing it across the bar. Austin did the same and got off his stool. He turned toward the dance floor and noticed that while many people continued dancing, there were also quite a few who had begun moving through the crowd toward the back of the room. Regina took his hand and pulled him in that direction.

Apparently, this was not a 'club-wide' event.

They walked through a doorway and down a short hall before descending a set of stone steps to a cool antechamber below. That room was filled with black candles; the scent of burning wax was heavy in the air. The light reflecting off of the dark walls was almost blinding.

There were several people loitering there, talking in couples and trios in low tones. But most of the people walked straight through the heavy dark wooden door to pass into what Austin assumed was their destination.

Regina squeezed his hand and pulled him through the door as well, and as soon as they reached the other side, leaned in to proclaim, "Welcome to the Sacristy!"

The room was wide and windowless; the walls were made of mortared stone, and the floor was also stone – wide, irregular slabs of polished limestone. Most of the light in the room came from candles burning in small insets in the walls. There were a half-dozen low divans around the room and people gathered around each of them, as well as a bar on the far side. Austin had to stifle a laugh when he noticed the statue in the centre of the room.

A satyr. The goat man sported a visible erection as it raised one hand in the air, as if to invite the start of revelry. He wondered if the nuns would dance around it, like the covens of old.

Regina led him to the bar but stepped in front of him when he was about to place his order. "I need one Evil Sacrament and one Dark Desire, please."

"I just wanted a beer," he complained.

She shook her head. "This is a ceremony. You need the right drink."

He looked at her sideways as if to say, *Are you serious?*

She ignored the look and handed him a silver goblet a moment later. "You're going to like this, trust me," she said.

He looked into the container. The liquid looked blood-red. Of course. Hopefully it wasn't actually virgin or goat's blood or something equally goofy.

She touched her goblet to his and smiled. He hesitated but, after watching her swallow hers, he went ahead and put the edge of the goblet to his lips. And took a tentative sip from the potion within.

When the heavy liquid hit the back of his throat, he almost moaned. The drink was like a heavy mead, filled with the thick sweet of honey and the bitter scent of incense or herb. His taste buds flipped cartwheels and he took a deeper draught almost instantly.

"Careful," Regina cautioned. "That shit sneaks up on you. But I was right, huh?"

He pulled the goblet away from his lips and nodded. "What's in it?"

Regina grinned. "Oh, the usual things. Bats' wings, the hair of a murderer, virgin blood…and lots of alcohol."

"You're not serious," he said. She didn't answer.

"I don't care what it is," he said and lifted the goblet to take another drink. "This stuff is amazing."

The buzz of conversation in the room suddenly quieted, and Austin turned to see a procession of nuns walking in from the main entry. They were led by the Irreverent Mother. The women filed around the room and after circling it once, took up positions around the statue of the satyr.

"Tonight is a special night," the Irreverent Mother announced. "We are gathered here to celebrate the needs of the flesh. We will perform the sacrament of Letting Go. The gods and demons will be jealous of your loins, my children. Hold nothing back. Give and take until there is no more.

"Let the ceremony begin."

From the corner of the room, a slow drumbeat began, and Austin peered into the shadows there to see a dark-skinned man sitting on the floor surrounded by handmade drums with wooden shells and white skins. He was setting a tribal beat, in stark opposition to the electronic techno music of the main room of the club. This was organic, and ancient.

The sisters in the centre of the room began to writhe in a very non-nun-like fashion, the black film of their habits moving and shifting like shadow play against the swaying curves of their hips and jiggling outlines of their breasts. The candlelight gave everything a weirdly shimmering quality, as if the room was seen through a fever dream.

All around them, small crowds of people gathered around the divans and knelt. They appeared to be praying. One by one, the sisters touched the prong between the statue's legs and then danced away from the satyr to take up positions at the front of each divan. The Irreverent Mother then walked up to each and undid the clasp that held her vestments on. One by one, the garments fell to the floor, and the sisters stood naked and exposed at the edge of each divan.

A man in a bishop hat – though one that looked to be decorated with satanic symbology – walked behind the Irreverent Mother and removed the headgear from each stripped nun. Then he held out a small black wafer – as if he was giving communion. The sisters each stuck out their tongues and took the wafer into their mouths before bringing it back inside their lips to chew and swallow. After they accepted his sacrament, they lay down on the divans and held their hands over their heads, exposing themselves to the kneeling crowds around them.

"Blood of our blood, life of our life," the Irreverent Mother said from the side of the room. "Remove the costumes and masks that you hide behind and show your true selves. Only in our nakedness can we share truth and the nature of what we are. You are not salesmen and accountants and cashiers and mechanics and electricians and web page designers. You are members of Equinox. You are our brothers and sisters, and you know the power that we hold in our chests, power that only in our unity can we set free. Stand up, watchers, and divest your impediments now."

All around the room, the kneelers rose and began to undress. In moments, nearly everyone in the room was nude.

"Come," Regina said, and led him to stand near one of the divans. She began to strip her own clothes off, tossing her blouse and bra to the floor behind the divan with the clothes of eight others. Austin was slow to follow, but she returned to him and took the goblet from his hand. "It's an all-or-nothing thing," she said.

He got it.

The room was feeling hot and thick anyway, he thought, as he pulled the shirt over his head. Regina's hands were on his belt buckle then, and before he knew it he was kicking off the pant legs. When he could feel the air suddenly slipping between his legs, he knew that he was fully nude, and blinked back a wave of fuzziness to see what was going on around him. The alcohol of the Dark Desire drink was suddenly hitting him hard, he realised. He felt buzzed and half out of it.

Regina picked their goblets up from where she'd placed them on the floor and handed his back to him. He took a sip, and the power of the drink took an even deeper hold. He felt his spine growing liquid. The Irreverent Mother was giving instructions from somewhere in the room behind him, and he watched as one by one the people around the divan leaned in to kiss the nun lying prone before them.

Regina guided him closer and then she herself leaned down to kiss the woman on the low divan. Their lips locked and held for what seemed like five minutes to Austin. But then the room pulsed, or at least his vision did, and Regina was pressing him to bend and kiss the nun as well.

He did and found the woman's lips hot and swollen. They felt like they would burst as his own touched hers, and the wetness of her tongue slipped into his mouth to tease him. The throbbing rhythm of the hand drums only seemed to heighten the eroticism of the moment.

The nun was not shy.

Regina's hands pulled him back and he stood then and watched as the girl kissed three more comers.

The drumbeat changed. Suddenly it became more staccato. More intense. Rougher.

The Irreverent Mother said something from behind him. Everyone in the room seemed to come to attention. And then the bishop was walking around again, handing out something to people at each of the divans.

When he reached Austin's spot, a balding man with a hairy paunch that nearly obscured a thick, stubby turtle's head of a penis took the offering from the bishop.

It was a ceremonial knife. The haft was decorated with coloured stones, and the blade was at least eight inches long. And curved.

"The ultimate union is to share all that we are, not simply spit or cum but blood and life itself, my children. Undo the boundaries of your flesh and let yourself out. Let go. Be one with a bride of Equinox. Let the letting begin!"

The balding paunchy man took the knife and pressed it to his chest, drawing it across his skin. Where the blade passed, a thin line of crimson revealed itself. A line of life.

The man took the blade and pressed it in the matching spot on the flawless white skin of the girl below. She did not flinch or move her arms from over her head. Her eyes followed the arms of the man as he drew the knife across the skin just above her breasts. Then her eyes rolled back and she let out a low cry of pain. Maybe. Austin wasn't sure if it was pain or pleasure, honestly. But she did not seem unhappy about the violation. She was not restrained, and yet she lay there and let him do it.

The man lowered himself until his wound was over hers. He eased his chest down on top of hers, briefly touching his whole body to hers until the blood of their mutual wounds smeared together across their chests. He lay there and gyrated for a moment. Then he raised himself back up, stood, and drifted away.

A woman took his place. She used the knife to slice across the top of her thigh, and then, just as the man had, sliced a wound in a corresponding place on the girl below. When she lay on top of the girl to share wounds, the two kissed for several minutes before the woman pushed herself away and handed the knife to another man.

Austin leaned in to Regina's ear and whispered, "This is kinda fucked up."

She shook her head. And then turned to him to whisper back, "This is Letting Go. Blood and kisses. They bind us. Here we share everything about ourselves with each other. And at the end, we all are one."

Austin closed his eyes for a moment to clear his head, and took that thought in. He didn't really buy it, but he got the symbolism. Still, the 'bride' on the couch was soon bleeding from a handful of wounds, while everyone else escaped with just one. It hardly seemed fair.

The drumbeat had begun to take on a different vibe again, more slow and throbbing. More sensual. And now the Irreverent Mother began to speak again.

"There are initiates among us," she said. "And this ceremony is for them. We take them inside ourselves and they bring us into their very hearts tonight. Make room, and celebrate their Letting Go."

The bishop was walking around the room again and handing out black wafers once more. But this time, he gave them not to the nuns lying prostrate, but to people at each of the divans. When he approached their group, he went unerringly to Austin. The people around him all fell back, and Austin was suddenly acutely aware that he was standing naked in front of a man in transparent vestments, who held out a black host. The Devil's communion? What made it black?

Austin felt the room swim for a second. Then he opened his mouth and accepted the host. What else could he do? When the bishop nodded and moved on, Austin turned to Regina. "You didn't tell me," he began.

She only smiled. And handed him the knife.

"Share your blood with us," she said. "And we will share a new life with you."

"Where," he asked. "I don't know where...."

He held the blade over his body, moving it from his chest to his belly to his legs and then back up. Cutting himself was not high on his list of things to do.

"Share the blood where you run hot," Regina suggested. And even as she said it, he felt his erection growing beneath the blade. Almost begging for the knife.

He nixed that idea right away. He would not cut his cock... but he *could* cut above it. Austin went with that idea and drew the edge of the blade along the top of his pubic hair. Blood instantly welled up atop his groin.

"And now take her in the same way," Regina prodded.

He frowned but brought the knife to the faint down that was all that remained of the nun's pubic thatch. She clearly did not believe in 'wild and wooly' and was almost as clean as a girl.

Austin touched the blade to the spot where the stubble ended and drew the knife across.

She bled, another line of pain on a body smeared with her own and others' blood.

"Take her as yours now," Regina said. When he didn't move immediately, she put her hand on his arm, and took the goblet from him. "Lie with her," she demanded. "Give yourself completely to her. I'll be right here behind you."

Austin climbed onto the girl, who accepted him easily, drawing her arms across his shoulders and pulling him down into her embrace. He could feel the heat of his blood seeping across the base of his penis and dripping down his testicles, but somehow that only made him more excited, as he kissed the ceremonial bride and felt his erection slide easily into the wetness of her sex. Blood or excitement, he wasn't sure, but he was suddenly surrounded with heat, and it drove him to an instinctual thrust.

The drumbeat in the corner of the room had become purely sexual and when Austin took a second to look up, he saw that every divan had people writhing in passion on it. When the girl beneath him grabbed his ass and drew him fully into her, he surrendered completely to the situation.

Regina stood to the side of the divan. She'd drawn something out of her handbag. It looked almost like a small doll, he thought, noticing that it seemed to have two arms and legs as she held it to her lips and spoke something that he couldn't hear over the volume of the room.

His blood suddenly felt on fire as it never had before and Regina faded into the background like smoke. Austin saw the room in almost a skein of raw colour. The girl beneath him was a fuzzy shade of passion red, the walls beyond were only shadows of another place. There was a burning in his throat where he had swallowed the host, and the fire from his centre seemed to spread, emanating to his hands and spine and most of all, his cock. Which only wanted to bury itself into the very core of this woman.

He did his best to answer the primal need growing more and more violent inside him. He could feel dark, angry electricity throbbing in his bones now; with the release of his passion, he seemed to be feeling the release of all civil inhibitions. The room grew indistinct around him as his thoughts became strangely savage. He'd never felt this way before, drunk or sober. He thrust and ground against the nun beneath him, and she cried out as he did – the first real sounds he'd heard from her all night, despite all the knife cuts – which only drove him to faster and harder motions.

Regina came closer and knelt at the head of the divan, coaxing him to continue his descent into dark passion with wicked whispers in his ear. She held the dark doll in one hand as she urged him with violent words to spend himself in the girl. And then as he drew near his orgasm, she held the blade up to the nun's flushed throat.

"She is your sacrament," Regina whispered. "Take and eat."

With that, she drew the knife over the woman's throat and a splash of blood suddenly hit Austin's face. The girl shifted and shook beneath him, and Regina pressed the knife into Austin's hand.

"She is yours now, every heartbeat is yours."

Austin didn't know what that was supposed to mean. But he could barely think coherently now regardless. His head was awash in a kaleidoscope of colour. Every flash brought a strange, powerful ecstasy. The girl beneath him was bleeding on him, all over him thanks to the wounds that others had made, as well as the cut in her neck. And yet somehow the smears of crimson across his chest and arms and face didn't faze him, but rather, turned him on more.

His heart seemed to pump faster than it ever had; he could hear it like a jackhammer in a tunnel as his hips moved. The girl's blood beneath him oozed like oil, coating them and making their congress ever more fluid. It was the most amazing, psychedelic, erotic moment he had ever experienced. For a few seconds, there was nobody else in the entire room but him and the bride, her luscious naked body a gift for him to suck and bite and eat and love all at once.

Regina was whispering things in his ear. Words he didn't understand. And then English phrases too. "Take her. Do it. Her life is yours."

He wanted to slow his motion, prolong his orgasm, but he couldn't hold back. Austin held the knife close to the girl's neck as he drove himself harder inside her. The blade pressed down on her skin as he felt his own rush build. Blood streamed out along the knife's edge and he felt a horrible excitement build as it did.

He screamed out at the end, unable to process the intense build of emotions and adrenaline and pure pleasure. He was lost in a place he had never imagined. Lost in blood and perversion. Something had changed his brain and he couldn't, didn't want to fight it.

The girl beneath him was no longer matching his thrusts, but Regina's face hung just above the girl's eyes. "Don't stop," she insisted. "You are one with life and death in this moment."

He couldn't close the loop in his brain with what that meant in that second, but he didn't stop. Couldn't have stopped if he'd wanted to.

Austin fell away from the girl finally, coated in her blood and completely drained and sated in every way. His limbs hung at his sides like lead weights. "Oh my God," he whispered. "What did we just do?"

"Drink this," Regina said, holding his head up until the edge of a metal goblet touched his lips.

People encircled the bed, and lifted and moved the bride away, carrying her to somewhere Austin didn't see. He collapsed back into the spot she'd occupied. His tongue was thick and his mind barely able to track what was going on around him. Regina pressed him down to the divan, and straddled him presently, teasing his still-erect member with the down of her own sex. She kissed him, and he surrendered to her tongue. He felt barely conscious, but the heat of her mouth woke him again.

When she pulled back, she whispered, "You are one of us now. You have sacrificed to Satan."

"Sacrificed?" he whispered, his heart constricting in fear. His voice seemed like it came from far away. "She's not dead?"

"We are all more alive than ever," Regina answered. Her words confused him.

"I don't understand," he said. "I never wanted anything like that before. It was like I was someone else."

"You let the Devil inside," she said. "It's the moment of transcendence that we all come here seeking. You're a true member of Equinox now."

"So...no more blindfold?" he asked. He had just fucked a masochist almost to death in a bloodthirsty haze and that was the thought that came to his head.

"No more blindfold," she agreed. "You have seen, you can't unsee. You have taken blood. You can't untake. You are part of Equinox now."

"That was ... amazing," he breathed, remembering the completely paralysing impact of the orgasm. "And ... wrong," he added, as he remembered the spurt of the nun's blood at the end. "She'll...be okay?"

"There is no wrong in Club Equinox," Regina said. "We all come here by choice. We all leave here forever changed."

"You didn't answer…" Austin said. He could feel his tongue slurring.

"I wanted you to be with me in this life," she said. "I hope I wasn't too fast in bringing you here."

He could see the troubled look in her eyes and the image of blood faded from his mind for a moment. She had brought him into the most secret of inner sanctums. He wasn't sure now that he wanted to be here, but everything was strange in his head. He didn't want her to be upset with him.

"No," he said. "…wanted to be with you."

She smiled faintly, and shifted her hips slowly against him, working him up again. "I really need your help, Austin," she said. "Will you help me?"

He nodded drunkenly. "Yes, anything for you," he said. His body moved but no longer seemed under his control at all.

She raised herself up on her arms then, so that her full weight was now driving down on his hips. Her breasts shook as she moved above his face.

"Anything?" she asked. There was a tremor of something deeper than sexual need in her voice.

"Yes," he whispered. "Anything."

In the back of the room, the drummer still played, but his beats were almost inaudible as Austin stared into Regina's eyes. He could not see anything beyond her; the world had constricted to be her and her alone. But it was increasingly difficult to focus on her. The edges of her face began to swim and flutter. And then she asked him a question.

"Would you give me your baby?"

He smiled and tried to move harder inside her. But he couldn't even feel his lower half. His whole body was strangely numb. "I will… make a baby with you," he whispered. He wasn't sure if he could do that now, however. His lips didn't move right and there were colours leaking across his vision. He felt as if he might slide down an angry rainbow into an ocean of winking stars at any second. He had given his all to the bleeding girl. Thinking of her made him smile and for a moment, he lost track of the woman he was with. His mind was swimming in a strange haze of pleasure.

"I don't want to *make* a baby," Regina breathed, looking down on him with eyes lit bright. Seeing her eyes brought him back to the moment. She was still somehow using him with short rhythmic hip motions. "I want *your* baby. I want Ceili. I want to bring her to the club for the Devil's Equinox. It only happens once every dozen years, and we need a child for the ceremony."

Austin wasn't sure what she meant, but through the haze, he felt a sudden strong intuition that it would not be good for Ceili. He moved his mouth and at first nothing happened. A moment later the words appeared.

"No," he murmured. "I can't let you have Ceili. This isn't … a good place for babies."

His words were a terrible slur, but Regina clearly understood him. Because when he finished speaking, her mouth split into a smile as wide as a shark's.

"You said you'd give me anything," she said. "I want you to give me Ceili. You've let me take care of her these past few weeks, and now I'm like her mother."

Austin shook his head. The room spun when he did. "I don't think so," he slurred. "Not for here. Not for this."

"Give me your baby," she urged again. "Say you will." She ground against him low and slow now, her lips just inches from his own. He realised that he could not feel her legs, though he knew they were still on top of his own. She watched his face with an eerie concentration.

"No," he said. "You can't … I wo' let you brin' her here."

"I thought you'd say that," she said. "But I wanted to give you the chance. I know you haven't had enough time here to understand and to give her freely, and the ritual would work better if she was given freely. But…we don't have enough time for me to make that happen. I wanted you to agree to do this voluntarily. If you were really part of Equinox, you would. But it doesn't matter. I claim Ceili tonight in exchange for granting your wish."

"Wish?" he mumbled. He could barely move his lips.

"Your wish that your wife was dead."

With that, she suddenly levered herself off of him, and stood next to the divan, smiling sadly. "I really did want this moment to be different," she said.

And then she walked away from him. Austin tried to sit up, to follow her. To stop her. And realised then that he couldn't move. At all.

His arms, legs, neck…they were all heavy as concrete blocks.

He couldn't move a muscle.

"Regina," he tried to call. But his throat only made a weak hiss.

He tried to turn his head to see where she'd gone, but the orange flickers of the candles only twisted in the shadows on the ceiling above him. His eyes focused briefly on those, as he realised the heat of his passion had suddenly grown grave-cold. Whatever she had given him to drink after he'd been with "the bride" had done something…

The lights grew dimmer and dimmer in his eyes. And finally went out.

CHAPTER EIGHTEEN

There was ice in his brain.

Or maybe it was steel. A blade pressing right behind the base of his neck and up and in. Austin was aware of the feeling for minutes before he was fully awake. It coloured his dreams, though the content of those faded as soon as he opened his eyes. Ice in his head. Ice on his body. He was cold.

Austin opened his eyes and knew immediately he was not where he should be. The ice in his brain instantly turned to pain as he blinked and turned his head. The room swam into focus and he realised that he was lying on the floor in what appeared to be a warehouse space. The ceiling looked a hundred feet away, but on the one side he could see large pallets stacked with boxes all along the corrugated metal walls.

The events of the night before suddenly all came back and he blinked hard, trying to put the room into full focus. This was not where he had been last night.

He pushed himself off the floor and shards of glass seemed to fall across the inside of his head, scoring the naked folds of his brain. He groaned and looked around, propped up on one arm.

He was lying naked on the floor of a large warehouse. A pile of clothes lay to his left and he reached out and lifted the pair of jeans. They were his. And the lump of his wallet was still in the back pocket. He checked it and his money and credit cards were still there.

Small favours.

His skin was covered in goose bumps and he shivered slightly in the early morning cold. Austin reached over to grab and pull on his underwear and socks as he considered the situation. He'd been abandoned in a strange place after being drugged by his girlfriend after holding a knife to a girl's throat in a sex club. And her last words had been to threaten his baby girl.

Austin's heart leapt. He'd been out all night. And Regina had been the one to bring in the babysitter – another member of Club Equinox.

He swore out loud and slipped one foot into his jeans. He had to get home. He feared what he might find there. A lot of emptiness.

Shit.

Austin pulled the shirt over his head, moaning as the ice knife moved back and forth in his brain. Whatever had been in that drink…or 'communion' was brutal.

He sat down again to pull on his shoes and then took a deep breath and walked toward a door to the right. There were loading bay entrances on one wall, and a small white door to the right of them. He moved in that direction, groaning with every step. He felt like hell.

When he turned the knob on the door, he found himself stepping into a wide-open faded asphalt parking lot. Austin walked outside. The door clicked shut behind him as he blinked hard against the glare of the sun. It was still early morning, and the air held the heavy scent of dew and dawn. He turned away from the orange globe and looked instead at where the boundaries of the parking lot were. The place had a silver metal fence that ran around the perimeter, keeping the bushes and trees of an old neighbourhood at bay. He had no idea where he was.

Austin walked along the structure to the front of the building. As he passed the corner, he saw that he was in one section of a long industrial complex. The structure went on and on, with nondescript grey siding the only constant. Doorways with address signs and small branded logos interrupted the building at regular intervals.

He was probably somewhere along the railroad tracks, he surmised, since that's where most of the industrial complexes in Parkville were built. Warehouses that led along the tracks and on out of town.

How far was he from the place that held Club Equinox?

Impossible to guess. Maybe close. Or maybe they'd dumped him on the other side of town.

Either way…he had to get home.

Austin began walking down the driveway toward the street.

He reached into his jeans and found the hard rectangular lump of his phone.

So, they had even returned that to him. He pulled it out and thumbed it on. He pulled up Google Maps and saw that he was just a mile or so from the centre of town. And then he looked up a taxi. He needed to get home. As soon as possible.

★   ★   ★

On a Saturday morning, Parkville was pretty quiet. The cabbie had picked him up within fifteen minutes of him calling, and Austin said nothing on the short ride home. All he could think about were the words that Regina had said a few hours before.

"I claim Ceili in exchange for granting your wish. Your wish that your wife was dead."

He pulled a twenty-dollar bill out of his wallet as soon as the cabbie hit the entrance to his subdivision. "The one with the grey shutters, there on the right," he said, as they pulled onto his street. He pointed toward the driveway and the cabbie turned in slowly. The meter said $12.60 as they made the turn but Austin wasn't going to wait.

"Keep the change," he said as they came to a stop, and dropped the bill over the front seat. He was out of the cab and punching in the entry code to the garage in less than thirty seconds.

The house was completely still.

He walked through the kitchen and into the family room. The couch was empty. Regina wasn't there, as she almost always had been over the past month.

There was no journal sitting next to the old bronze base of the light.

Austin didn't spend any time on the lower level; he ran to the stairway and vaulted up it. When he reached the landing, he turned left and pushed through the half-open doorway into Ceili's nursery.

It was empty. Just as he'd known it would be.

Austin stared at the white cotton blanket and the empty brown eyes of the teddy bear that lay discarded next to the silent pillow and began to cry.

Regina had taken his baby.

His head was throbbing, but he shook it anyway as the tears streamed down his cheeks. What did they want Ceili for? What could he do to get her back?

He took a breath and forced himself to stop staring at the empty crib. She wasn't there. But was Regina nearby still?

He ran down the stairs and out the front door. If the neighbours were watching, they must have thought he was crazy as he vaulted up the steps to the old house next door. The door was dark blue, with a small window in it, but it was covered with a curtain. He couldn't see inside.

He rang the bell and banged his fist on the door over and over again, but there was no answer. As he had known there would not be. Regina had stolen his baby girl; she wasn't going to answer her door and say, "Hey, what's up?"

Austin walked away from the old house and stared up into the curtained vacancy of the upper-storey windows. He could feel the tears streaming down his cheeks, but he couldn't look away. She'd taken Ceili.

She'd taken his wife *and* his baby from him.

Austin felt his legs give out, and he sat down on the white concrete sidewalk in front of the house next door and began to bawl.

*   *   *

"Where is he now?" the Irreverent Mother asked, carefully placing an unlit black candle in a canvas sack.

"He's back in his house," Regina answered, wrapping the ceremonial candelabra in a small towel and adding it to the bag. They were packing up Regina's secret altar, now that there was no further need to occupy the house. Everything she needed for the Devil's Equinox was at the club now. It was hard to believe that she could count the time until that long-awaited night in hours rather than months and weeks. She had been preparing for this time literally for years.

The older woman nodded and set down the increasingly full sack to stand on one side of the altar. Regina took her lead and moved to the other side, and together they lifted and began to fold the black silk that had covered the table beneath the candles.

"We have a problem," the Irreverent Mother said.

"What do you mean?" Regina asked.

"Jilli texted me while I was on the way over here. You know she's been translating a grimoire of Felida de Seantia."

Regina shrugged and folded an end of tablecloth silk over. "She is all about researching Felida's life."

"She ran into something this morning in the grimoire that might impact our ceremony."

Regina stopped moving and looked hard at the Irreverent Mother. "Like what? Felida was an Elementist. Her coven would never have gone near rituals like the Devil's Equinox. She worked with herbs and calling forest spirits. Not in our wheelhouse at all."

"That's where you're wrong. Apparently, Felida's coven *did* attempt a Devil's Equinox ritual… and it failed."

"Seriously?" Regina asked. She looked confused for a moment, but then rolled her eyes. "Even if it's true, I'm not surprised she failed. Felina was all about herb and nature spells, not rituals like this."

The Irreverent Mother shook her head. "That's what we always thought. Because that's what she became known for. But… she wrote at one point about the Equinox ceremony she attempted. And how they failed – she said because they did not have one of the child's parents there to perform the sacrifice."

Regina paused in her folding.

"We need to bring the father back to Equinox."

Regina shook her head angrily. "He's not going to agree to be part of the ritual, so he's useless to us," she complained. "We have what we need. I tried to seduce him into being a part of it, a part of us. But… there just wasn't enough time to bring him all the way along."

The Irreverent Mother said, "I know that you hoped that he'd be swayed by temptations of the Letting Go ceremony and the taste of the Devil's communion last night. At least long enough for him to fall into that moment of weakness and give the baby to you of his own free will. But you knew going into it that this was a longshot at best. I agreed that taking the child was a reasonable course, but…after what Jilli has translated, I'm not sure that we *can* do this successfully without him at least being present. It sure seems like we have more chance of success if the father is present at the Equinox. There may be an aspect of complicity that is part of what draws the power."

"I can invoke the ghost of the mother," Regina said. "I already gathered her hair and blood so that I could call her if I wanted to. I thought it might be amusing to have her witness what we do. Her anger may add fuel to the spell. I even have a spell that could fully incorporate her in the end, if the ritual goes the way I think. I could make her my servant, with no ability to say no."

The Irreverent Mother frowned. "I like the intent, but I don't know that a spiritual witness will help in His eyes. I think we need the father to be there, in the flesh, even if he doesn't raise the knife. And we might be more sure of success if he was the one to spill her blood."

Regina said nothing for a minute as she took the silken covering from the other woman and stowed it in the bag.

"He'll never agree to do it," Regina said. "I haven't had enough time to make him one of us."

"When he is faced with two bad choices, and neither of them is desirable, he'll choose the lesser of the two evils," the Irreverent Mother said. "He must be made to see that Ceili's sacrifice is the lesser of two horrible evils, and the best course for both him and her."

Regina considered. "That's a tall order," she said. "But you may be right."

The Irreverent Mother smiled. "I'm always right when the subject is about doing wrong," she said with a grin that dripped of wickedness.

CHAPTER NINETEEN

The police made him feel very nervous. But he had to call them. His baby was missing, how could he not? But once they began swarming his home, Austin felt as if he'd made a mistake. There was one, Detective Wolff, who seemed to be heading up the team; he asked Austin all of the questions. He arrived at the front door within ten minutes of Austin calling the police. Wolff carried an old-fashioned notepad and had a head of curled, silvering hair. He was no stranger to the force, and his eyes looked both sad and tired as he ran through his litany of standard questions. But as Wolff rattled off a list of 'where were you at the time of the crime' and 'who was the babysitter you left in charge' kind of questions, Austin felt increasingly uneasy.

At first, he figured they would accept that Regina was the prime suspect. But as he spit out answers to all of the questions, he realised that his own motives sounded sad and pathetic. He'd let a relative stranger move in with him right after his wife died, and he'd given her the charge of his child, even letting her hire the babysitter, so that they could go out to a club and 'party' on a Friday night. What must they think of him? Did they believe him at all?

When they asked him the location of the club, he almost choked. Could he really say that Regina had blindfolded him? What did that make him sound like?

"She wanted it to be a surprise," he said, after stumbling over his tongue. "I didn't realise what this place really was."

"Had she taken you there before?" the detective asked.

Another quandary. Did he admit that last night had not been the first night he'd been to Equinox? He didn't want to be caught in a lie. But he didn't want to tell the truth either.

"Yes," he said. "But she never took me deep inside the club to the place we were last night."

"Did she blindfold you before?"

He nodded. "She said that once I wasn't just a visitor, that she could take the blindfold off."

The detective looked at him quizzically. "And you didn't think this was unusual?"

"It seemed like a game, so I played along."

The detective nodded and wrote something on his pad.

One of the other officers walked up then and tapped Wolff. "Excuse me," the detective said and got up to confer with the other cop at the side of the room. Austin couldn't hear what they were saying, but he did hear the detective say, "Really?" in a rather surprised tone. Austin's attention perked up; maybe they'd found something out about Regina that would help.

Wolff's face said otherwise. The detective returned and sat down across from Austin and simply stared at him for a moment. Then he asked, "When was the last time Regina had you over to her house?"

Austin shrugged. "Never, actually. She always came here."

"You never went next door to pick her up for a date?" the detective asked. "She never had you over for dinner?"

Austin shook his head. "With the baby, she always came here. That's how we got to know each other – she was babysitting Ceili every day."

"Did you ever see her go into the house next door?"

Austin frowned. He didn't understand where Wolff was going with this.

"I've seen her there over the hedge."

"Have you seen her go in or come out of the house?"

Austin racked his brain. Had he? "Yeah, I think so. I'm sure I have. Why are you asking?"

"Because, Mr. Everett, nobody has lived in that house for the past seven years."

Austin said, "I know it was empty most of that time. But then Regina moved in."

The cop shook his head. "We checked with the bank. It hasn't been sold or rented. We've also just sent an officer inside. He says the place is mostly empty. There's a front room couch and a few other furnishings left from the previous owners, but that house has been basically empty since a baby – Carolyn Jones – disappeared seven years ago. The parents claimed the infant was kidnapped, but the Joneses themselves disappeared a few days later. The case is still listed as an open homicide investigation."

Austin frowned.

"Did you know about that case, Mr. Everett?"

"No," he said. "We just moved in here last year. The neighbours told us that that house had been vacant a long time. But then Regina showed up and said she was living there...."

Wolff shrugged. "The house is actually still on the market," he said. "We checked. Someone put the For Sale sign in the garage, but it's still listed with the realtor."

Austin wasn't sure what to say. It sounded ridiculous. He was sure he'd seen Regina go back there before she'd basically moved in with him.

"Is there anything else you can tell us about her, to help us try to trace her? Anything personal she might have left here with you? She left no personal belongings next door."

"I'll look," Austin said. "She has clothes here, upstairs, but really that was about it. She didn't fully move in with me."

"Though she was sleeping here."

Austin nodded. "For the past couple weeks, yeah."

"Did she talk about her family or friends...did she say anything that might give us a lead on where to look for her?"

Austin struggled to think. What did he actually know about Regina? The silence drew out as he thought about all of their conversations.

What did he know about her?

Nothing.

Where was the club she'd taken him to?

He didn't know. He realised he sounded like a nutjob.

After more questions that Austin could not answer, the detective finally stood up and handed Austin a business card. "We'll be back in touch soon," he said. "In the meantime, call me if you think of anything – *anything* – that might help us find her."

Minutes later, Austin was standing on his porch, watching Wolff get into a squad car as two other officers closed the door to the house next door and returned to their own car.

His head was pounding. There was a weight on his chest that felt as if it were crushing his lungs. He took deep breaths to try to force it away, but it did no good. He felt sick and helpless and completely alone.

Austin slowly went back inside the house to get a drink of water. He saw Ceili's bottles in the fridge and tears immediately began to leak down his face. He went back to the couch and sat down to really let out his pain. His baby was gone and there was no way for him to find her.

And then he felt his phone vibrate in his pocket.

There was a text notification. From an unknown number.

He clicked it open, and a photo suddenly took up his screen. It showed the stark image of a girl with wide-open eyes…and a wide-open neck, where her throat had been slit. There was blood all over her neck and chest. At the far left of the frame was Austin's shoulder and face in profile, looking down on the girl in an expression of orgasm. He was clearly on top of the girl, who appeared dead. The text accompanying the photo was short and heart-stopping.

I think the police would be very interested in this. Don't you? I wouldn't call them again if I were you.

Austin began to cry in earnest.

CHAPTER TWENTY

He knew the search would be fruitless, but he went anyway. He couldn't just sit in his house and wait for the police to call. And after the threatening text, he didn't dare call them now to ask what they were doing. He was obviously being watched. Plus, the police had a hundred cases to deal with. He only had one. And it meant the world to him. To the police, finding Regina and Ceili was just a job. They would clock out at the end of the day and not feel a thing if they didn't turn up a clue. So he was not just going to sit and wait for them to help him. But he didn't even know where to begin. The best way to find Regina would be to go to Club Equinox, if he only knew where it was. He had a vague idea of which direction Regina had headed in when she'd driven him there but really, that directional sense only extended to the end of his neighbourhood. Past there, she could have gone in any direction. He knew she'd passed over the tracks at one point, but those tracks cut all the way across town.

Austin decided to start at the only place that he knew Regina had gone to outside of his house. He drove to the place where he'd woken up this morning. Maybe Equinox was actually close to there. Of course, he could be standing right next to it and not know – there certainly wasn't going to be a big marquee sign on the street proclaiming *Club Equinox – your darkest desires unleashed!*

But maybe…if he found some likely buildings, he would hear the distant pound of club beats. It was nearly dusk, so it was a good time to go out looking for a dance club based on ears alone.

When he arrived, he pulled up in front of the large loading-dock doors and got out of his car. The place looked much the same as it had this morning. Sprawling and empty. He walked around the building to the back parking lot and shook his head. This was definitely not where the club was hidden. There were no cars here, no sidewalks and no sounds really, aside from the wind whooshing across the open field out back. When Regina had led him from the car to the club he knew that they had parked on a downtown street – he could hear distant traffic and they had walked down a sidewalk for a block before arriving at the club. He had this mental image from his time walking around blindfolded that the club was in a downtown kind of area with curbs and old sidewalks – he remembered stubbing his toe a few times on uneven concrete slabs.

He walked back to the car and drove slowly along the road back toward the centre of town. There was an old downtown area just a few blocks from here, so he followed the parallel run of the old train tracks for a couple minutes until the road curved away, and then he found himself waiting at the light to drive over the tracks. The intersection just beyond them marked the centre of the old Parkville downtown; the one nice thing about living in a small town was that you couldn't go too far before ending up in the centre of things. While there was a growing array of suburban sprawl developing all around the downtown, the old area itself was not that extensive. He turned right at the main intersection and drove slowly down the side streets. The restaurants and bars and grills of the main drag quickly turned into large old brick buildings with no commerce evident. Originally built as warehouses and factories, the Parkville downtown was now a mix of converted residential and office space. There were business signs on some of the buildings, but not for much that would draw consumer traffic. This was wholesale row. He noted a carpet warehouse, an electronics supply business and a hair salon in between buildings with no signs at all. Those unmarked buildings had likely been converted to condos.

He drove in a widening square around the centre of town, noting possible areas that seemed like places Club Equinox could have been located. He stopped a couple times, and walked for a couple blocks, looking and listening for potential hidden locations in unmarked old brick buildings.

All he could hear was the distant sound of a freight train running along the tracks on its way through town.

Every now and then he thought of Ceili's cherub face and a

particular look that she got when he kissed her or fed her. And instantly his throat grew thick, and tears fell from the corners of his eyes. He had failed her. Utterly failed his baby. He couldn't forgive himself. And he didn't know what to do to make it right.

He nearly tripped on a broken sidewalk slab and grew hopeful for a moment – could this have been the same sidewalk where he'd stubbed his toe when blindfolded? He walked up to a large red-brick building with tall stone pillars and decorative window facades. There were gargoyles on the corners of the roof where the gutters hung down. This was an old building with classic architecture. The kind of building that they used to construct when people actually cared about architecture versus simply creating tall pillars of steel and glass.

It might have been a bank at one time, but today it appeared untenanted. He walked up to a ground-floor window and looked inside. There were empty white marble counters within and broken tile floors. It looked as if several things had been removed from the wide room, given the state of the floor, which was strewn with crumbled papers and chunks of debris. The room he could see appeared long abandoned.

And as he stood still and listened, he couldn't hear any sounds of inhabitants.

Depressed at the futility of this search, Austin walked back to his car. He could hear the distant sounds of cars and the hums and mechanical clanks of fans and air conditioners: the background noise of any town when all the people are inside for the night, and the air holds the fading heat of the day, but not much more.

Austin drove home, more depressed than ever.

*　　*　　*

When he walked into the house through the garage entry door, he kicked his shoes off in the mud room and opened the inner door to the kitchen. And instantly had a sudden, overwhelming feeling that something was wrong.

The hair on the back of his neck suddenly stood up, though he heard no noise at all in the house. He entered the room and flipped the lights on.

The cabinet doors over the stove were both open, and there were bottles and baby formula cans sitting on the counter.

Austin frowned. He had not left the kitchen like that. Somebody had been here. He took a deep breath and considered. Had Regina come back secretly to get Ceili's things?

He cautiously walked through the family room and paused at the landing to listen. What if she was still here?

He crept up the stairs slowly, pausing at every step. He realised at the fifth step that he was holding his breath. He forced himself to let it out, and then drew in a new breath until his chest stopped burning.

The upstairs was as quiet as below, and he peered around the doorjamb into Ceili's room. It, too, was not the way he'd left it.

The closet doors were open, and the drawers to the small bureau were all open as well. He stepped inside and confirmed that Ceili's clothes were missing, not simply disrupted.

Regina had been here, he knew it. And he'd been gone, damn it! But the fact that she'd been here meant that she was still close, right? And that Ceili was okay if she was grabbing food and clothing.

Austin went to his bedroom and retrieved the card that Wolff had left him. Then he went downstairs and picked up the phone. When he heard the dial tone, he began to punch in the numbers on the card. He didn't want to touch anything else in the house until the police had been notified. Maybe they would find a clue somehow in the mess she'd left.

He paused mid-dial without completing the call. The image of the girl with the cut throat played over again in his head. He couldn't call them. His finger hovered over the keypad, frozen. He didn't know what to do. If the police could find anything here that would help locate Ceili…. He shook his head and hit the next number. He was calling them, to hell with Regina and her photos.

The line went dead.

He pressed the number again on the keypad and there was no beep. He pressed the receiver to his ear and heard only silence. *Damn it!* Fine time for the phone to go dead. Austin got up and started to walk toward the kitchen to get his cell phone.

Before he could reach the door, three men in black bodysuits came through it from the other side. Two of them grabbed and pinned his arms, while the third dove for his feet.

Austin tried to break free of their grasp and started to yell but something was suddenly shoved in and around his mouth. A gag. He grimaced as his tongue pushed against the cotton. Before he knew it, both of his hands were tied behind his back and something was cinching at his feet. He wrestled against the men but after they pulled his bonds fast, they stepped away from him and Austin fell to the floor.

He kicked and jittered there, rolling onto his side and then facedown in the carpet, before rolling back to his side. He screamed in frustration, but the gag kept most of his anger contained in his throat.

The men in black stood around him, arms crossed, watching his reaction. Austin continued to thrash around on the floor for a bit, struggling to loosen the bonds on his feet or hands to no avail. When he finally stopped bucking and shifting, and lay still for a minute, looking from one captor to the next, one of them finally took pity and bent down. One of them reached over to the phone and picked up Wolff's business card. He shook his head sadly.

"If you yell, I will kick you in the balls," the man said. He held Austin's gaze for a minute as he said it, as if to underline his point. *Cross me and you're fucked worse than you are already,* that look said.

Austin nodded, and did not try to scream from beneath the gag.

The man reached down and with both hands undid the knot that held the gag on. When Austin looked up, the man grinned.

"You obviously didn't understand the text you received," he said, waving the card in front of Austin's face. "It's really best for everyone if you don't make any calls right now. We're here to take you to Equinox. The ropes are just a precaution. Maybe you want to go. But we do not take chances."

"I want to go if my baby is there," Austin said. His voice caught and he almost choked as he said it. His mouth tasted awful now that the gag was removed. He swallowed and blinked hard, clearing his throat and his vision. "Do you have Ceili?"

The leader of the trio nodded. "Your baby is safe. She's waiting for you in the secret heart of Equinox."

"Will you take me to see her?"

The man grinned.

"Not only will you see her," he said. "but you will eat of her flesh at the height of the Devil's moon."

CHAPTER TWENTY-ONE

They didn't blindfold him. Which meant that they didn't expect him to ever leave the club once they reached it.

That was one of his first thoughts as they pulled away from his house in a large SUV. They had parked it in the open space in Austin's garage and had quickly muscled him through the door and into the middle seat in the back. Two of the three men in black sat on either side of him, while the third took off his mask and drove.

Austin watched as they turned right out of his neighbourhood and then shot down 8th Street toward downtown – he'd guessed that the club lay in that direction, when he'd tried to retrace Regina's route to Club Equinox earlier.

They crossed the tracks at Nineteenth and turned right, moving into one of the blocks that Austin had been to just an hour before. And then they parked in front of a nondescript brick building. It might have been one that Austin had walked in front of earlier, but he couldn't be sure.

The man nearest the sidewalk opened the door, stepped out and then reached back into the car to pull Austin after him. The other two joined in, and together they steered Austin through an unmarked wooden door. As soon as it shut behind them and they moved past a second, inner doorway, the familiar club sounds assaulted them.

Heavy pounding beats, flashing blue and white and red lights. Austin saw the undulating bodies on the dance floor ahead of them. A DJ stood on an elevated riser with a stack of black electronic equipment and a microphone to the right. But the men in black weren't interested in that side of the club. They pressed Austin to the left, and in moments, they were past the throng and moving through a narrow hallway in the back.

The hall emptied into another large room, but there was no modern sound system or electric spotlights here. They were back in the candlelit section of the building. Every few feet, one extended up from an inset in the stone face, and the flames flickered upward to throw orange shadows on the ceiling. A larger, singular torch lit the centre of the room, in front of a large stone statue of a goat's horned head.

Around the centre, a series of crosses were anchored in the ground. In front of each one stood a naked man or woman, with chains leading from manacles on their wrists to hooks in the arms of the crosses.

Behind each nude figure stood another, each of them brandishing leather whips. The sound of their tips cracking against the damp flesh of the chained subjects echoed through the room. The snap of whips against skin was the music of this club within a club.

Austin looked at one of the crosses and saw a woman with shoulder-length black hair and arms completely sleeved in tattoos literally dancing as the woman behind her snapped the whip. As her flogger snapped the leather, the girl bent forward, absorbing the lash, and then came up to grin and laugh.

He stared hard across the room at her tattoos, trying to make out what the designs represented. He could see the eye hollows of a skull on the shoulder closest to him, but there was a rich tapestry of vines and thorns and who knew what else around it. The creamy globes of her breasts bounced in front of those tattoos, yet he barely even noticed as he stared at the design. The artistry fascinated him for some strange reason. But before he could decipher its meaning or inspiration, a hand slapped the back of his head.

"Eyes on the prize, pervert. This is not the room we have in mind for you," one of the black-garbed men chastised. "Maybe you can come back here later, but there are darker things for you ahead."

"Much darker," one of the others laughed.

They walked through the undulating bodies writhing beneath the horsewhips of black-clad men, and suddenly the debauchery that Austin had seen in this club seemed somehow laughable. He realised that it was merely window dressing for a darker heart within, as they left the room behind and entered another hallway beyond, where

Austin was pushed down a flight of rough-hewn stone steps. As he descended, the flight spiralled to the right and around. He didn't count, but after a couple dozen steps, they finally reached the floor at the bottom.

It looked like how he imagined ancient Roman catacombs had been. Stone-floor hall. Torches on the grey block walls. Shadows in every corner. They walked for several yards, footsteps echoing eerily in the passageway. And then they reached an entryway. Heavy granite pillars flanked the opening, and the men in black pushed Austin through them.

The air inside was cool and damp. The light was low. Austin blinked after they entered, struggling to take it all in.

There was smoke in the air, maybe incense. He could smell a strange, pungent odour of burning. And as he strained to make out the layout of the room, he could see in the faintly blue light that there was a small crowd of people at the far end. And candles burning. A man wearing a tall ornamental hat and a vestment around his shoulders raised his arms and as he did, Austin could make out the fact that there was an altar beyond him.

And a nude figure upon it.

A familiar tableau from his past visits here.

"Where are we going?" he asked. But his question was only met with an elbow to the back.

"Just walk," one of the men said. "You'll get your answers soon enough."

They walked through the blue gloom of the subterranean room, and then, when they reached the stone altar at the front, Austin gasped.

Brandy, his babysitter, was the naked figure on the altar. And his baby was lying there, also bare, in her arms.

Austin leapt forward, but six hands grabbed and held him back.

"Uh-uh-uh," one of them cautioned. "Not until they're ready for you."

At that moment, there was a stir in the crowd beyond the altar, and sisters shifted and moved aside as someone pushed forward. Austin's heart sank as he saw who it was.

Regina.

She stepped through the crowd and reached the altar with a wide grin on her face. She wore next to nothing – a sheer black vestment that draped across her shoulders and served not to hide, but to accentuate, the swell of her breasts and the shadowed *V* of her sex. Her bare skin glistened with the sweat of exertion. What exertion, Austin didn't think he wanted to know.

"Necromancy told me you would return," she said, leaning in toward him.

"You didn't need magic to figure that out," he said. "You took my baby; of course I'm going to return."

Regina smiled. "I knew you would come. In fact, I banked on it. Because for the ceremony to be successful, we need your participation."

She stepped past Austin and touched one finger to his lips. He could smell the sweat on her. The steam of sex, maybe.

"What ceremony?" he asked.

"The rite of the Devil's Equinox."

Austin didn't like the sound of that.

"I just want my daughter back," he said. "Just let us go and I won't tell the police anything. I'll say you left her on my doorstep and that will be the end of it."

Regina walked past the altar and ran her hand across the baby's head. Ceili lay quiet on Brandy's breast; it could have been a Madonna and Child picture. Except that they were in a room with a demonic goat's head as the centrepiece.

"You'll make no deals with me now," she said, holding up one hand. "Now is when you pay back your debt."

"What debt?" he asked.

"You wanted your wife dead," she answered. "And I delivered. Now it's your turn."

"What do you want?"

"The price of your wife's life is the blood of your daughter."

"No," he said, straining against the hands that held him back. "I never asked you to hurt Angie. And I won't let you hurt Ceili."

Regina shook her head. "It won't be me that holds the blade," she said. "Ceili's blood will open the door. Her flesh will bring us to the heart of dominion. And our power will grow deep in that moment when she transcends. But your blood will draw her blood. Your hand will give her over. That's the crux of the ritual. And it is the only route to her salvation."

"You're insane," he said. He spit the words at her. But she only smiled.

"I didn't make the rules," she said. "But I will do my best to enforce them."

One of the 'sisters' walked up at that point holding a ceremonial dagger in her open palms. The knife was shiny silver, its haft encrusted with red and green jewels.

"At the height of the Equinox, you will enter Ceili's heart, and release her life to us all. When the moon moves away from the centre of the sun, the power of Selene will be ours. Your debt will be paid, and you can walk away free."

"I don't think so," Austin whispered. "I won't kill for you."

Regina laughed. "You already have. Or didn't you understand the photo I sent you?"

"You drugged me," he said. "I would never hurt anyone intentionally."

"Drugs, magic, your own brutality finally set free...it doesn't matter why," she said. "The point is, you have killed for me. And tonight, you will do it again." Regina shrugged. "That's the best thing that you could do. But there is another way."

She walked over to Brandy and lifted the child in the air. As she looked up at Ceili's face, the baby gurgled and smiled, her lips glossy wet and her eyes shining with happiness. The baby knew Regina.

"We can tie your life to hers," Regina said. "It won't bring as much power, but it should be enough. In that scenario, however, you do not walk out of here."

"I am not walking out of here without Ceili," Austin said.

Regina shrugged. "You might reconsider when you know more."

She pointed and from the crowd, four women in black silk robes stepped forward.

"Take him downstairs," she said.

Austin leapt toward Regina, struggling with all of his might to reach out to Ceili, but the women anchored him easily. The baby laughed and chirruped, thinking her daddy was performing some kind of joke for her.

And then a collar snapped around Austin's neck. He felt them thread the strap through the metal hook, but he couldn't lift his arms to stop them.

"That's better," Regina said. "You aren't fit to be a master. So you can be a dog."

Someone yanked hard on the chain, and Austin staggered backward choking.

Before he could regain his balance, two hands grabbed his arms and held them together behind his back. He felt the rope slip around his wrists but could do nothing to stop it from cinching tight.

One of the sisters took the leash and pulled on the chain, leading Austin through the throng of onlookers and out of the room. He tried to look backward, to see Ceili, but the woman only yanked harder on the chain, and he staggered and struggled to stay upright. Thick hands gripped his shoulders and pushed him forward. Seconds later they were walking through a dark empty passageway. And then he was pushed through a doorway and into a shadow-filled room. The visual echoes of orange flame flickered against one wall, illuminating an upside-down cross and several strange geometric designs that he knew meant something...but had no idea what. A woman attached his chain to the end to a metal hook sticking out of the wall. He heard something click.

His captors stepped back but did not instantly leave. Austin pulled as hard as he could on the chain, but it didn't budge. He looked up to see that it was fastened with a padlock to the wall hook. Lovely. He was caught fast. He sat down on the low cot beneath the hook and stared back at the false nuns and priests gathered at his cell door. One of them – a broad woman with large nipples and an even larger mouth – stepped forward and spoke.

"The way is hard," she said. "But the rewards are great. Reconsider, and remain alive with the power of Selene at your call."

"I don't want power," he said. "I just want my baby girl."

"Then you will have neither," the woman said, and turned away. The rest moved to follow her, and a moment later the heavy door slammed shut. He heard the key turn in the lock. It wouldn't have mattered if they had left it unlocked; he couldn't walk more than three feet from the small cot. He shifted the heavy iron chain attached to the collar on his neck so that it wound around his shoulder. Then he stood on the cot and turned his body slowly, wrapping the chain around to his other shoulder. He couldn't give much pressure pulling with his neck, but with the weight of his full body?

Austin threw himself hard away from the wall, absorbing the tightening of the chain on his shoulders.

The metal dug into his arms but did not budge from the wall above.

Fuck.

He tried again, throwing himself against the chain with his right shoulder. He felt his skin crease and crimp and stifled a yell at the pinching pain.

Nothing.

Austin stood on the cot and twisted his body clockwise one more time, and then steeled himself to literally run off the edge of the bed. He could put his full weight into the action and bear the stress on his arms versus his neck. If that didn't work....

He silently counted to three. And kicked off the wall.

The chain snapped hard against his shoulder and he lost his balance, falling off the bed. His body turned and twirled like a top. Austin's hips hit the floor, but his neck yanked up instead of going to the ground. He choked and screamed with a throaty gasp. He had no hands free to grab the chain to relieve the strain. He pushed with his feet and flopped his body around until the pressure eased. When it did, he laid his head down on the cold cement ground and coughed until he thought he would puke.

When the stars cleared from his eyes, and his breathing eased, he finally lifted his head and looked up at the eyebolt that held him locked to the wall.

"You win," he whispered. Slowly, he drew himself up and crawled onto the cot.

He stared at the flickering light on the ceiling. Candle fire. Hypnotic and eerie. He was chained to a wall in a room beneath a building where a coven of witches performed sex magic around a goat's head. And just down the hall from where a cadre of BDSM worshippers played whip the body with each other for kicks.

All behind a façade as bland and innocuous as possible. A two-storey brick industrial building in the old part of town. All because one night, after a fight, he sat in a bar at midnight and wished that his wife was dead.

In front of a witch.

Be careful what you say because you never know who is listening. He could have used that advice a couple months ago and his life would be very different now. Austin cursed himself again and again but it didn't matter. It didn't bring Angie back and it didn't loose the chains that held him. Hindsight was both 20/20 and more painful than any of the whips being used in the club outside this room.

Austin looked around the room and without thinking, let out a whistle. The walls were covered in graffiti. But it wasn't the usual kind. Some of it looked like mathematical hieroglyphics, but some of it he recognised. Like the pentagram. And a pentacle. And intricate drawings of a ram's head. In one instance, the head of a goat appeared inscribed at the centre of the star that was drawn inside a circle. There were words written near the symbols, but they were words in a foreign language, something far older than English, he thought.

The longer he tried to decipher the black scrawls and drawings on the walls around him, the more uncomfortable he felt. Not that being chained to a wall was comfortable…but his stomach and chest tightened the more he stared at the walls. He was in a *bad* place. There was no other way to describe it.

And it was all his fault. He'd had bad thoughts about Angie and his life and sent those thoughts into the world. And the world had answered him in a way he could never have imagined. Wicked karma. He had found himself free of his perceived problem…and 'gifted' with a new partner who made him feel more like a man than he ever had before. Regina had driven him to heights of lust and ecstasy that he had never experienced with Angie. And because of that, he'd trusted her with everything that was important to him.

Exactly as she'd wanted.

Now he was here. And his lover…and his babysitter…were going to take everything from him that he had left. Including his life, apparently.

Austin felt tears roll down his cheeks. This was all more than a little insane.

He spent the next four hours staring at the evil symbols painted on the rough rock walls all around him…and pulling on the bonds that held him to the walls of the Devil. But nothing moved more than a few inches. He couldn't stop thinking about his baby. And he couldn't escape.

He was a rat in a trap. And unless he could chew his arms off… he wasn't going anywhere.

Austin could hear the thump of the drums out in the club area and the hum of voices; but as the night went on, both sounds faded until eventually, he realised that he was chained to a satanic wall in silence.

The feeling had long ago left his arms, and his eyes had begun to close of their own accord. And soon, the world simply disappeared into a vapour dream of anger and depression. He struggled at first, trying to stay awake and keep the Devil's symbols in view. A reminder of how fucked his situation currently was. But at some point his eyes closed and didn't reopen. Austin was exhausted and succumbed to sleep no matter how his heart bled.

The silence was the sum of his dream.

Black. Lost. Silence.

And then…

…from somewhere…

He heard the toll of an ancient bell.

The slow, steady clang of a bell ringing far away in the dark.

Austin opened his eyes.

The room was almost black…but not completely. A candle flame still guttered in an inset in the wall across from him. Another candle still flickered down the wall a couple yards away. Beyond those, and a couple other tiny candle lights farther away, the room was a study in black.

The hair on the back of his neck stood up.

Austin was barely awake, but something made him realise he

needed to be awake. A bell tolled somewhere, a slow, relentless echo. The sound was sad and slow…and undeniable. He struggled to keep his eyes open and take in the room. Something didn't feel right. And after looking into the shadows for a bit, he realised what the problem was.

He wasn't alone.

There was a pale figure on the far side of the room. He could barely see it in the dark, but it looked like a woman. She moved slowly, shifting one strange step at a time across the long black space. Any sleepiness left him then, as he began to track her across the room. She was coming his way.

The clock struck again and again, and Austin wondered what time it really was. He had lost track. He didn't know if he'd even heard the first chime.

As the figure drew closer, Austin found his eyes growing larger. He didn't want to admit it to himself, but as he watched the shuffle of her feet and the movement of her hips, he couldn't deny that… he *knew* the woman walking across the room. Only…it couldn't be.

He stared and squinted and then shifted his gaze again trying to convince himself otherwise.

But there was no denying it.

The woman walking toward him – the woman who wore a rotting blackened blouse and stained skirt – was his wife, Angie.

He could never deny those eyes.

And now, they looked at him with a gaze that said, *"You are dead."* They stared at him unblinking…filled with a dangerous intensity.

He watched helplessly. Step by step she drew closer to him. He pulled on the chains that held his arms, but he knew it was a futile gesture. And indeed, his wrists did not slip out of the bonds or pull loose the chains from the wall.

Austin was held fast. Stuck.

Angie was now just four feet away from him.

"You … can't be here?" he whispered, but even at a whisper his voice cracked.   She was dead. How the hell and why the hell was she standing in front of him?

Angie kept coming. Slowly. Relentlessly. Austin pulled again against his bindings, but to no avail. He could not break free. His wife was free to exact whatever punishment she cared to dole out. He was at her mercy.

Angie moved closer, one slow step at a time. And then she was right there in front of him. As she approached, he could see how the flesh of her cheeks had rotted, turning black and suppurating, sliding like burnt grease down the face he knew so well. She was a hideous thing, ghoulish and dead...but he couldn't deny that it was her.

His dead wife was touching him.

"Did you miss me?" she whispered. Only...her voice sounded cold and dead, not at all like the soft, easy tones of the woman he'd slept with for the past seven years. Austin wanted to scream...and cry...and draw away...but he could not retreat. Angie had him at her disposal.

She drew her fingers across his face and he could feel the sticky cold rot of her flesh as it passed. A part of him wanted to throw up.

"Why are you here?" he whispered.

When she smiled, the sides of her mouth rose up beyond where they should have. And he could see the roots of her teeth, like the skeletal bones that they were. She was rotting away, and yet she was here, touching him.

"Your girlfriend brought me back," she said. "She thought it would be amusing to have the ghost of the woman she killed around to do her bidding. But at the moment, she doesn't need me. So, for a few minutes anyway, I'm free to do as I want. Why am I here? I'm here for you. I'm here for Ceili. Is she okay?"

The question sent a pang of pain down his spine. It stabbed his heart. Was she okay? No, she wasn't okay. If he didn't kill her, someone else was going to. There was no upside here for his baby.

"No," he gasped. "They want to kill her for some black magic ritual, and I don't know how to stop them."

Angie's eyes widened, and she pressed a slimy finger to his lips. "You are all she has now," she said. "Figure it out."

"I don't know what to do," Austin said, as tears began to run down his face. The ghost of his wife was not conciliatory. She stood now right in front of him, the strange white-blue complexion of her dead face hard to ignore as she prodded him.

"She needs you now," Angie said. "Get over your stupid, selfish bastard self...and save our daughter."

"I can't do it alone," he complained.

"Let me help you," she said, and reached out both of her hands to touch his face. When he felt their cold, slippery touch, Austin couldn't help his reaction.

He screamed.

That only gave room for her tongue to slip into his open mouth.

He gagged, and then screamed again. But her body pressed close to his own, and her mouth soon completely engulfed his, smothering his terror. He felt as if her kiss was choking him. But that didn't stop him from screaming. His voice disappeared down her dead throat. He couldn't breathe. But still he screamed. Eventually, his fear lessened as the darkness came and overwhelmed his sight. He struggled for a moment, trying to hide from the glare in the eyes that stared bitterly into his own. The world grew foggy then as his chest burned with desperate fire and his mind slid down into the dark to escape.

CHAPTER TWENTY-TWO

There were candles all around him.

That's the first thing Austin saw when he finally returned from the blackness. As his eyes fluttered open, he saw the orange glow of flames everywhere. Candles guttering.

And bare legs all around.

There was a circle of women looking down on where he lay.

Brown legs and white, smooth skin and stubbled. Knobby knees and sensually curved. There were all types, but the common denominator was they all wore the black gauze of the sisterhood across the delta of their thighs. Which barely hid anything. He could see the dark delta shadows between their hips as he looked up from the couch he lay upon. It was a very strange vantage point. His neck was sore and when he rubbed it, he realised that they'd removed the collar. He was out of his chains and his hands were free, but there was nowhere for him to run. There were too many of them. Too close.

"You're awake," Regina said. He felt his heart sink as he recognised her voice. "We've been waiting."

"What do you want?" he asked.

"We want you to do what must be done," Regina said. "We've taken off the bindings and set you free. Ceili's soul is now in your hands. You can choose whether her essence lives on in ecstasy or eternal agony."

He shook his head. "No," he said. "You can let her go home with me, and she'll be spared any of this."

Regina smiled. "If you perform the ceremony, her soul will escape the bounds of earth without pain. She is still an innocent. Only her bones will be left behind, and those will become the third totem of Club Equinox. They will hold great power, because of what her father – you – did. But you have to be brave and not stray. You must take her heart quick and clean and set her free...and in doing so, we all will be set free."

"You're free right now," Austin said. "Taking my baby's life won't free anybody."

"That's where you're wrong," Regina said. "Her bones will be a tool of immense power – but only if you, the man that made her, release her."

"You mean if I kill her."

"Release her," Regina said. "We are all prisoners on this realm. Haven't you learned yet that Equinox is all about release? The power of an innocent can bring us things you have never imagined."

"So, it's really all about you?"

Regina smirked. "Isn't that every human relationship? Haven't we talked about this before?"

Austin started to sit up, but the bare foot of one of the sisters pushed his chest back.

He let his head fall back, but as he stared up at the wood-beam ceiling, he asked, "And what happens if I refuse?"

"We'll take your life as her substitute," Regina said. "It won't provide us with the same power, but it will provide us with revenge. And Ceili will then grow up a member of the coven, and will lose her soul to the power of dark magic – if that's the kind of thing you're concerned about."

"Why would you want to raise a child here?" he asked.

"Because we can guide her from infancy on to the way," Regina said. "And the child she could birth someday could bring us more power ultimately than she will right now. But I don't particularly want to wait another generation to find out."

"I will never kill my baby," Austin pledged.

Regina shrugged. "Then you will doom both yourself *and* her."

She reached out and took the hand of the woman on the left, next to her. And that woman in turn took the hand of the woman to the left of her. A moment later, there was a ring of women standing in a circle around him. Two remained within the circle, one on either side of him.

Regina said something in a foreign tongue. The words were strange and guttural. It sounded exactly like what he'd expect a satanic spell to sound like. Dark. Evil.

He couldn't believe that her sweet voice was uttering such things.

After all of the nights he had kissed those lips and touched her body with passion. And trust.

It was like seeing an angel lick a pile of excrement and grin, with vileness smeared across her lips.

"*Burunte, kiemu vrzimente schutonge!*" she said. And the sisters around her all repeated the foreign words in unison.

More words followed, syllables filled with the bitterness of the gutter and the dark sheen of something foul. The sisters bowed after every sentence, never breaking their contact. But then Regina looked up at the ceiling and shouted something that sounded like a command. Or a curse.

"*Erudactus Comi Dei Vol!*"

The two sisters on the inside of the circle suddenly lifted instruments from the floor, where they had apparently been lying unseen by Austin. He saw them bend, and the silver glint in their hands when they stood up, only knowing at first that the sisters had grabbed something metallic. But then they lifted the tools above their heads and held them pointed toward the ceiling and he saw that he was in trouble.

They had raised long silver blades from the floor.

Deadly, curved blades.

Austin began to sit up, but a hand grabbed his hair from behind and kept his head pressed down to the stone he lay upon.

He reached behind him but as soon as he touched the wrist of his captor, more hands suddenly gripped his arms, and pulled them back to rest on the dais. The alien words of Regina rose in volume, and the entire sisterhood answered her invocation with a single word.

"*Nevtlets!*"

The blades came down then. Slowly. The sisters touched the tips of the wickedly curved knives to his nipples and held them there.

Austin found himself holding his breath. His arms were held fast, and he didn't dare move.

Regina said something then that sounded more like a command than a prayer, and the two women holding the knives nodded in unison. A moment later, he felt the cold bite of steel pressing upon... and through...his flesh.

The women dragged the knives down across his chest, opening

blood lines that led from his two nipples to meet at his belly button.

They stopped when the blades met there, and Regina spoke in English for the first time in several minutes.

"They could end it all here," she said. "But that would be pointless – at least at this moment. We need your participation tonight. Let this be a lesson, though. In a heartbeat, your life could be ours. Sacrificed for power. Or spite. Your life is ours to use as we wish. Please us and live. Displease us...and you will regret it as you die."

The sting of the cuts hit him then. Austin looked down and saw the red beads welling along the tracks they'd cut through his skin. The cuts were not deep. But they would hurt for days.

"These are the final hours," Regina said. "We will take you to a room to think things over. When the moment comes, you will act as one of us...or you will die and Ceili will grow up as a sister of Equinox. And she *will* lose her soul, if that is something that truly matters to you."

Hands grabbed him then and pulled him upright from the cold stone. The sisters broke apart from their circle around him and scattered. His hands were pulled to his back, and Austin was pushed to walk forward.

The hallway was short and dark and then he was back in his cell, with symbols of dark magic all around him. Illuminated by candle, not electric light.

Austin drew a fingertip across the trail of pain that led from his left nipple to his belly button and grimaced as the nerves registered his finger's passing.

He raised a fingertip dripping with red and closed his eyes.

He was not mortally wounded, but he was bleeding. And it stung like hell.

Austin walked the room, staring at the weird symbols and foreign words scrawled across the rock. His cell was akin to being imprisoned inside a devil's spell. He could see the magic, but didn't know what it said. Or how to break it. Finally, he lay down on the cot and closed his eyes to think.

He was a man in a snow globe.

The Devil's snow globe.

CHAPTER TWENTY-THREE

Something tickled his ear.

That was the first thing Austin recognised as he began to wake from a sleep so deep he felt drugged. He'd lain down on the cot after pacing the prison cell, and surprisingly, he'd dozed off. It was difficult to shake off the torpor of the dark place his mind had just been moving in. He didn't remember any dreams, only a thick, heavy darkness that even now was calling him back.

But something cold and wet circled the outside of his earlobe. When that unpleasant feeling registered again, Austin finally opened his eyes and began to raise his hand to push whatever it was away.

His fingers connected with a lock of greasy hair and then he saw the whites of human eyes on the pillow right beside him. They were inches from his own, and despite the darkness, he recognised them instantly.

Angie.

"Good morning, lover," she whispered. Only her whisper was more like a grating rasp. As if her vocal cords were rusted. "You passed out the last time I visited, before we were through."

Austin jumped and instinctively pushed himself back from her.

"What's the matter?" she asked. Her eyes flashed in the darkness. "You used to want me to come on to you when you were asleep. You used to always say I could wake you up any time."

"That was fine when you were alive," he said without thinking.

Her eyes narrowed. "So, there were conditions?" she asked. "You never said that before. You always promised you'd love me forever."

Angie raised herself up from the cot on one elbow. He could see that she was naked this time. Her nipples were wide and dark; he'd always loved that about her. But instead of her normal creamy complexion, he could also see purple and blue blotches covered her skin. And blackened places.

She was rotting.

Angie's fingers reached out to wrap around his back, and he shivered as their cool, wet touch slid across his skin. Her touch made his skin crawl; he wanted to vomit.

Austin scooted backward on the bed and Angie's teeth flashed.

"I was good enough for you before the bitch," she whispered. "Wasn't I?"

She moved her fingers across his cheek, and he saw that her nails were now yellow atop blackened fingertips.

He stifled the feeling in his throat.

"Why are you here?" he finally managed to say.

"I'm here for Ceili," she said. "I'm here to make sure you do the right thing."

He considered that for a moment and nodded. "I don't know what the right thing is now," he admitted. "I want her to live. But I don't want her to be damned."

"Then get her out of here," Angie said. Her voice was like a file across rough metal.

Austin flinched.

"How can I do that when I can't get out of here myself?" he asked.

"Figure it out," she demanded. Then she slid her body across the cot and over the top of him. She was a cold, horrible, naked weight on top of him. And he wanted to dissolve into the sheets beneath him. His wife was lying on top of him, and he was disgusted beyond words. She was slimy, decaying and…dead.

"Tell me what to do," he said.

Angie laughed. "Oh, now you want me to give you the answers. I was always the last person you'd listen to…you could never admit when you were lost."

"I'm not lost," he said. "I'm trapped."

She ran a cold finger across the cut in his chest and traced the scabs down to his belly button. When she reached the end he suddenly flinched. He couldn't take her touch anymore and he instinctively threw her off of him.

Angie responded with a backhand to his face. He tasted something foul and then her fingernails gouged their way down the path that Regina's witches had carved. Angie opened his wounds with blackened fingernails and then pushed herself up from the bed to stand.

He could feel the blood welling hot from the scabs she'd broken.

"Get over yourself," she hissed. "Our baby needs you. She needs you to get her out of here. She doesn't need your pathetic whining. And she doesn't need you to kill her. She needs you to be a man. Grab your balls and pull yourself up and find a way out of this room so that you can protect her. She can't walk. She can't do anything yet. But she has a whole life ahead of her, and it shouldn't be lived here."

Angie put her hands on her hips, a disconcerting picture. A naked corpse, showing her unbridled disgust.

"You let me die. Don't make the same mistake again. Don't let her die too, just because you were too much of a selfish bastard to find the way to save her."

Angie's head suddenly tilted the ceiling and she frowned. "She's calling me, I have to go."

With that, Angie turned her back and moved toward the steel door on the other side of the room…and when she reached it, her body suddenly grew foggy, translucent. He could see the door through the black curls of her hair, and then she passed through the barrier and disappeared.

Austin wiped the place on his face where she had touched him… and then moved his hand across his chest as well. It came back sticky and warm and wet with broken scabs and blood.

But it didn't come back with an answer. What was he supposed to do? How could he save Ceili from this place? How could he save himself?

Angie's appearance hadn't served to help him at all. She'd only made him feel more helpless.

Austin lay back on the bed and stared at the ceiling. He realised there was a witch's star there, tucked within a satanic circle.

He was lost. Broken. Trapped.

And he didn't know what to do to get out of this one.

Eventually, he fell back asleep, the trail of wet, salty tears streaming across his cheeks.

CHAPTER TWENTY-FOUR

The night passed like a century. Minutes stretched into hours, hours into years. Austin lay on his rock-hard bed staring into the darkness above, struggling to find answers. What could he do to save his baby? Why was his wife appearing to him now as a rotting, hideous corpse? What was real? Was he slowly losing his mind?

Something spoke from far away and stopped him from idly musing. He couldn't hear what the voice said, but he couldn't deny that someone was speaking somewhere nearby. Someone in the hall just outside his cell?

He rolled off the bed and tried to follow the sound. But the closer he got to the door, the farther away the words sounded. The voice wasn't coming from the door where Angie had disappeared. It was behind him. Which made no sense.

It was coming from the wall behind his bed.

Austin pulled the cot away from the wall and stepped into the gap left behind. He could hear the voice a little clearer. It spoke words of prayer. A familiar cadence. He struggled to place it, pressing his ear against the wall and closing his eyes. He still couldn't hear the words clearly, but he heard the rhythm. And then it clicked as the words started over....

"Our Father, who art in Heaven...."

It was faint, far away, but someone was on the other side of the wall, reciting the Lord's Prayer.

Austin pressed his hands against the wall and felt along the rough surface for...something. He couldn't be hearing voices through rock, could he? There must be some kind of entryway to another room beyond his.

And then his fingers reached the area just a couple feet above the ground and found the hard, metal ridges of a vent.

That's how he was hearing the voice. Through a duct.

Austin knelt down and felt carefully along the edges of the vent. It wasn't simply an air duct. It was the ventilation grille on a full metal door. His fingers found the edges and traced it carefully all the way around. It was about two feet tall and more than two feet wide. The vent was just a small section of a much larger entry.

A door that he needed to open.

Austin traced all of the lines in the metal, trying to find the spot where he could force the door. There was a small lock in the right side.

A keyhole.

Only…he didn't have a key. Or a paper clip. Or anything really that he might use to pick a lock.

Shit.

He pressed his ear to the vent and could hear the words a little louder and clearer. This was definitely where the voice was coming from. It sounded like a man praying, very far away.

Austin needed to make those prayers be closer.

He moved his fingers along the floor, searching for something that he could use to pick the lock and open the door.

It was bare.

Then he traced the underside of the cot. It had wires and springs; surely there had to be something there he could bend and adapt?

Something gouged his finger, and Austin winced. He withdrew it and sucked a drop of blood from a small nick in the tip. *Damnit.* He lay down on the floor and looked under the cot to see what was there.

The thing that had gouged him was obvious. There was heavy spring that held the wire mesh supporting the mattress to the metal frame. He'd poked himself on the end.

Austin ran his finger down the frame of the small cot, looking for something else that could help him. He came back to the twisted metal wire of the spring. Maybe there was something he could do with that?

Austin tried to unwind the piece that had stabbed him…but it didn't budge.

He risked breaking the skin again and finally pulled away. He wasn't going to move that bit of metal with his bare finger.

Footsteps sounded from the hall outside and Austin rolled back onto the top of the cot. He didn't need anyone seeing him investigating the underside of the bed.

A moment later, something metallic clanked in the door and he heard the lock click. Austin forced his head to lie back, though he kept his eyes open. Someone entered the room and set a tray down on the floor near his bed. One of the nuns. She leaned over the bed and he could see her nipples pushing against the translucent black film she wore. It was a strange look for a prison warden.

"This might be your last supper, so try to enjoy it," she said.

She didn't stay to hear his response. The door rattled closed before he could sit up. But when he did, there was a metal tray with a plate of Thai Pad Prik sitting next to his bed. He knew that Regina had sent it…she knew that he could eat Thai food every day. She was taunting him.

Bitch.

He didn't turn down her offer; he was starving.

For a moment, he considered that she could be poisoning him… or at least drugging him…with the food. But he ate it anyway. The lure of jalapenos and wide noodles and onions and sauce was just too much. It tasted awesome and he was starving.

It was after he'd eaten his fill that he realised what he'd been given. A fork!

Austin thought about all the times Angie had complained about him bending the tines on their forks when he'd cut his meat with too much 'brute force' and bent her precious silverware. This time though….

He lifted the thin excuse for a mattress and wedged two of the prongs of the fork into one of the springs. And pushed. The spring didn't budge, but the prongs on the fork bent.

Austin smiled. And pulled the bed out from the wall. He found the lock in the small door, and pressed the now-isolated tines in.

Nothing happened.

He twisted the fork, but there was no click.

Austin swore, and jiggled the metal again, twisting his wrist back and forth trying to feel for a connection.

When it happened, he wasn't prepared. The fork suddenly

turned, and he opened his eyes in surprise. But he didn't lose his cool; he pulled the fork toward him and sure enough...the vent door creaked outward.

All right then.

Austin walked to the door and tried to look down the hall. He couldn't see anyone. He returned to the bed, pushed it out farther, and took a deep breath. Then he put his arms into the opening and felt ahead into the darkness.

There was only cold metal around him. Austin shrugged and launched himself inside. He didn't know how often they'd come to check on him, and he couldn't hide the evidence of where he'd gone once he'd ventured into the vent. So...he went.

Austin wriggled his way down the vent, his shoulders hitting and moving him down the shaft. He wished he could make his feet pull the vent door closed, but that wasn't going to happen.

He moved down the shaft as quick as he could; he worried about cutting himself on metal edges, but he shimmied ahead carefully. The passage stretched out in front of him in utter darkness. He placed his hand on the cold metal and pulled himself forward, a foot at a time. It was eerie because he couldn't see anything. The path ahead was unknown, a dark shadow that he could crawl through... but couldn't see through.

Little by little he inched forward; the darkness stretched on and on. He was completely alone in the dark. He couldn't see ahead or behind...but he had to keep going. Every time he put his hand down, he feared that he'd impale himself on a rusty screw or shard of glass...or something worse. But he had to keep moving through the black. Moving on faith.

Until he suddenly saw an orange glow. Evidence that he wasn't completely lost in the dark.

Austin moved faster toward the light. It was good to be able to actually see what he was moving toward. Even if he didn't know what the light held. It had to be better than the black.

The light was streaming in through a vent in the duct he crawled through. He arrived at it and could look down through the grates and see a hallway below. Which made him feel better – he could see something! But...he couldn't get out there.

He paused at the grate and realised quickly that unless he wanted to unscrew the vent with his fingernails, he wasn't going to get out of the tunnel here. He at least felt better that he could see something. He took a deep breath and forced himself to begin crawling again. He needed to find a way out, and this was not it.

Austin moved slowly, relentlessly, forcing his fingers to crawl forward into the pitch-black dark.

He could taste the dank air. He could feel the sweat trickling down the edge of his spine. But he continued forward.

And then he came to another place in the metal tunnel where light trickled in. It wasn't much, but he could see the tips of his fingers. And the small mounds of dust and dirt that coated the surface he crawled across.

When he reached the source, he pushed his fingers in the grates and tried to lift the vent cover.

The edge of the metal moved.

A grin slipped across his face. This might be the way out.

The vent caught, but he slipped his fingers under the gap and shoved.

There was a screech – the sound of stripped screws catching on metal – and then the vent lifted.

Austin pulled the grate aside and looked down through the hole. There was a cement floor below, and a faint yellow light. Just barely enough to see the walls and floor. He didn't know where it was…but he couldn't be choosey either. He needed to get out of this vent.

He slid his feet through the opening and wedged his hands on the corners of the vent, bracing to hold his weight…and let his body slide through. He hung in space for a moment and took a breath. Then he let go.

Austin's feet hit the cement below hard and gave way. He instantly fell on his ass and rolled. A moment later, he was back on his feet in a dark corridor. He walked a few steps and the hall ended in a doorway. He stood at the threshold a moment, hesitating. And then took a breath and stepped inside.

The room beyond was apparently…a museum.

Or maybe a shrine.

He wasn't sure which. There were wooden pedestals and stands spaced around the long room, against the walls, and in the centre. Atop each stand was a glass case. There were some cases also hanging from the walls, with costumes displayed inside – long white vestments encrusted with rubies, violet sashes with the symbols of moon and star stitched into them in gold thread.

The room was lit with lanterns inset every few feet along the walls. There were also candle stands in the front of the room, with small flames gently flickering. Austin walked to one of the cases – a small glass box at the top of a one-foot-wide wooden pedestal. He refrained from whistling, but just barely.

Inside were the bare bones of a human hand. They lay on black velvet, finger bones perfectly aligned, as if the flesh had simply melted away while the hand had been sleeping.

Austin stared at the yellowed bones for a moment, as if waiting for them to suddenly spring to life. And then he shook his head, and moved on to the next cabinet, against the wall. There was something dark inside. It was small and round, but its surface was wrinkled and uneven. It lay atop the same black velvet that the hand bone case had, and with the low light and dark background, Austin could not tell immediately what it was. It could have been a large tree knot for all he could tell.

But then he stepped back and saw the plaque on the outside of the case.

Heart of Berniece D'arcy
Saint of Seduction
November 3, 1993

Okay. He didn't know what that meant, or why the heart of Berniece D'arcy deserved preservation and display, but the idea of a shrivelled heart lying in state in front of him made him shift backward a half step.

Austin looked at the case next to this one and his eyes widened for a moment. There was no mistaking what the contents were, though the object was blackened and curled. This case held a human ear atop the black velvet.

Ear of Renaud Merilee
He Heard The Call
June 23, 1982

He stepped past it to the next, and it held the mummified but still identifiable tube of a human penis. The caption read:

The Best of Dennis Jones
Ceremony of Selflessness
March 13, 2007

He could see the curled, ragged edge where the thing had once connected to a man's groin and Austin shivered and almost crossed his legs. He shook his head and stepped away. He understood being selfless… but whatever that ceremony had been, it was not about selflessness.

There was a larger box near the back of the room, flanked by two candelabras. Part of him knew what he was going to see before he peered over the edge, but he was still shocked when he looked within.

The naked corpse of a woman lay within, her skin shrivelled and brown, the pits of her eyes sunken and skull-like, though the bone was still covered in a layer of dried flesh. The skin looked ancient – brown and leathery, with wrinkles throughout. The puckers of her nipples appeared almost black, and the thatch of hair at her groin, though matted, appeared full.

The thing was…she had no hands. And only one foot.

After seeing first the mummified grimace of her face and shrivelled chest, Austin's gaze broadened, and he realised that her arms had been severed at the elbows…and her left leg at the knee. He grimaced as he took in the ragged blackened flesh that hung free over the white nub of a bone on the arm nearest him. She hadn't been born without limbs, clearly. From the look of the shards of flesh, her arms and leg had been torn off.

Sister of Suffering
Stretched in Sin
June 21, 1893

He didn't like the implication there. His mind instantly drew an image of a naked woman on a wooden rack, arms and legs chained to giant gears, as a cruel hooded torturer drew the chains tighter and tighter while she screamed, her body stretching like human taffy until...

He shook away the thought and turned away from the corpse. Austin looked around the room, and saw more items hung from the walls. Iron masks. Curved knives. Long handled pincers and medical instruments. There were also garments and leather things – straps or codpieces or...he wasn't truly sure what.

This was a chapel of torture. And it suddenly occurred to him that it might not be the best place to be discovered in.

He looked around for an exit and saw a doorway in the back to the left of the Sister of Suffering. He tried not to look at her again when he passed by, but the leathery folds of her desiccated face flashed before his eyes from memory anyway.

The doorway led him to a small antechamber, and then another room, this one smaller and darker than the chapel. He heard the murmur of a voice somewhere near. Austin stopped to listen and recognised again the familiar cadence of the Lord's Prayer.

He pivoted slowly, trying to place where the sound was coming from, as his eyes adjusted to the dark of the room. And then he saw that there was another door in the back of this room. He walked through it. There, chained to a stone wall, was a nude man kneeling in the corner, head bent and facing the wall. His voice continued to pray the familiar syllables of the Lord's Prayer. There was an air vent over the man's head. That's how the words had travelled so easily to Austin's cell.

He didn't want to break the train of the man's prayer. But after a moment, Austin cleared his throat to gently signal that there was somebody else in the room. The prayer stopped, and the jangle of chains rippled through the room as the man turned.

"Who are you?" the man asked. His face was wide and wrinkled, his eyelids heavy and drooping over a deep-set gaze. His hair was silver and thick; tufts stuck out mad-professor style from around his ears. "You're not one of them."

Austin shook his head. "No," he said. "I was a prisoner, like you. But I managed to get away."

"You're not away if you're here," the man said. "You're in the deepest hole of a prison. This is where they put people just before they sacrifice them to Satan. You've escaped to Death Row, my friend."

"Well, it sounds like I better get you out of here then too," Austin said.

"I'd be happy if you did," the man said. "But don't risk your chance. You should go back down that hallway and get as far away from this room as possible. Hurry before they come."

Austin ignored the advice. "Do they keep a key for your chains down here somewhere?"

He searched the dark wall for a key ring. Nobody would want to carry that around with them all the time; they'd probably keep it near the prisoner, but far enough away that he couldn't reach it.

"On the other side of the doorway, maybe?" the man answered.

Austin nodded and stepped through the threshold, scanning every surface of the walls. Then he grinned and reached out to his left where a dark metal ring hung from a bolt in the wall. There was a rusted key at the end of the ring.

He grabbed it and rushed back to the dark room. He traced the chain up from the man's wrists to an eyebolt in the wall. It was a similar situation to the way they'd locked him up earlier tonight. A large padlock gathered and connected the chains to the hook. He slipped the key into the lock and twisted. When it didn't open immediately, he jiggled it again and then gave a firm tug. That did it. The lock snapped open, and he pulled it free of the bolt, releasing the chains.

"You are a man of miracles."

"No, I'm just a guy named Austin," he said.

The older man stood and extended his palm. "My name is Father Perry Vernon," he said. "Please excuse my lack of uniform."

Austin's eyebrows rose. "You're a priest?"

The man nodded. "They stripped me of everything I had."

"I could say the same," Austin said. "They killed my wife and stole my baby. But I'm going to get her back if it's the last thing I do."

"Then we'd better get out of here quickly," the priest said. "If they catch us here, *this* will be the last thing you do."

The priest held out his hands. "Can you help me with these quickly?"

Austin pulled the chain through two metal rings attached to leather bracelets strapped to the man's wrists. He quickly unbuckled the wristbands and dropped the chain to the ground. Father Vernon rubbed his wrists and grimaced. "I've got a case of pins and needles that feel like fire," he complained.

"Are you okay?" Austin asked.

"Better than I was five minutes ago," the priest answered. "C'mon, I know a way out."

The priest took the lead and Austin followed. They threaded through the museum of mummified remains, and then took a passage that Austin had not been in before. It wound around in the darkness until it emptied into a brighter hallway. There were candles burning in the walls here, and Father Vernon held up his hand. He put a finger to his lips and peered down the corridor before nodding. Then he motioned for Austin to follow and ran quietly down the hall. He stopped at a wooden door halfway down the passage and turned the knob. The door opened with a faint squeak, and Father Vernon stepped inside.

"Where are we?" Austin asked, once inside. The place was pitch-black; he couldn't see where the priest had gone.

"Just getting something so I can go outside," Father Vernon whispered. "Stay quiet. People do walk these halls."

Austin nodded, not that the priest could see him in the dark. A moment or two later, he felt a hand on his arm, and the priest led him back to the exit. He was no longer naked, but instead wearing some kind of dark robe, though he was still barefoot. And then they were softly padding down the stone hallway, darting from one passageway to the next. They went down a stone stairway at one point. Father Vernon motioned for Austin to follow him farther down the hall, but then Austin saw a room with floors covered in old linoleum through a doorway to the left. It looked like the floor of an office building from the 1960s.

And maybe it was.

"This way," Austin whispered, and ran into the room. Everything was shadowed, but Austin could see streetlights beaming in through tall glass windows at the front of the room. He stole through a room filled with cubicles and a large wooden front desk at the entryway.

"That's not the way I was going to take you," the priest argued, but Austin pointed out the window.

"There's a street right there," Austin said. "Come on!"

He turned a simple lock on a steel-and-glass door and stepped outside.

Father Vernon followed him and looked around as Austin took a long, deep breath of air. They were in downtown Parkville, but off the main drag. The street was quiet; in the distance, he could hear the faint sounds of traffic. Behind them was a dark, nondescript office building. He couldn't believe that in the bowels of that place, there were satanic rituals going on. And a coven that wanted to sacrifice his baby daughter.

The priest seemed to grasp his thoughts. Father Vernon put a hand on his wrist and gripped tightly. "I know you want to find a way to rescue your baby. But you're going to need help. Come with me now, and we'll think of a way to prepare."

Austin shook his head and ignored the image of the slit-throat girl that passed through his mind as he thought of what to do. "I know how to prepare – we need to call the police. They're planning to kill my baby tonight. Now that I finally know where this place is, I can bring them here. They'll throw everyone in jail and this club will never open again."

Father Vernon stopped and grabbed Austin's arm. "No, my son," he said. "I know that sounds like the right thing to do. It's a very tempting idea, but if you ever want to see your baby alive again, it would be the worst mistake you could ever make."

"What do you mean?" Austin said. "We need reinforcements! The police have guns. And there are more of them than there are of us."

"I know," Father Vernon said. "But this needs to be a covert operation. If you bring the cops to the door, your baby will be gone from that building long before they get into the first room. The people who run Equinox are ready for things like that. They have escape tunnels and all of the leaders will be gone with the baby a minute after a policeman crosses that doorway with a warrant.

Speaking of which…the police would *need* a search warrant before they would go inside, and we don't have time for them to get that if we need to stop a ceremony that's tonight."

The priest nodded sadly. "I know how you're feeling, but we need to do this ourselves. I can get us back in through a back entrance, once you're ready. We *will* get her back. We just have to be careful. I promise you will hold your baby again."

Austin frowned. He didn't want to do anything that would risk Ceili's life further.

Father Vernon squeezed his arm. "C'mon, let's get out of sight before they realise we're gone and start looking around out here."

The priest led the way down the street. Austin kept his eyes on the sidewalk in front of them carefully, worried that at every step he was going to slice his bare foot open on a piece of broken glass. He hadn't been wearing shoes when they'd grabbed him from his house and this was not exactly a clean, modern area of the town. The sidewalks were crooked and broken, and the parkways littered with debris, from crushed pop cans to foil gum wrappers to broken beer bottles.

But as it turned out, they didn't end up walking far. He looked up from staring at the back of Father Vernon's heels when the priest's feet stopped moving. They were standing at the side entrance of a church. They'd crossed through an alley and it was as if the church simply appeared out of nowhere. The priest reached down to a small statue of the Virgin Mary in a flower bed next to the entryway and twisted one of her praying hands until it rose upward. Then he retrieved a key from a hollow that was revealed in the centre of the statue.

"You can always trust the Lord's mother to keep a secret," Father Vernon joked, and used the key to unlock the side entrance. Before they went in, he secreted the key back in the statue, and pushed the arm back into place.

Austin followed the older man inside. They walked through an empty antechamber, and then down a short hallway to a sitting room. Father Vernon flipped a switch and two table lamps flickered on across the room. It was a cosy, if terribly dated room. The lamps stood on end tables near a couch that looked as if it had been there since 1955.

The priest gestured to the couch and two burgundy recliners. "Please," he said. "Have a seat and make yourself comfortable. Can I get you something to drink?"

Austin sat on one end of the ancient couch as Father Vernon walked across the room to a sideboard near the television. When he opened a wooden cabinet, Austin saw an array of bottles. "Whiskey, Scotch, vodka?" the priest asked.

Austin's face must have looked surprised, because the other man laughed. "What, are you shocked that a priest drinks more than Eucharistic wine? Trust me, the nights get long when you're alone here in the rectory. Prayer and Netflix can only take you so far." He bent down and opened a small refrigerator tucked below the level of the counter. "I have beer too," he said. "There's a Killian's here, and a couple of Lagunitas."

Austin caught a glimpse of a familiar beer label inside the refrigerator. "Would it be wrong if I asked a priest for a Lil' Somethin' Somethin'," he joked.

"You can ask me anything," Father Vernon said. "I won't judge. That sounds like a fine choice, however."

He pulled out two bottles, and used a bottle opener to pop the tops before handing one to Austin. He upended the bottle and closed his eyes as the hoppy wheat brew poured down the back of his throat. His eyes teared up as the ale coated and excited his taste buds. It felt as if he'd been locked away for weeks.

When he finally set the bottle down, already half emptied, on the end table next to the lamp, he realised the old priest was looking at him intently. The man had thick grey caterpillars above his eyes, and jowls that spoke of many nights in this room tilting back a glass while watching the tube. His face seemed a little flushed where it wasn't obscured by unshaven stubble.

The silence between them grew uncomfortable, as the priest absently sipped from his bottle. His gaze didn't falter.

"Why did they have you chained up?" Austin asked finally.

Father Vernon smiled sadly before answering.

"Let's just say that a den of Devil worshippers are no friends of a neighbourhood priest," he offered finally. "I had heard one too many stories about Club Equinox in the confessional, and I finally decided to do something about it."

"I thought the things said in confession are private," Austin said. "Just between you and God."

"Private, sure," the priest said. He took a drink and then gave Austin a wide eye. "But that doesn't mean that I can't try to do something about things with the information that I have." He winked. "I was pleased to know that at least some of my parishioners felt guilty about the sins they committed there, and I asked enough questions to slowly piece together exactly where *here* was. Imagine my chagrin when I realised that this bed of sin was literally right here in my backyard."

"I'm surprised that any of these people would ever come here to confess," Austin said.

The priest shrugged. "Not the worst offenders, to be sure. Some of the new initiates have doubts though. They watch those sexual ceremonies and get their hormones racing, and then later feel guilty for enjoying the perversion. They haven't given over their souls completely to Club Equinox, and I'm thankful for that. I tried to plant the seeds in their minds to come back to the Lord, but at the same time I knew the only way to save them and so many others was to destroy the source of their temptation. I had to stop the rituals if I was ever to save my flock."

The priest paused and took a sip of his beer. Then he looked at Austin pointedly and asked, "How did you end up in that place?"

"I picked up the wrong woman at a bar," Austin said. He quickly explained his meeting with Regina and the events that came after, though he didn't linger long on the details of his time with her in Club Equinox when he had not been a prisoner. His heart felt sick when he thought about the things he had witnessed and ignored. He was as guilty for Ceili being in danger as anyone, because he had agreed to be part of the evil that eventually stole her.

"The Devil wears the best makeup," the priest observed. "You can't even tell she's wearing any, but at the end of the day, it's all fake. All a lie."

Austin hung his head. "I can't believe I was such a fool. But when Regina came over, everything felt right in my world again. And then when she brought me to Equinox it was exciting. I'd never been in a place like that. I knew it was all dark and wrong…I just didn't want to see it. I only wanted to see her."

"And you were never seeing her anyway," Father Vernon said. "All you saw was the mask. The glamour."

Austin hung his head in shame.

"Are you sorry for the things you did with her in Equinox?" the priest asked.

He nodded. "I wish I could forget them."

"Repeat after me," the priest said. "Bless me Father, for I have sinned...."

Austin repeated the first words of the penitential rite.

"How long has it been since you last confessed?" Vernon asked.

"I don't know," Austin said. "Years."

"It's okay, my son, you're here now. Tell me what you would ask the Lord's forgiveness for."

Austin described the rituals he had aided Regina with, omitting some of the more erotic details. He began haltingly, but soon the words were racing to come out; all of the guilt and shame poured out in a torrent. When he was done, the priest put a hand on his shoulder and looked at him with wide, understanding eyes.

"The Lord knows the depths of our weakness," he said. "What matters is that you recognise it and commit to doing better. It's that action that brings his forgiveness. In the name of the Lord, I offer you his forgiveness and absolve you of these sins. I admonish you to go out and sin no more. For your penance, I ask you to say the Hail Mary and Our Father here with me now."

The priest began reciting the Hail Mary out loud, and Austin joined in. It had been a couple years since he'd been in church, but the prayer fell from his lips like an old habit. He found himself saying the words in tandem with the priest without thinking.

When they were finished, Father Vernon smiled sadly and patted Austin's shoulder. "Your soul is free, my son. Now we have to find the way to do the same thing for your daughter."

"I don't want her *soul* to be free," Austin said. "I want all of her to be free! And there isn't much time to find a way to get her out of there. The ceremony is tonight."

Father Vernon nodded. "The Devil's Equinox. It's a rare event, and something I know they've been planning a ritual around to increase their power for a long time now. They need the blood of an innocent to be spilled during the height of the Equinox to open the death portal – the pathway that souls take to leave this world. If that blood is spilled by the child's mother or father, the gate will be thrown open all the way, and the power of the Devil himself can be harnessed and brought to live in the flesh of those who participated in the sacrifice."

"Well, I'm not going to stab Ceili, or whatever they want me to do to her. So, their spell is not going to happen. If we can't get the cops in there over the next couple hours, I'm just going to have to find a way to get her out of there myself."

The priest nodded again. "We don't have much time. They don't need you to complete the sacrifice, but it would bring them more power if you did. So, the ritual will go forward with or without you. And the murder of a baby isn't the worst of it."

"How could it get worse than that?" Austin asked.

The priest looked up at the ceiling, not meeting Austin's eyes. "If they eat the flesh of your child in the Devil's Banquet after she's killed on the goat's altar…everyone who tastes her will gain the power of glamour. Whatever story they tell someone after participating in the ritual, they'll find the person hearing them believes."

"That's ridiculous," Austin said. "Because they eat a baby, people will suddenly believe everything they say?"

"That's the power the Dark One grants in exchange for the abomination he seeks," the priest answered. "It's a great talent to have if you plan to rob banks," he joked.

Austin shook his head. "Regina took me in easily without killing Ceili," he said. "I don't think she needs any more help."

"No," the priest agreed. "We need to find a way to save your daughter."

Austin was silent for a minute as he thought about the past few days. He remembered reading Regina's journal the night she'd left it out. She had written about the importance of the bones of the dead in creating both protection spells and building an arsenal of power. It was the whole reason she had taken up residence in the house next to his. Her need for the bones of a child was really why he had run into her in the first place. If he was right, he might be able to pit her own magic against her.

"I have an idea," he said. "But I need some time to prepare."

"We have a little time," the priest said. "I don't think they'll begin preparing for a couple more hours."

"Perfect. I need to go home for a bit," Austin said.

"I'm not sure it's a good idea for you to go far from here," the priest said. His face looked concerned. "What are you thinking of doing?"

"I'm not totally sure yet," Austin said. Actually, he had a good idea of what he wanted to do, but he didn't want to admit to the priest what the idea was. Not yet. Not until it was time. It wasn't the kind of thing a priest would condone or help with…and he definitely needed the priest's help right now.

"It's just an idea," Austin said. "But I want to check it out. Would you be able to keep an eye on the Equinox building to make sure they don't take Ceili out of there while I'm gone?"

Father Vernon gave him a questioning look, but ultimately nodded. "That's not a problem at all," he said. "I'm happy to be on the outside looking in, rather than the way it was before you found me. I can keep an eye on them for you."

"Thanks," Austin said. "Could I use your phone to call a taxi?"

Father Vernon shook his head. "No need for that," he said, as he pushed himself upright with a groan. "You can take my car. Lord knows it could use a few miles to be put on the odometer. All it does is sit in the parish garage."

He walked out of the room before Austin could answer, but returned a moment later holding a key ring.

"Here you go," Father Vernon said. "Go home and get what you need. I'll stand watch out back and make sure they don't all decide to run off somewhere. But I don't think there's any need to worry. They'll hold the Devil's Equinox ceremony inside Club Equinox. I'm sure of that. They're not going anywhere."

The priest pointed at a clock across the room. "It's after seven o'clock now," he said. "Do you think you can be back by nine? I would think they'll begin to prepare for the ritual by then. That's three hours before midnight, the moment of change. It's the time they'll try to hold a final ritual using your baby. And they'll surely know you've escaped by then. Which may change some of their plans."

Austin nodded. "I don't need that much time."

He accepted the keys from the priest, who then led him out of the room and down a back hallway to a door that opened on a garage.

"Hurry," the priest warned. "I'll keep an eye on things until you return."

"Thanks," Austin said, and stepped down into the cold garage. He pressed the button on the wall and the door opened. Then he got in a long black Buick and put the key in the ignition. He wasn't completely sure where he was, but he knew that as soon as he started navigating through the streets of downtown Parkville, he'd figure it out. The place simply wasn't that big. He couldn't go more than two or three streets without running into some place that he'd been before. He turned the key and the car sprang to life. Austin pulled out onto the small street outside of the parish garage and turned left. He drove for three blocks and then he saw Park Avenue and smiled. It was one of the main drags through town, and he was instantly oriented. He made a mental note of where he needed to turn when he came back. Then he turned left again and gunned the engine to start down the road toward home.

CHAPTER TWENTY-FIVE

Sometimes your view on life changes overnight. Last week, Austin would have laughed at anyone who tried to tell him that witches were real. That magic was real. That the Devil was real.

But tonight?

Austin was driving a priest's car home to gather materials for a magic spell. It sounded ridiculous, even to him. But he was now operating on the 'if you can't beat 'em, join 'em' philosophy. Or something like that. He'd read enough of Regina's journal to remember some things. He hoped he remembered enough. In particular, he knew the power of bones. And he knew from her writing where there were bones of power.

He pulled into his driveway and thumbed the remote to lift the garage door. He wasted no time inside, but slipped on a pair of shoes, ran up the stairs, opened the medicine cabinet and grabbed a razor blade from inside. He tucked it carefully into his jeans inner pocket and then hurried back downstairs to the kitchen to grab a small candle and matches. Then he grabbed a light jacket from the hall closet. The night wasn't that cool, but he needed pockets to carry things in. In the garage, he found a roll of galvanised wire and a flashlight. Then he walked down his driveway and headed to the house next door.

He walked around the side of the garage, and used the steps in the back, hoping to stay out of sight. He didn't need anyone calling the police and accusing him of breaking in.

Though that was exactly what he intended to do.

Austin looped and crimped the wire, and then slipped the makeshift 'key' into the lock. He turned his hand, but instead of tripping the lock mechanism, the wire just bent. He pulled it out, added a third strand of wire to the hook and put it in again.

Then he shifted the 'key' inside the doorknob and slowly moved it side to side, searching for the right fit.

When he turned it this time, something inside the lock clicked. Austin smiled and turned the knob on the door.

He was inside.

He flipped the light switch on the wall, but as he suspected, nothing happened. If the house had been vacant all this time, there would be no electric. He pulled the flashlight out of his pocket and flipped it on. When the light guttered to life, he walked down the hall to find the door to the basement.

What he needed was down there.

One by one he descended the steps. The flashlight flickered eerily against the walls in the dark, and he moved slowly, worried about tripping on something and braining himself by falling down the stairs in an abandoned house.

He remembered the description of the basement from Regina's journal. Or maybe 'spellbook' or 'grimoire' was the more accurate description of her secret book that he'd read. Either way, he knew that he needed to walk through the underbelly of this house and find an oven or old hearth on one wall.

It was damp and smelled of old mould as he walked through the silent space. Somewhere water dripped periodically. He felt as if he should be able to hear anything within a mile radius of here…it was so silent. Even though he had on rubber soles he could hear every step he made…he could actually feel the hair rise on the back of his neck as he walked under the floor joists beneath the kitchen above. He could imagine someone rushing him from the dark; he'd never see them until he was down.

The thought made his heart race and he walked faster, bobbing the flashlight from side to side as he searched for the place Regina had described.

It didn't take long to find; it wasn't a large house. The flash trailed across the old iron vent and door embedded in the wall, and he brushed his fingers across the surface, tracing the edge of the door down to the latch.

He gripped the latch between his fingers and pulled; the door creaked open with a hideous squeal. Austin trailed the light across the space inside. The hearth was maybe four feet deep and three feet high before it constricted into a funnel to the flue. There were blackened bricks that served as the floor, and a grate for ashes in the centre of them. According to Regina's journal, there was a shovel for ashes nearby....

He looked around and located it, lying in the concrete corner of the basement a few feet away. Austin grabbed the shovel and brought it to bear in the same way she had described. He pushed the edge between the bricks and tried to pry them loose. The iron clanged and scratched against the stone, but after a few misses, he was able to move a brick upward enough to reach forward and hold it with his fingertips. Once he had a touch on it, he let go of the shovel and grabbed it with his other hand as well.

It took some massaging, but gradually, he was able to shimmy the brick upward, pushing against the edges until it moved. Once he was able to grip it on both sides with his fingers, he grabbed the ash shovel again and dug it against the edge of the brick. He pushed on the handle, levering it up, while holding the top part with his fingers to ensure it didn't fall back in the hole.

In a few seconds, he'd lifted the thing out. And once he had that edge...the process went quickly. He pulled out a half dozen bricks and set them to the back of the hearth. And then he looked at the grey sediment beneath. There was a pile of grey and white ash there. And gravel.

And as he brushed the top bits aside....

Bone.

Austin reached down and lifted a small white thing that looked like a twig and held it up in the light of the flash. It was the bone of a human baby; he had no doubt because the round dome of a tiny human cranium was lying in the gravel just above it. The telltale eyeholes and tiny jaw and teeth were facing him. The piece he held should be the child's upper arm bone. The skeleton was fragmented, not perfectly formed in the gravel – after all, he wasn't the first to disturb it – but he could make out the tiny shards of fingers on the left, and the lower bits of the spine to the right.

There was a foot at the bottom of the bones that almost made him cry. Unlike the rest, it seemed to have held its shape perfectly.

The thought of that tiny heel and ivory toes once having flesh upon them instantly made him well up. This had been someone's baby. A tiny helpless child.

But it had ended here. In the ashes of a firepit. Its life snuffed out and its flesh and bones buried for use in dark spells to bring some gain of evil power to someone else. It had never grown up and gotten the chance to live its life. Instead, the child had been used as someone's pawn. The thought made his stomach churn.

And the worst part was, he was here to continue the trend of using this infant. The only reason he was here was to mine this baby's bones.

Austin closed his eyes and took a breath. Then he reached down and removed the small skull from the gravel. As he picked it up, some of the gravel around it moved, and he saw a narrow, oval stone with a round hole bored through it on one side. It would make a perfect top for a keychain, but Austin knew better. The stone was a hagstone. He'd read about them on the Internet while doing some research about witchcraft, after he had realised that was something Regina dabbled in. He had seen a diagram of what one looked like. It was a totem of protection, according to witch lore. He raised an eyebrow, surprised at himself for even being able to recognise it. But the stone was unlike all of the other gravel near the baby's bones. He had no doubt that it had been placed here by the same witch who had killed this child. He picked it up and added it to his pocket collection, along with a few of the other larger bones. He stuffed them all in his pocket, and then picked up the flashlight. He could obsess about how unfair it all was, but that wouldn't change anything. This baby was dead.

His was alive.

He would use the remains of the other child to make sure Ceili stayed that way.

There was nothing he could do for this baby, other than make its sacrifice mean something positive. So he tried to make himself feel good about disturbing its remains. Lord knows they'd been used to drive dark magic in the past. He needed to use them for a positive force today.

Austin bit his lip and shone the light around the gravel pit beneath the bricks. He saw the tiny finger bones of the infant and shook his head. Then he backed away. He wasn't going to sift through the gravel to take every piece of the skeleton with him.

He took a breath and reached out to move a handful of other larger bones into his pocket. He didn't want to think any more about what those tiny white shards represented. Austin turned away from the hearth and began to walk out of the basement. He needed to get back to where this child's life could help save another's. His child's.

He walked the silent steps back up from the abandoned basement and exited the house, pulling the door shut behind him. The neighbourhood was silent…and he was thankful for that. Nobody asked him what he was up to or how his day was going. Instead… it was just the dry rustle of leaves, and the distant moan of traffic on Eighth Street.

Austin half ran across the yard to his garage and looked around for something he could use as a weapon. He didn't keep a gun in the house. There was a hand ax hanging above his garden tools, but he shook his head at that. Instead, he grabbed for a crowbar. Easier to swing, and he could use it to jab. Then he pulled open the door to the car and tossed the crowbar on the passenger's seat. He reached into his pocket for his keys and cringed; he had to sift his fingers through bones to find the car keys. But he did. Because…he needed to leave.

The engine revved to life a minute later and he pulled out of his driveway, barely pausing to make sure the garage door started to shut.

There were bones rattling in his jacket pocket. Hell…there was a baby's *head* rattling in his jacket pocket.

That was all kinds of fucked up.

When he pulled up to the curb by the church, he looked at the roof and saw the deep blue of the night over the shingles. He leapt out of the car and ran up the concrete steps to the door. Before he could even raise his fist to knock…the wooden door opened.

"I've been waiting," Father Vernon said. "I didn't want to leave the foyer until you returned."

"I'm back," Austin said. "Now we need to make something happen. Any thoughts on getting into the club without being seen?"

"We go in the back door," the priest said.

"All I could find at home to use as a weapon was this," he said, brandishing the crowbar. "You don't happen to have a machine gun or something lying about the rectory, do you?"

The priest smiled and shook his head.

"The Lord will provide."

"I hope so," Austin said.

"Did you find what you were looking for?"

Austin nodded, but did not elaborate. He actually had no idea what he was going to do with the things weighing down his pockets…but he thought they would help…somehow.

"Yes and no," he said. "It's just us, and I obviously didn't find a gun or anything." He shook his head and put up a hand. "Just get me back inside."

"I know a way," The priest said. "Wait here. There is one thing we'll need."

He disappeared back into the rectory and left Austin alone. The minutes seemed to stretch out into hours as Austin waited, looking around and hearing nothing but silence and the creaking of an old building around him. It was an eerie few moments. Was the priest coming back? Where had he gone?

And then Father Vernon stepped past Austin and down the rectory steps. He was holding a metal tool. It had handles like a tree branch clipper and looked like some kind of jaws, or clamp, at its end. "Don't ask," he said. "Just follow. Stay quiet."

Austin followed the priest down a stone path that led across the rectory yard and into a back alley. The night air moved with a sour force against the back of his neck as they walked; the alley was like a wind tunnel and the scent of old garbage wafted like a sick perfume.

Father Vernon put up a hand to tell him to stop. They were in front of a nondescript steel trap door in the ground next to the brick wall of a building along the alley. "This will lead us inside," he said quietly. "But you must be quiet from here on. There are guards in some of the back halls. Just follow my lead."

"My lips are sealed," Austin said. "Just get us to Ceili."

The priest reached out with the tool he'd grabbed at the rectory. He put the business end on the chain that locked the door from uninvited visitors like themselves…and pressed the arms together. With an easy snip, the chain separated and fell away. Father Vernon dropped the metal cutters to the asphalt ground nearby and pulled open the metal doors that led to a stairway down. It looked like a storm cellar below. The priest met his eyes. Then without a word he began to descend the metal steps.

Austin turned and put his foot on a rusted metal step and followed the other man's black robes down into the dark. When the ladder ended, he reached out with one foot and shifted it around until he found the ground beneath. They were in some kind of underground room. The floor was old, rough concrete. The walls appeared to be the same, at least from the one wall that he could see. Vernon moved quickly through the dark, and he struggled to follow, not wanting to trip, but not wanting to lose sight of the priest either. The only light in the place glimmered in from windows near the ceiling – well, glass that let in the distant glow of streetlamps, nothing more.

It was enough. They walked carefully in the near dark until they reached a heavy wooden door. It had a black iron handle with a thumb latch as an opener. "Here we go," Father Vernon said.

The older man pressed the latch down and pulled the door open. It moved slowly, with a faint but angry creak.

And then the priest made a sound that caused Austin's stomach to shrink.

"Uh-oh."

CHAPTER TWENTY-SIX

The door that Father Vernon had opened led to a dark chapel. Austin recognised the stations of the cross instantly – he had been here before. It was the Chalice Hall. Within, along the walls, there were eyehooks that had chains linked to the wrists of a series of naked and subjugated victims. They were kneeling or standing all along the wall. At the front of the room, an altar of rustic wood held the form of a nude woman. A man wearing only a bishop's hat stood between her legs. An upside-down cross hung from the wall behind them.

A woman clad in black silk and silver chains stood behind the altar and directed the bishop in his fleshy impaling; Austin only had a second to take in the woman arching her back on the altar before he realised that their entrance had evoked an immediate response.

The door released a stream of silken black. As soon as Austin glimpsed the room beyond, figures from within moved out to surround them. Before he could react, they were circled by a crowd of nuns who looked like they had walked off the set of a pornographic movie. They pressed in close, acting as a wall of flesh, leaving them no room to move. He tried to use the crowbar to force them back, but he couldn't lift his arms at all. Warm flesh shifted almost provocatively against his own, but in this situation, the touch of feminine breasts and thighs did not serve to excite him. Hands gripped his arms and wrists and waist and pressed him back against the stone wall. The crowbar was pried from his hand.

As the depth of the mob grew, he lost track of Father Vernon, who was pulled in another direction. Tongues licked at his lips and cheeks, and women crushed his body to the wall. One by one, they ground hips against his before shifting to the side as another woman moved in to take her place. It was as if they all needed to physically touch him, just once. He was meat in a blender of dark sisters. Their eyes flashed with secret thoughts. Red, wet lips parted and touched and moved away from him like a kaleidoscope.

And then he was dragged into the chapel beyond. The scent of human copulation and the sighs of passion and pain surrounded him like a fog. Entering the chapel was like diving into a pool of sex. Not exactly the expectation when you walked into a room with paintings of stained-glass windows and a cross. For a moment he wondered if they intended to add him to the throng of bodies being flogged against the walls.

But instead of chaining him with other victims, a group of sisters held on and led him through a narrow door at the back of the room behind the altar.

The sister guiding the insemination on the altar didn't acknowledge their presence at all. They moved past her as she flipped her arm and flogged the breasts of the woman before doing the same to the ass of the man joined to her. Austin could see the flesh redden as her black strap connected and withdrew with wet, sharp snaps.

Somewhere in the room a male voice screamed, and a woman laughed.

And then they were through and into a narrow space beyond.

"Welcome home," a familiar voice said from behind him.

Regina stepped around his captors and smiled. Her hair was wild, curls loose and uncombed, strands twisted and rising above her head in a way he'd never seen. She might have just risen from her pillow, except that the makeup around her eyes was dark and perfect. She wore the costume of all the sisters here, and he could see the excitement of her nipples as the filmy material moved and shifted as she walked.

She was excited at the opportunity to dole out pain.

"Tonight is the night of the Devil's Equinox," Regina said. "Tonight is the night that Ceili will become one of us. The only question is how. Will she bring us power as her soul passes, or will she become one of our acolytes, using her flesh to open our sisterhood to more interest from the devils we indulge? Have you decided? Will she become a pure sacrifice, or a devils' whore? Those are your only two choices."

Austin shook his head.

"She will be neither," he insisted. "Because she's leaving here with me tonight."

"You say words that are both false and foolhardy because...." Regina pointed at the women all around him. "There are all of us, and one of you. You can't stop all of us. You can only choose how much you will try to get in our way. I know you will. But I have to tell you this – in the end, all of your efforts will not matter. Ceili is ours. She will always be ours. So, I will ask you to consider – do you want her soul to bring us power as she moves on to her own afterlife...or do you want her to become one of us, using her body for Satan?"

Austin glared at her but refused to answer. He accepted neither of her two alternatives. But he also didn't know how he was going to change fate, given that his arms were currently held tight between the hands of six different women in Regina's army.

"You have three hours left to decide," Regina said. "And I want you to think about this carefully. If you release her soul, she'll leave this earth and move into her own life beyond. The power of your sacrifice will give us what we desire. And it will set Ceili free to seek the next stage of her soul's path."

She leaned in to Austin's face, so that he could see the strong determination in her eyes.

"If you choose to not set her soul free, we will sacrifice you. But your daughter will not go free. She will be raised here as a daughter of Satan. She might go out and do exactly the same as what I did to you. Meet men in bars. Promise them their most secret desires, and then take them to bed again and again. Always despising them... but using their weak, desperate needs to bring the sisterhood what we all truly need. More sacrifices. More power. No matter what you do tonight, we will grow in numbers. All that you decide here is whether Ceili will become one of us, or whether you will set her free."

She leaned close and touched her tongue to his lips. "Think about it," she said. "This time we'll make sure you don't go roaming until we need you." Then she moved away.

The hands on his arms gripped him harder then and pulled him toward a doorway. When they reached the threshold, he tried to resist, digging his feet in and struggling to reach out to grab at the dark wood slats that bordered it. But to no avail. A heavy hand pushed hard against the small of his back, and another pounded against the place just beneath his left shoulder blade. Someone else dug a finger into his side just below the ribs and in seconds Austin's attempt at resistance failed. He fell forward into a small room, and someone lifted and clasped his wrists in cold steel cuffs.

A sister with a curled wisp of blond hair escaping her wimple to trail across her cheek reached above his head to secure the left arm, and when she was through, she let her body slide across his. Her eyes lifted toward the ceiling as her breasts rubbed across his chest, and she licked her lips as her cheek touched and pulled away.

Then she met his eyes and her lips spread apart into a wicked grin.

She laughed. An ego-crushing cackle of victory. Her tease was just that – a challenge won. She knew she'd had him, if only for a second. She had roused him and imprisoned him in the same moment.

"See you later, stud," she whispered, and pulled away. When she turned, the rest of the sisters went with her, and in seconds Austin was left in the room alone.

Austin found himself hanging, arms above his head, in a small dark cell. A prisoner again. Déjà vu. Three times, you're out. So much for escaping. He stifled the urge to cry in frustration and tried to think of his next move.

His mind came back blank. After a while, he fell back to the only thing that he could think of to do. It had been years since he'd said the words in earnest before tonight, but he meant them more than ever before in his life as he spoke them for the second time in as many hours.

"Our Father, who art in heaven, hallowed be thy name...."

CHAPTER TWENTY-SEVEN

The dark felt like a blanket. Thick and warm. It held Austin close against the wall. He waited and prayed. Prayed and waited. He could hear sounds from beyond the room, faint laughter and music. The throb of drumbeats striking again and again somewhere far away. He murmured every prayer he knew and then repeated them all. But eventually, his whispered prayers fell to silence and he struggled to hear what was going on beyond this room.

His eyes grew heavy after a while. This day seemed to have lasted forever. And he couldn't bear to face the moment at its end. A moment that grew closer with every breath. How was he going to find a way to save his baby?

Something creaked. It sounded as if it came from the direction of the doorway. In front of him. He couldn't make out anything, however, in the dark.

"Who's there?" he asked softly, but there was no answer.

He heard the sound again. A faint slap on the ground and then a slow drag. The sound of halting footsteps.

It was closer now.

The air near his cheek grew cold, as if a gust of winter air had suddenly filled the room. He wanted to rub the chill away, but his arms only rattled the chains above his head. And then a whisper spoke straight to his ear.

"You are a disappointment in so many ways," the voice whispered. The chill slipped across his lips and touched his neck on the opposite side. Austin shivered involuntarily.

"How does it feel to be a prisoner?" the whisper asked, in his other ear this time. "Do you like being the one trapped in a place where you can't escape?"

He shivered again but didn't answer. The voice laughed.

"You're pathetic," it said. And then the chill shifted, and the edge of his chin suddenly felt wet and cold – as if it had been dipped in a bowl of ice water. The chill slid up to his nose and down to his throat.

"I wish I could watch them make you suffer," the voice said. "You deserve everything they could do to you. But I need you to survive. I hate it that I need you to get out of this…but apparently, I do. You need to save Ceili. And you can't do that while you're chained to a wall, as satisfying as this position may be for me."

Twin pinpricks of light ghosted into view inches from his face. As he struggled to see through the suffocating black, the angry eyes of his dead wife looked back at him from the darkness. She seemed to shine with her own internal light, a ghoulish blue-white glow that was faint as smoke, but solid enough to show form. Seeing Angie's face made his heart constrict.

"How are you even here?" he asked.

"You don't want me to be here?" she asked. "I'm hurt. You said you'd always want me by your side." He could hear the sarcasm dripping from the whisper of her voice.

"You're dead," he said. "I buried you."

"And your girlfriend killed me and then brought me back as her plaything," she said. "Most women would have been happy that the ex was dead and buried, but not your little witch whore. Oh no, she didn't just want to steal my husband and baby, she wanted to steal my soul. She wanted me here to see her kill my baby. So here I am, thanks to her spell. She pulled me back from somewhere else, and when she calls, I have no choice but to answer. And if she has her way, after tonight, I'll have to serve her fully."

"What does that mean?" he asked. "What does she want from you?"

Angie shook her head. "It doesn't matter. All that matters is that you get Ceili out of here. Which means I can't enjoy watching you get what you deserve tonight."

"Can you get me out of these chains?" he asked.

"I don't know," she answered. "I have moments where I can move and touch physical things…but it's not consistent. I'm like a wave, I come and go without warning. Unless Regina calls me. Then for a little while, I'm solid."

"I can't get out of this on my own," he said.

Her eyes flashed and she moved back from him. Suddenly he could only see the blackness again. "Angie?" he whispered. "Are you there?"

There was silence.

Shit. He didn't want her anywhere near him. But…she was the only chance he had right now.

Austin pulled on the chains that held his arms above his head. They had very little give. They were threaded through an eyehook, so he could stretch one arm up and allow the other to come down, but the clasps around his wrist were tight. He couldn't slip out of them.

Something metallic clinked several times on the stone floor, as if something hit the floor and bounced several times. The sound came from the direction of the entrance of his cell.

Austin froze.

He could see nothing through the dark. But after a moment, there was a faint sliding sound. Again, it sounded metallic. But small. As if a small bit of chain or something was shifting across the floor, one inch at a time. It happened again and again. A faint, repetitive rhythm. After a minute, he realised the sound, albeit faint, was drawing steadily closer. It would make a soft clink, then a sound of shifting across stone.

Then silence.

And then he'd hear it again. He tried to judge the distance, but in the dark, it was impossible. All he could be sure of was that something was shifting across the floor toward him, though. And it sounded very close now.

The sound stopped.

He cocked his head, trying to hear.

"Kick off your shoes," Angie's voice suddenly whispered in his ear. Austin jumped.

"I can't do everything for you," she said. "You're going to have to do some of the work."

"What do I need to do?" he whispered.

"The key is at your feet," she said. "You're going to need to kick off your shoes, and use your feet to grab it, lift it and get it into your hands."

"I'm not a monkey," he complained.

"And I'm not alive," she countered. "Suck it up. Unless you

want to be just like me, you better tap into your inner ape and do this. I was able to knock the key off the ring and push it across the floor…but I can't levitate the thing. If Regina has her way, after tonight's ceremony I'll have a real body again, be able to pick up the key, unlock your chains and kick you in the balls. But by then it won't matter."

Austin touched his toe against the back of the sneaker on his other foot and pushed. It took a couple times, but eventually the heel of the shoe slipped off and he could kick the shoe to the floor. Then he repeated the process with the other shoe. With his toes, he then pulled down his socks.

Once barefoot, he carefully felt along the cold stone for the small metal object that he knew was there.

"To the left," Angie whispered.

His toe found it, and the key shifted away from him.

"Careful," she warned.

Austin dragged it back toward him until the key was positioned between his feet. Then he had to somehow get it from lying flat on the floor to standing up between his feet so that he could wedge it between two of his toes.

The key shifted and clinked on the floor in the dark. He used one foot to hold it in position and tried to use his big toenail to get under and lift it from the floor. Just when he thought he had it, the key fell back.

"Damn it," he complained after several failed times. "I can't do this."

"That's why our marriage fell apart," Angie taunted. "I had to do everything for you."

"Bullshit," he said, "I think it's the other way around." But her words enraged him and gave him the energy to try even harder. And then with an invisible shift, the key suddenly was tucked in between the big toe and second toe of his right foot.

He tried to lift it and pull down one arm, and almost lost his balance and fell.

"Just as coordinated as ever," his dead wife's voice whispered with unveiled disgust.

"Shut the fuck up," he said.

Slowly, he dragged one arm down as far as it would go and then began to lean on the chain to help maintain his balance as he lifted his foot. His finger touched the end of the key, and he felt it loosen and begin to slide out of his toes.

"Damn it," he swore again and scooped down with his hand as hard as he could.

He caught the key just before it dropped to the floor. Then his whole body collapsed. He gripped the key tightly as he fell back against the wall and quickly stamped his bare foot back to the ground to halt his fall.

"You should have been a dancer," Angie said. He could see the glimmer of her body nearby, but he could no longer make out her form.

"I hope you've got this from here," she said. "I don't think I can stay."

Austin stood on his toes and put both hands up as high as they'd go, holding the key between his fingers. He didn't answer her but worked on finding the correct way to slip the key into the lock without losing it. When the metal of the lock suddenly clicked and the chain unravelled and fell to the floor with an iron clank, he looked back to where Angie had been.

There was only darkness.

CHAPTER TWENTY-EIGHT

Eventually, they would discover that he was missing. Austin knew he needed to get away from this place as fast as possible. He needed to find where Ceili was being held before they realised he was loose. His only hope was that they wouldn't come for him until they were ready for the ceremony, which should buy him some time. Regina had mentioned midnight…if that was the real time, he should have a couple hours yet before they went to his cell. That was resting on a lot of assumptions though.

Austin released the cuffs and dropped those and the chains to the floor. Then he navigated his way across the dark room to where he knew the doorway was. He could see a faint illumination from that direction. Once he passed into the hallway beyond, the light grew stronger, and he began to move faster. He could see the flicker of a torch in the next passageway. He hurried to the end of the short corridor but then hugged the wall and carefully peered around the edge once there. He didn't need to walk into a trafficked hallway and immediately get nabbed ten yards from his cell.

There was nobody in the passage beyond. He had no idea which way to go. Austin flipped a mental coin and decided to go right. He passed three white steel doors on the right side of the hall and tried the handle of each one. They were locked. He wondered if this corridor was a wraparound passage on the outside wall of the building. That would suggest that all of the doors on the right side led inward, and thus were locked from the inside to keep traffic on the perimeter out. That might also explain the lack of doors on the left – if it was an outer wall.

Following that assumption, when the corridor reached a T, he turned right. He didn't need to find the exit right now. He needed to find a safe entry into the heart of it all.

He was definitely below ground here. There were heavy pipes

and ducts that crisscrossed the ceilings above him. He could hear the hum of water and electric and at one point a small steel ladder led up from the cement floor through a square hole in the ceiling. He passed the ladder and could see another corridor branch ahead when he suddenly stopped. There were voices from up ahead. He flattened himself against the wall and listened. They were coming closer.

There was no place to hide. There were no doors at all in this section.

He started moving back the way he'd come – he might be able to duck into another hall before they discovered him. And then he saw the shadow of a figure walking on the wall at the end of the hall.

Shit.

Austin did the only thing he could – he grabbed a rung of the ladder and hauled himself up. He had no idea where he was going but he couldn't stay here.

He pulled himself above the edge of the ceiling in a heartbeat and looked around. It looked like some kind of boiler room, with large steel reservoirs, presumably for water, and pipes leading in from all directions.

Nobody else was there. He pushed off from the ladder and lay down on the floor, peering over the edge to watch if the person or people he'd heard passed by. Had they seen him? Would they follow him up the ladder? He glanced right and left at that thought, wondering what his options were for escape if they did.

Other than hiding behind a giant reservoir…his options were not great. There did not look to be any doors or hidden spaces in the room. He had to pray that they had not seen him and would not look up as they passed.

A moment later two men in long black robes and pointed hats passed through the hall beneath him. They were talking animatedly – one gestured in the air with his hands and Austin was struck by the strange thought that the man looked like a prophet. But what was the message he was trying to spread now, in this place?

He stifled a laugh and watched as the two continued walking and passed.

He'd lucked out.

But it only underscored the need for him to find a disguise. If they were looking for him, he was going to stand out here like a sore thumb.

A black robe would do him well and probably get him into the places he needed to go without question.

But where to find one?

He lay on the floor and considered that question before looking up and realising there was a clock on the wall behind one of the tanks. The red LED numbers said 10:47 p.m.

He needed to get moving.

Austin hung his head over the edge and confirmed that nobody else was walking down the hall before he let himself back down the ladder and hurried down the corridor in the direction he'd been walking before this detour. This time, when he turned the corner, he knew right away that he was in a more populated area. The torches were brighter, there were more doorways, and the floor turned from bare concrete to a rough brown tile.

He turned the knob on the first door that he came to and this time it opened. He stepped inside and found nothing of use. It was essentially a broom closet, with boxes, odds and ends and an actual broom. He exited quickly and moved to the next door.

This one…led to real room.

There was a film playing inside. And it was really a *film*, not a DVD projection. He could see the projector in the back of the room nearby, with a reel of film propped up high on an arm, feeding the brown film stock into the slot where the light projected it to the far wall. There were a couple dozen chairs in front of the projector; about half of them had people sitting in them.

He realised that he would be obvious if he stood in the back of the room, so Austin walked to the last row of seats and slipped into an empty one on the far left.

The whir of the projector provided a low hum beneath the soundtrack of the film itself. Which, once Austin sat down and actually focused on the screen, was…obscene.

A woman occupied the centre of the frame. She wore fishnet stockings and bright red lipstick…and nothing else. She straddled a horse – the construction kind, not the animal. It was made of two-by-fours and was low – she had to squat slightly to touch the top bar of wood. But, that was by design. Because there was a rubber representation of a human phallus secured to the centre of the horse…. And she was using it as if she were having sex with a man. There was a semicircle of people standing around her, all wearing robes of black. Some had hoods covering their heads. None moved at all; only the woman on the horse shifted, rhythmically, back and forth, up and down. The image and expressionless faces of the onlookers were oddly unsettling.

He looked around at the others in the room. There was a single man in his row on the right side. The guy looked older, with silver curls and black-framed glasses. Austin quickly scanned ahead, not wanting the man to turn and catch his eye. In the row in front of him, a man and a woman sat close together. Both wore black robes suspiciously similar to the outfits of the crowd in the film. The woman leaned forward slightly, her shoulders shifting back and forth as if pushing at something in front of them with her hands. The man, meanwhile, leaned his head back periodically, as if he felt the occasional need to study the ceiling.

Austin leaned to his left and caught a glimpse of what was really going on.

There was a man kneeling in front of the couple. The woman's hands were on his head, moving it up and down with a particular rhythm.

Austin suddenly understood…and instantly looked away.

In the next row, two women dressed as nuns sat next to each other. There were three men sitting in front of them, all of them wearing black shirts with white strips around their collars.

Austin knew that none of them were priests and nuns ordained by a Christian church. No, just the opposite. They were anti-priests and anti-nuns. There were moans coming from the front of the room, and he turned his attention back to the screen. The woman riding the horse had somehow acquired leashes, or reins. The crowd now used her like a sick marionette. A dozen silver chains pulled taut against hooks in her skin. Each chain was controlled by one of the black-robed audience members. As the woman bobbed above the phallus of the horse, the skin on her breasts and belly and back pulled and stretched as she shifted her body toward orgasm. The pain of the hooks presumably kept her motions as tightly controlled as possible. She was not bucking with the same abandon as before, and with every motion she alternatively squealed in complaint and excitement.

Austin felt eyes on him then and realised the man to his right had noticed his presence. And was eyeing him with an odd look. He was suddenly conscious of the fact that he was the only person in the room not wearing some iteration of a black robe.

It was maybe time to leave.

And he knew what he needed to find, first and foremost.

A black robe.

Austin slid his butt off the seat and slowly pushed himself upright holding his hand on the back of the chair. He nodded politely at the man watching him, and back stepped toward the door. He knew when it was time to leave the party.

This was something of a toga party and he wasn't wearing a toga.

He closed the door behind him carefully, and then moved quickly away from it. The next doorknob he tried led to a small chapel.

And more black robes. A priest with a tall hat – maybe he was supposed to be a bishop – stood at the front of the room before an upside-down cross, holding something up in the air. Austin didn't stay to find out what it was. He didn't need to be noticed again.

He kept walking and turned a corner. The smell of incense was suddenly strong in the air. Maybe it was just the effect of smoke, but the temperature seemed slightly warmer here too. He could hear voices nearby. There was a hum of talk from one direction. And the distant echo of both laughter and shrieks.

A man turned the corner at the end of the hall and began walking toward him. Austin didn't wait to see the man's reaction. He decided to go back the way he'd come. He walked past the chapel room and as he was passing the film room he heard the man call out to him.

"Hey there, wait a minute."

Austin didn't answer but increased the speed of his feet. And as soon as he did, he heard the sound of footsteps running. He didn't dare enter the film room with all of the people in there. Instead, he sprinted around the next corner and toward the broom closet. Maybe he could duck in before the guy saw him.

He pulled the door open and stepped inside, flipping the light switch near the door. A bulb flickered on overhead. In addition to the broom and boxes he'd seen earlier, the room had several shelves with everything from coils of electrical wire to screwdrivers and wrenches to aluminium ductwork. There was even a stack of metal pipes on the floor next to the wall. Seeing no other easy options, he reached down and picked one up. A second later, the door opened, and the man came charging in.

Austin didn't even think about it; he swung the pipe at the back of the man's head. The guy went down, fast and hard.

Austin grabbed at a coil of white electrical wire and wound it around the man's ankles before he could recover. He only had seconds – the guy was already starting to moan.

Speaking of which…he looked around for something to gag the man. He didn't need a screamed alert going out.

There was a stack of duct tape on one of the shelves and he grabbed a roll, pulled a segment loose and ripped. Then he slapped the tape over the man's mouth. That would solve the immediate problem. The man was blinking rapidly and lifted a hand to feel the back of his head. Austin knew he only had a few seconds before the man was fully in control of himself again. He grabbed at the black sleeve of the man's robe and pulled it free. Then he yanked it from the other arm and reached again for the wire. The man began to struggle when Austin brought his wrists together, but he was still fuzzy and Austin had the strength of desperation on his side. In just a few seconds the man's wrists were bound. Austin pulled the robe free. After considering for a second, he shook his head and began to strip off his clothes before slipping the robe on himself. He frowned when he looked down at the way it clung over his groin and thighs. The nun and priest outfits here were not designed to conceal much. But if he was going to look like one of the club's members… he had no choice but to let it all hang out. Luckily, the side panels of the robe were not only not transparent, but they included pockets. Even devil worshippers needed someplace for their wallets! He quickly transferred his phone, the bones and other implements from his jacket to the robe.

There was a smear of red on the cement floor from the back of the man's head. Austin felt bad for hitting him but...the man's eyes were bulging angrily and he appeared fully conscious now, yanking against the bindings and grunting behind the tape.

"Sorry," Austin said. "But you came after me. You should just leave people alone."

The man flapped his bound arms at him accusingly.

"I need you to stick around here for a while," he said, and grabbed the roll of wire. Then he looped a length of wire through the binding at the man's ankles and tied the other end to a large pipe that ran floor to ceiling through the room.

"If I don't get a chance to come back for you, I'm sure someone will need supplies in the next couple days," he said. "See ya."

Austin slipped out the door and back into the hallway beyond. He hoped the guy would be okay. But at the moment, he cared more about blending in until he could track down Ceili. Now he should be able to slip in and out of rooms without attracting attention.

He retraced his steps back to the area where he'd heard voices. The incense seemed even stronger now, and he soon found out why. The first doorway he came to was an arched entryway to an ornate room beyond. He stepped through and saw gold gilt columns reaching to a vaulted ceiling and murals of debauched scenes panted on the ceiling just above.

He stood in an antechamber above a large hall. There were theatre style seats to his left, with just a narrow walkway between here and there. He had entered the balcony section of the hall. He walked over to a balustrade and looked down. A procession was going on down below. Black-clad figures wove in a serpentine line around a series of round tables. The smoke streamed steadily from a gold box. A man dangled the box from a chain as he walked.

He was calling out words in a strange tongue as he led the procession, and every time he stopped speaking, the crowd behind him answered, with a single, guttural syllable: "*Goi!*"

The procession wound around the edges of the room, and then when the man yelled out "*Parlay avun das erunt al interogattan deo dua*," most of the people behind him answered, "*Goi!*" and the line continued to move.

He watched as they completed a full circuit of the room and then turned down the centre aisle and began to move toward the main entrance on the level below. He was just about to stop watching when he realised that the back of the line was made up of a handful of young women…one of them carrying a baby in her arms.

Ceili? He squinted and leaned over the edge, trying to see better. The baby lay on a black pillow, wrapped in a black sheet. Probably a piece of one of the nuns' robes, he realised.

He could only see the white of the child's face, but as the procession moved past his vantage point on the rail, he saw the baby's eyes open and look about.

It *was* Ceili. Her eyes were wide and bright as the nun passed below him.

He needed to follow them to wherever they were going! But first he had to get out of this balcony. He looked around for an exit, and saw an arched doorway covered in black drapery near the seats to his right. He rushed over and poked his head through the dark velvet curtains.

It led to a carpeted circular stairwell down. He took the stairs two at a time and found himself at the back of the main hall just as the last of the procession exited. He didn't slow but hurried after the last person in line. He fell in step just as the final people left the room and began to march down the long dark hallway beyond.

If the person ahead of him noticed that they were no longer last in line, they gave no indication. His timing couldn't have been better. Nobody seemed to notice that the procession had grown by one. And why should they? The whole group continued to walk down the corridor until they came to a room at its very end. The glow of red flickered from inside, and the leader simply turned and put up his hand.

"Only one may pass," he said. "The chosen one."

With that, the nun toward the back of the procession moved forward with Ceili and disappeared into the room beyond.

"The preparations are complete," he told the group, holding the incense container in the air and clanking its body against the chain.

"In one hour, we will meet in the Sacristy and complete the ritual of the Devil's Equinox."

With that the crowd began to stream past Austin, and he fell in step behind a blond woman in the translucent black silk of the sisterhood of Club Equinox. He could see almost every movement of her muscles through the garb as she walked. He forced his eyes away and looked for a place to sidestep the crowd. He didn't want to get too far from the room where Ceili had been taken, but at the same time he didn't want to suddenly be the sole person left standing right outside it as the priests kept an eye on the area. He couldn't afford to stand out, not when he was this close.

He stopped along the wall when the corridor zagged left and waited until the throng passed him by. There were a host of conversations going on between the sisters and priests about tonight, and in their excitement, nobody paid any attention to the guy leaning against the wall. Which suited him just fine.

Once the hall was clear, Austin walked back toward the end of the hall. He had not been able to get close to the room before. Now, he should be able to walk right in without anyone noticing.

He put his head through the arch.

There was a black crib at the end of the small room. Candles guttered from every place you could think to look. They flickered and bathed the room in faintly moving shadows. Austin could see Ceili lying in the crib atop a black sheet. But before he could move farther into the room, a man in a black robe carrying a long staff with a curved blade set atop it stepped in front of him.

"No one may pass until the Equinox is upon us," the man said. "The child must not be disturbed."

"I just hoped I could see the baby before the festivities," Austin said.

"None shall pass!" the man said again.

He didn't have a pipe handy this time. And the guard had a very dangerous-looking staff. Austin needed a new plan.

He nodded and backed away. "I'll see you in the Sacristy," he said. And began to walk away. He could feel the man's eyes boring into his back. It took everything in him not to look back, but he kept his eyes straight ahead.

Once he was out of sight of the room, he stopped and leaned back against the corridor wall. So, he'd found Ceili. Now what? He apparently had an hour to think of a way to get past the guard and get her out.

He needed a weapon. And help.

He needed Father Vernon. The priest had to be nearby, chained up again no doubt just as he had been when they'd first met. The plan clicked into place like a gear. He would find Father Vernon, who would help him find a way past the guard.

There was suddenly a renewed fire of hope in his chest, and Austin began to walk hurriedly down the corridor. He stopped and opened every door, peering inside of each room and quickly backing out when he found either nobody…or groups of people performing decadent rituals that he did not wish to become part of. He had no idea where they had locked up the priest, but he had to find him. And fast, before they realised that Austin himself was loose again.

In his mind he could picture a giant clock with its minute hand clicking steadily toward the toll of midnight. He could almost hear the seconds ticking by.

When he'd exhausted all of the corridors of the level he was on, he found a narrow stairway that curled around and up.

"I'm coming for you, Ceili," he whispered to himself. "Just hang on a little longer. Daddy's going to get you out of here."

CHAPTER TWENTY-NINE

He knew where he was almost as soon as he left the stairway. He'd been here before, with Regina. He recognised the painting of a coven holding hands in a circle around a burning fire. He knew the one that depicted a nude woman lying spread-eagle on an altar. Another woman, with an unfastened black cape and a knife tucked like a phallus between her legs knelt above her with her arms in the air. The blade of the knife curled upward to its tip – a deadly penis ready to slide inside the woman on her back. The kneeling woman appeared ready to fall forward to embrace the woman below her. It would be a deadly embrace for the girl beneath.

Austin remembered the first time he'd seen that painting and how nonchalant Regina had reacted. "Underground art," she had said. "People here like to push the envelope."

At the time, he'd thought it was kind of cool. Dark fantasy. But now he knew that for the people in this building, those paintings were depicting reality. Those things actually happened here. The thought sent a chill down his spine.

He moved faster down the corridor. Despite now having a 'costume' that should protect his identity, he still didn't want to be seen. And sooner or later, an alarm was going to go out when they discovered he was gone – or once they found the guy he'd left in the broom closet.

Austin passed the hall to the front bar; as he did, he could hear the thumping bass of whatever the DJ was playing to draw people to the small dance floor. He was sure the room was crowded; it was prime time on a weekend night. And while everyone wouldn't be clued in to the ceremony that was happening in the bowels of the club tonight, there were surely more people here because of that than usual. Certainly, the sounds of laughter and chatter were at a higher pitch than usual; the buzz of dozens of conversations rode the air above the music like a haze of smoke.

He passed by the corridor quickly and remembered the rooms on his left and right just ahead. He'd seen people gathered in those places before. And he knew that just to the right he'd find the entryway to the Sacristy. But he didn't want to go there just yet. Father Vernon wouldn't be there. Most likely, he'd be chained up in the 'prison' area that Austin had found him in before. And that was down a side path at the end of the hall. He stepped quickly past the Sacristy, noting a loud buzz of voices from inside there as well. And then he came to the museum place. There were three nuns inside. They stood near the coffin at the front of the room. Austin hesitated, and then entered the room anyway. He couldn't stay waiting in the hall outside, so he moved to the far end of the room and pretended to be studying one of the display cases with what looked to be the bones of an infant on black velvet inside. He could hear the women talking but could not quite understand what they were talking about.

"...after the *frileu* the Mother will come out..."

"...and the ninth Resurrection will bring us the *gentrilex!*"

"Only if you are bad enough," one interjected, and they all laughed.

"Define bad enough," another said.

"Bad like this?" the other said, and Austin snuck a look over his shoulder to see one of the women bending forward to suckle the breast of her friend through the translucent habit.

The woman pulled her close and gave out a loud moan before the third sister slapped the suckling woman on the ass.

"Save it for later," she said. "I want to get another drink."

A moment later, the trio filed out of the room and Austin grinned and began to walk to the back door into the chamber he knew lay beyond.

He stepped through the doorway fully expecting to see the priest chained to the wall as he'd been the first time they'd met, but when he stepped inside, he found that the dark room held only empty chains.

Damnit.

He'd been so sure. He looked around the dark room and felt helpless. He didn't know where to look next; he hadn't thought of a backup plan.

And now he felt the pressure of the clock ticking...the night was moving on and he was wasting time. He had to find Vernon and get Ceili out before the ceremony began. Austin threaded his way back through the display cases and out into the hall. There was a throng of people now in the main hall, and he turned right and followed a group that way. If he had to check every room of this place for the priest, he would.

He followed two into a small side room where there was a bar and a myriad of red lights. The place glowed like hell. A woman mixed drinks, wearing nothing but a headdress that looked like butterfly wings and a set of chains that crisscrossed her torso and cinched through her crotch to hook somewhere across her back.

The occupants were watching a stage show. There were two men on a small elevated platform. They were naked but armed. Each held a small leather whip. The straps were only a few inches long, but had silver hooks at their ends. The men had to get close to hurt each other...but if they could connect without taking a counter blow from their opponent, they could rake a nice gash across the other's flesh.

As he stopped to watch, he saw one with dark black hair and a pot belly slap hard at the other, aiming for the man's midriff.

He connected, and the hooks ripped across the man's belly. One caught the skin of the other man's penis and blood suddenly darkened the hair around his belly button and glistened across his wild pubic patch.

The wounded man screamed in anger, but instead of moving away, he grabbed for the other and drew him into a bear hug. Austin thought it a weird move – hug another man while naked and bleeding? But then he saw the strategy. The proximity allowed him to slap his opponent down the back. The hooks of his whip caught his opponent – a silver-haired man with deep brown skin – in the ass. In seconds, there were rivers of blood flowing down the man's back and ass, and the first wounded man released his embrace and jumped back.

The crowd cheered, and some lifted their drinks in honour. Austin shook his head and started to back out of the room.

"Hey friend, don't leave now. We're almost ready for the main event."

Austin looked at the man standing beside him. The guy was in one of the ubiquitous black priest outfits, only, since it was made in part of the same material as the nun's habits, he could see that the man's chest was crisscrossed in leather straps. There were three that led from a silver ring on his chest to connect with another circle ring that hooped around his bare cock and balls. Austin closed his eyes for a moment, trying to erase the image. He knew instinctively that this was not a guy he wanted to get to know better. Not his scene.

"I'll buy you a drink," the man said.

Austin shook his head. "Thanks, but I was just leaving."

At that moment, a hand grabbed him by the arm. "Nobody leaves now," another man's voice said. "It's the time of the final act."

Austin looked to his left, and a large burly man with grey hair and silver skull earrings stood at his side, staring ahead to the stage.

"I need to meet a friend," Austin argued, but it was too late. Even as he said it, the large wooden door at the back of the room closed, and he heard a heavy iron lock snap into place.

"What do you drink?" the leather strap man asked.

"Beer," Austin said. "IPAs usually."

"I think we can set you up," the other man said, and flashed him a grin that made Austin's cock shrivel. The man turned to the bare bartendress and a moment later handed Austin a pint. "Cheers," he said, and clicked the rim of a martini glass filled with something clear and an olive against Austin's pint.

"Cheers," Austin said and took a sip. The bitterness of the hops slid down his throat with a welcome jolt, as in the front at the stage, the men who had been wrestling now lay down on the floor.

"It is the time of the becoming," a voice called.

At that, a man in a tall black bishop's hat walked onto the stage. "In just a half an hour, in the Sacristy, we will celebrate the Devil's Equinox. But here, in the next few minutes, we will witness the dark joining that will bring the Devil closer to our midst. The men are the beginning. The child is the end."

Austin considered the words. They seemed to omit the women, however, the men on the stage, in all honesty, did not seem to need a woman. Bloody and glistening with sweat, they were no longer trying to rip each other open. At least not with whips and barbs. The silver-haired one held the other down on the floor with his hands on the other's wrists and threatened anal defilement as he straddled him with an obvious erection.

Austin looked away. The two men who had kept him from leaving before now flanked him, and each of them pressed close. He was their meat sandwich and it was making him very uncomfortable. They clearly did not intend for him to leave and he didn't want to make a scene…but he needed to go. The sound of the lock he'd heard on the doors behind them also led him to believe that leaving would be difficult at the moment. He guessed they were locked in for the current show. There were moans now coming from the small stage in the front of the room, and nearby a flurry of catcalls grew all around.

"And the winner was…" a voice nearby called out.

"Bartholomew!"

The crowd cheered and the dark-haired man looked around with an angry scowl. "No way, I scored more than he did. Look at his back."

He pushed for the older man to turn around, but a half dozen men streamed onto the stage from the bar and grabbed at a series of chains with hooks that hung from the ceiling. Hands held the man's legs and arms as the others grabbed at the chains and pulled them to bring the hooks into strategic positions. And then, one by one, they pressed the hooks to the loser's flesh. He screamed out with each one, as barbs infiltrated the flesh of his palms, his calves, his ass and his back.

The worst was when one long thin chain was brought around to his front, and a grinning blond man slid the barb beneath the thin skin of his penis and yanked it forward.

"Raise him up," a voice cried, and that voice was quickly followed by a chorus of men. "Raise him up!"

And suddenly a team of men stood on each side of the hooked man and pulled on the chains. In seconds, his body floated up and off the ground, suspended by all of the hooks in his flesh. Austin had to close his eyes when he saw the skin stretching from each place where the hooks dug deep beneath the skin, especially the man's penis, which was yanked to his left, his cock head stretched sideways. The man shrieked with the first pull, and then cried again with the second. But when he was three feet above the floor, he stopped crying, and the other man took a stance between his legs.

"Let it begin," a deep voice called, and with a thrust and a groan, it did.

Austin took a deep swig of his pint, refusing to look forward. And after a few minutes, he realised that his 'friends' had become entranced by the foul acts performed on the stage to the hanging man. He felt a hand slip across his back and work its way down to cup his ass. And then another moved across his chest.

Austin swivelled, pirouetting out of the embraces of the two men beside him.

"I'm sorry, but no," he said, and started walking toward the door.

"You can't leave," the leather strap man insisted.

"I can't stay," Austin insisted and walked to the door as behind him a horrible shriek came from the stage. A crowd of men cheered and then a shriek came again, this time with a heavy, guttural undertone.

When he reached the door, a man wearing only chain mesh across his chest and waist blocked his path, but Austin wasn't having it.

"I have to leave, I'm sorry," he insisted. "Let me go." When the man stood fast, Austin pointed to the door lever, "I have to prepare for my part in the Devil's Equinox ceremony. Let me go."

The man looked surprised, but then nodded and opened the door.

Austin slipped into the hallway and took a deep breath of cool air. Then he gave out a sigh of relief and began to walk toward the end of the hall. He still needed to canvass the rooms and find Vernon, and the hour was growing late. He looked at his cell phone and the clock on the home screen read 11:33.

He was running out of time.

CHAPTER THIRTY

The torches flickered and crackled as he walked down the empty corridor. With each room that he poked his head into, his panic grew. He was going to have to turn back, and try to save Ceili himself, without help. But he knew that was going to be a losing proposition. There were too many of them. There was no way he was going to get the baby out of here alone.

Austin stopped and took a deep breath. He could keep walking for the next hour and not find anything but empty rooms. This was an industrial complex; he could wander forever.

He considered turning back, but then said to himself, *One more room.*

And just after he did, he heard footsteps in the hall behind him. There was a room a few yards ahead and he moved toward it, turned the handle and ducked inside. He didn't want to deal with another situation like he'd just escaped from.

"So they set you free?" a voice asked from the dark.

"Father Vernon!" Austin cried out. In the shadows, he could see the priest, stripped to the waist, chained to the wall.

He hurried over and ran his hand up the chain, looking for the lock.

"The key is over there," the priest said, gesturing with one cuffed hand.

Austin followed the priest's direction and quickly located the key on the wall. In moments, he'd set Father Vernon free.

The priest pulled up the back of his vestments and slipped his arms through the sleeves. Then he rubbed his wrists for a minute, shaking his head. "I'm getting too old to be chained up like this," he complained.

Austin laughed. "Have you had a lot of experience?"

The priest smiled. "Some would say I've been in chains since I joined the priesthood. But I don't look at it like that."

"That's good, I guess," Austin said, and then abruptly switched subjects. "The Devil's Equinox ceremony is in just fifteen or twenty minutes…we need to get Ceili away from them before it begins."

"Whatever you need," Father Vernon said, still rubbing his wrists. "Just tell me what to do."

"She was downstairs, before," Austin said. "I was hoping we could get her from the room they had her in before they took her to the Sacristy. You could be a distraction while I grab her."

"Well…then we'd better go."

Austin nodded, and led the way out of the room. They turned left and started walking down the hall. The priest seemed to be limping slightly, hanging back.

"Are you okay?" he asked. "Did they hurt you?"

Father Vernon shook his head. "I'm just old and stiff," he said. "Keep moving, I will keep up."

Austin began to walk faster, leading the way. They turned the corner, and ahead of them, he could see a stream of black-robed people filing into a doorway.

The Sacristy. They were already gathering for the ritual.

Austin put up his hand and they stopped, watching the men and women streaming through the doorway. There was actually a procession here – he could see a bishop's hat down the line, and the staff with an upside-down cross on it not far away.

"I think we're too late," Austin said.

They stood and watched for a moment, since the people made the hallway impossible to pass anyway.

And then the cross came into view, and Austin saw the blond nun behind it, long curls cascading out of the headdress of her false habit, her breasts bobbing obscenely beneath the black silk, a baby cradled in her arms.

"That's her," Austin whispered.

The nun and the cross and the bishop behind her all disappeared into the Sacristy. After a dozen or more people behind them filed into the room, the procession finally ended, and Austin and Father Vernon were alone in the hallway.

"Now what?" Austin moaned. "We're too late."

"It's never too late for hope, my son," Father Vernon said. "We must wade in where angels fear to tread."

"You sound like a bad scripture."

"There are no bad scriptures," he said. "Only bad people."

Austin grinned. "If you say so."

He reached into his pockets and withdrew the vial of holy water and the blessed candle he'd brought from home. And a silver crucifix that Angie had gotten from her aunt who had bought it at the Vatican while on a vacation trip to Rome. She had always kept them in a special box in her closet.

"I don't have much to go in there with," Austin said.

The priest looked at the items and nodded. "They will have to do. The Lord will provide."

Austin raised an eyebrow at that platitude but said nothing. Faith and prayer were the only tools he really had right now, and he had precious little of each. He pulled out a lighter and lit the candle, holding it in the same hand as the crucifix.

"I'm not sure what this will do, but it's all I could think of," he said.

The priest nodded. "It'll bring the eyes of God upon us and blind the minions of Satan."

"I think I'd rather have a gun."

"Violence is not the way of the Lord," Father Vernon pointed out.

Austin nodded. "Well, prayer alone won't get my baby out of there."

"Action is needed," the priest agreed. "But we don't have to take another life to save Ceili's."

"The point is moot anyway," Austin said. "I don't have anything that can be used as a weapon. We need to go in there and surprise them. I'll grab Ceili, if you can help me distract them?"

"I'll do my best."

Father Vernon held his hands out. "I can hold the blessed items so your hands are free," he offered.

"Good idea," Austin said, handing them over.

The priest took them and smiled thinly. He held the cross out in one hand and the candle in the other. "We will walk into the den of iniquity, with the Lord before us."

Austin looked at him, not sure what to say. The priest said it for him.

"Let's do it."

Austin nodded. He stepped forward, grasped the handle and pulled open the door to the Sacristy.

CHAPTER THIRTY-ONE

A cloud of incense hit them as soon as Austin opened the door. The air was ten degrees warmer than in the hall and filled with the acrid smell of burning herbs and the buzz of dozens of voices. A crowd gathered around the bar talking and drinking in small huddles, but a larger contingent had gathered near the altar on the far side of the room. They stood around highboy tables and left a centre aisle open, which led to the wooden altar itself. The Irreverent Mother stood behind the altar near the large upside-down cross, conversing with a man in a bishop's hat. At the front of the centre aisle, in front of the altar, a baby's wicker bassinet sat on a small table. The bassinet had been painted black, and a witch's star was painted in white on its side.

Lying in the centre of the basket was a tiny babe, eyes blue and wide, staring up at the painted ceiling above, arms reaching and fingers grabbing at the sky. She didn't make a sound, but Austin felt his heart crack in half when he saw her eyes darting this way and that.

Ceili just wanted to be held. By Austin or Regina or…. Someone who would love her and take care of her. Not someone who would sacrifice her to the Devil for black magic power.

Austin started to make a beeline to her bassinet, but just before he reached it two men suddenly blocked his path.

"In a hurry?" one of them asked. He was at least six feet tall with a haze of beard across his face. His shoulders and chest were broad; he looked like a linebacker.

"Just going to meet my friends," he lied.

The linebacker shook his head. "I don't think so. I don't know you."

"So…you know everyone here?"

The man nodded. "Pretty much. Nobody is allowed near the altar until the ceremony begins."

Another guy suddenly stepped up behind the linebacker. And then a woman flanked him on the other side. "Is there a problem?" the woman asked.

Linebacker shook his head. "No problem at all," he said. "Just a man who doesn't know his place."

There was a couch to his left, so Austin moved to the right, intending to get away from the linebacker and go around the woman. However, she stepped right with him, blocking him. He started to turn in the other direction, but then felt someone pressing against him from the other side. And then from behind.

It suddenly dawned on Austin that in a matter of seconds, he had quietly become surrounded. There were at least two dozen people now standing between him and the entrance. It couldn't be an accident.

He turned away from the linebacker and tried to face the back of the room. Where was Father Vernon? He couldn't see the priest he'd come in with, only the black robes of the imposters. There was a mob around him now three bodies deep. And they all were staring at him. Smiling silently.

"We've been waiting for you," a voice said from behind.

He turned. The linebacker had faded back and the Irreverent Mother now stood between him and the bassinet. She held up her hands to the air, as if calling on the gods above.

"You are a difficult man to contain," she said. Around her, there were cackles of laughter.

"But in the end, you are here with us, and that's what's important now."

"I am leaving," he said. "With my baby."

She shook her head, and the tall hat of her "office" wobbled so much that it looked like it would fall. "I'm afraid not," she said. "You're both part of our ceremony. For tonight is the Devil's Equinox. It's the night we've been waiting for for a decade. And you're here to share it with us."

"No," he said. "I'm not."

Austin slammed his fist against the woman who gripped him on one side, and then did the same against the grip of the man on his left. Both released him, and he found himself suddenly standing free in the aisle. But all around him were throngs of men and women in black robes. Everyone in the club must be here. They blocked any exit. He couldn't go forward, back or sideways.

"In just a few minutes, we will begin the ceremony," the Irreverent Mother said. "There are only two ways that this can go. You will either be the one who sets Ceili free, or you will be the sacrifice yourself."

Austin shook his head. "There's another way. Ceili and I leave here tonight and never come back. End of story."

Regina suddenly stepped out from behind the Irreverent Mother. Her face glowed in the dim lights like a moon. "This story never ends," she said. "And no matter what happens, you are now forever a part of it."

"And so is Ceili," the Irreverent Mother said. She stepped aside then, gesturing at the man behind her, a man who wore black priest vestments – the real kind, that weren't see-through. In his arms, Ceili shifted and cooed. Austin saw the white hair and wrinkled cheeks of Father Vernon and sighed with relief. Somehow the priest had gotten around the crowd to the altar and grabbed the baby. All was not lost.

"Thank God you got her," Austin said. He pointed to the door and yelled, "Don't worry about me, just get her out of here."

The priest did not move. All around him, people started to laugh.

Father Vernon shook his head slowly and began to stroke the face of the child with the back of his hand. The white tufts of his eyebrows shifted and his smile broadened. For a second, he reminded Austin of Clarence, the bumbling angel from *It's A Wonderful Life*.

"Ceili is ours now," the Irreverent Mother said.

Father Vernon held the child up, above his head. Then he brought her back down and kissed her forehead. And embraced her again in his arms.

"What are you waiting for?" Austin hissed. "Get her out of here while you can!"

Regina stepped back from her position next to the Irreverent Mother to put her hand on the priest's shoulder. She touched a finger to the baby's chin and Ceili's arms waved excitedly in the air. Then Regina looked up to catch Austin's eye and smiled.

"Father Vernon has been a child molester his entire life," she said. "He was one of the founders of Equinox. If we end up needing to make you our sacrifice tonight instead of her, Ceili will grow up here, in Equinox. But during the days, she will live with him. He will be the man who teaches her what it is to be a woman. Which death do you think will be worse?"

Austin's chest suddenly felt like a vacuum had touched his heart. All this time the priest had been a plant? A fake?

He let out a long wail as all around him, the laughter increased.

Father Vernon lifted Ceili up again, and this time bent forward to kiss her on the lips.

Austin leapt forward, fist outstretched, but hands grabbed him at the arms and waist and pulled him back.

"You asshole!" Austin yelled. "Don't you touch her again, or I swear I'll kill you."

The priest looked up from Ceili's innocent face and grinned. "I don't think you're in any position to do that."

"I will hurt you," Austin said. "I promise I will."

"He'll like that," the Irreverent Mother said. "Why do you think we keep him chained up? He enjoys being punished for his sins. And then…he sins again and again."

Tears welled and streamed down Austin's cheeks as hands dragged him around and away from the priest. Bodies pressed against him from behind and to the side as a band of nuns pushed him away from Father Vernon and Ceili toward the front of the room. Toward the altar.

A moment later, the priest passed them by on the side with Regina. She took a position in front of the altar and raised her hands.

"Sisters," she said. "It is the night of the Devil's Equinox. The night we have looked forward to for months. Some of us have been preparing for this night for years. At last, the moment is at hand. We have our child. We have our priest. We have the man who will either sacrifice his own life, or his child's. In a few minutes, the moon will begin to move into position, blocking the light of heaven and allowing the Devil's eye to see us clearly. We are ready for a night to remember. A night that will bring us…something amazing."

She picked up a book from the altar. Austin recognised the black leather cover, and silver half moon on the front. It was Regina's Book of Shadows. She riffled through the pages toward the back of the book and finally stopped on a page, a smile spreading across her lips.

"I have been researching the right way to draw the Dark Eye to our midst. I've visited the catacombs of Myridian in Ireland, and the secret library of Damascules in the Vatican. There are references to the Devil's Equinox, of course. But the words are always veiled and unclear. I have not been able to find clear evidence that anyone has successfully made the calling; it is a very rare opportunity. The last time the ceremony of the Equinox was attempted was 1963. At that time, the Bremen House coven in Bachelors Grove attempted the ceremony, but they were unsuccessful. If there were any survivors, they scattered, and did not leave an account of what went wrong. However, the place itself has been full of restless souls ever since. So, I'd say they were successful on some level. Something changed that place forever."

She looked at the throng of people gathered around her and nodded. "We will succeed where others have failed. Why? Because we have spent years making ourselves ready. We have defiled ourselves and danced naked beneath the light of the moon to draw his eye. We have followed the teachings of Sister Celestine, the original Irreverent Mother, who founded this order. We have drunk the blood of the innocent and the perverse alike and yearned for the day that we can demand that men fall to their knees simply by a whispered word of power. Tonight, we will have that power, and the word will be all of ours."

A cheer erupted from a group of nuns nearby, and Regina smiled and paused. Then she raised her hands and the noise quieted.

"In 1698, in a basement below a convent in Philadelphia, there was a secret society much like ours. They called themselves the Feet of Satan. The name was a reflection on the convent above where the order called themselves the Hands of God. And, in fact, the Feet of Satan were actually those selfsame nuns known during the day as the Hands of God. The entire convent was a sham, a front for the Dark Eye. The head of the order was a woman named Elizabeth, and she wrote hundreds of pages about the nights she spent prostrating herself to a man who exhibited the head of goat and the hunger to match. When she talked of the satisfaction he provided, her order grew, as more and more of the townswomen yearned to feel the orgiastic pleasures she described in page after page of poetry and drawing and prose. She was the Devil's pornographer, and her fame began to spread throughout the world in underground circles. In some places she was known as the Devil's Concubine. In others, the Whore of Satan. Witches around the world were envious and wanted to know how she drew the goat to her bed. She appeared ready to take on the full powers that the opening of Hell's Gate would provide during the Devil's Equinox. She would have become the most powerful witch in the history of mankind on that night. However, when she staged her ceremony of the Devil's Equinox, she miscalculated the loyalty of her coven. Just at the moment of the child sacrifice, the doors of the convent were breached, and a stream of men poured into the satanic chapel beneath the stairs. The sisters were killed with pitchforks and guns. The child was rescued from the altar and the entire building set afire and left to burn to the ground."

She paused and looked around. "You would think that that would have been the end of it," she said. "Every bit of evidence as to what Elizabeth had planned was burned in the fire. Or so everyone assumed. But decades later, one of her journals was discovered in the attic of a descendant of one of her coven. And while it languished unread in a museum for a century, last year, it was finally rescued. I have it here."

She held up another old book and grinned. "I have been introducing Elizabeth's rituals to you here in the Sacristy for months. It was she who wrote of the importance of sharing the darkest blood in nocturnal communions of the beast. It was she who described the power of the grave pearl. And I have devised our ceremony tonight based on some of her musings on the best way to attract the eye of the beast to our desperate bodies. Between the writings of Elizabeth, and Celestine, and a description I found in Durthy's *A History of Evil,* I think we will have a successful and exciting Equinox tonight. I've written down all of the steps here."

She held up her Book of Shadows and bowed her head. The

Irreverent Mother stepped forward and lifted the veils from Regina's head.

"You have done well, my child. You will lead us into darkness."

She raised her hands to the ceiling and looked around at the assemblage. "Tonight, we will brave the darkest ways. If you are not ready to give yourself completely, I would ask that you leave now. There will be no penalty. But we cannot have anyone in this room who is not ready to surrender everything in their heart and soul to this path. I will turn my back, so that you can leave with no shame."

The Irreverent Mother turned toward Regina and put her hands on the other woman's shoulders. She leaned forward and whispered something, and Regina nodded. Austin looked around the room but saw nobody heading to the doors. If you had been coming to these ceremonies for months or years, it was a little late to back out now.

"You have chosen the ecstasy of evil over the drudgery of good," the Irreverent Mother said, turned back to survey the crowd. "I am pleased that I have not been kissing and whipping all of your behinds for nothing these past weeks. And I am excited to share this forbidden sacrament with you. May your blood and devotion bring us all a new well of power. May we all become the true sisters of Satan tonight. I give the room now to Regina, our saint of seduction, our acolyte of arcane. She has given all that she has to bring us here. Hers is the ritual, and the sacrifice, and the mule."

When she said mule, Austin flinched. She was looking right at him as she said it. So, all he was in the end was a pack animal. A plaything for Regina whose only purpose had been to deliver Celli.

Bitch. He said the word over and over in his mind, but it did not resolve the red flare of anger in his soul.

"Please hold out your hands," Regina said, stepping forward again with a glow in her face that reminded Austin of the aftermath of orgasm. She was in her glory right now.

"Sisters, we are one in the blood of each other. We are one in the blood of our prince. To begin the night, we will share our blood and surround the priests with our circle. We are the womb that they came from. The womb that they yearn for. The womb that will smother their desperate stabbing for meaning. Move the priests to the centre now. The hour of the Equinox begins."

There was a shuffling and murmurs, and several men in black vestments and one in a bishop's hat moved to the centre. All around, the women – sexy, slovenly, fat, skinny, tall, short, old and weathered, young and smooth as plastic – took each other's hands to hem the men inside.

"There is no life without blood," she said. "Our circle begins with my own."

At that, Regina picked up a dagger from the altar behind her and held it up in the air for show. Then she brought the tip to the centre of her left hand and drew it across. She repeated the action on her other palm. She winced visibly, and the red quickly welled in the centre of both hands. She handed the knife to the Irreverent Mother, who stood next to her, and then held up her wounds to demonstrate her devotion. The flicker of the candles nearby flashed eerily across her skin, as if the fires of hell were licking at her wounds.

The Irreverent Mother repeated the act and passed the knife on to the next. Regina reached out and cupped one bloody palm in the hand of her superior. As they pressed their hands tightly together, a drip of blood fell between them to dot the floor.

The blade made its way slowly around the room, until the last woman to Regina's right sliced her hand. She reached out and took the final sister's hand and held it up into the air.

"We are now one," she proclaimed. "One in the service of Satan. One in the unity of our sisterhood. One in the joining of mouth to wound, wound to mouth. My blood is yours and then hers and again mine. My heart pumps its load of life into your veins. My sickness is yours. Your disease is now mine. Sisters, we are now one."

Their hands all rose in the air, and then came down to reach out and grasp and fondle each other's bodies. Almost instantly cries of ecstasy filled the room as fingers plumbed each other to release a wetness more primal than blood.

The sighs and moans increased, as the priests huddled inside the circle. Most of them watched, but a couple reached beneath their robes to follow the lead of the women, whose heads swayed and bent, as they pleasured themselves and others.

Austin was part of the inner circle now; his captors knew he could go nowhere and had abandoned him and taken up their positions as part of the blood circle. He couldn't escape, but he could at last move closer to his baby. Father Vernon had set the baby back down in the bassinet and now knelt at the waist of one of the gyrating nuns, his tongue outstretched as if awaiting Communion.

It all allowed Austin to move close to Ceili, and he bent and kissed his baby's cheek for the first time in days. "Daddy's here now," he whispered, and the look from her electric bright eyes melted his heart. "I'm going to get you out of here," he said. "I promise."

He had read enough of Regina's book to know that the sharing of blood was an important part of their rituals. It formed connections and shared power. It broke the seal on the visible shell of nature and released the secret energy within. It was the reason all of the witches around them had sliced their hands. He'd come prepared in his own way. He had decided to fight fire with fire. He did not have an entire circle to draw upon. But he did have one sacred font. He reached into his pocket and drew out a small razor blade. He had thought that he would have Father Vernon in his circle, but obviously that was not going to happen. Still, he had himself and Ceili.

Austin looked around and confirmed that all eyes around him were currently trained on Regina. He sliced a small cut on his left palm. Then he took the blade and held it to Ceili's soft perfect skin. He didn't know if he could go through with it then. How could he cut his baby? But around him the noise of perversion increased, and he took a deep breath and touched the blade to her palm. Her hand bled.

Ceili cried. Austin lifted the baby out of her crib, and then sat down with her on the floor. The nuns closest to him glanced over at the baby's cry, but quickly seemed content that Austin was simply trying to comfort his child as he sat on the ground. They turned their attention back to Regina in moments.

"I'm sorry, sweetheart," Austin said, and gripped Ceili's wounded hand tightly in his own. "Your blood to mine, my heart to yours," he whispered. "I call upon the spirits in this space to join my circle. Feel the blood in our veins, swim in our circle now. As we give you this taste of life, we draw from you the power to resist those that would break our circle. We offer blood for your protection now."

He didn't know if he was supposed to feel something change or not. If spirits truly did hear the words and enter their wounds... would there be a charge of electricity? Would there be a whisper in his mind of some ethereal creature? Regina's book had not said.

How long did he hold her hand? He had no idea. His inner critic laughed at him. *Who do you think you are, trying to pretend you can use witchcraft?*

He shrugged it off. This was the only chance he had right now. He couldn't beat them with force. It was just him and a baby against dozens of Devil worshippers.

But blood was not the only weapon he had. Austin reached into his pockets and began to draw out tiny shards of ivory. The bones of the baby that had been in the basement of the house next door. The hagstone. Ceili's brush.

The baby continued to cry in his lap as he arranged the bones of the dead child in a circle around him. There were long gaps between the tiny arm and leg and rib bones, but he drew a circle of bone around them.

Shape was important in magic. That's one thing he had learned from Regina's writings. Shape and substance and intent.

Here, he had made a circle of protection, from the innocent bones of a child. And his intent was to use that circle to repel any forces that gathered against them.

The philosophical arithmetic was there. Whether it meant anything really was another story.

Next, he took out the hagstone, which was hung on a thin strand of twine. He had a brush in his pocket that he'd taken from Ceili's dresser at home. He pulled three strands of hair from between its tines, and carefully weaved them in between the threads of the twine so that they held fast to the necklace.

Then he reached up to his own head and tugged loose a strand of hair. He felt the pinch on his skull as it let go. For good measure, he pulled two more. Once he had the hair between his fingers, he pressed one end into the twine, the same as he had with Ceili's. He wove it in and out of the necklace and when both of their hairs were securely threaded into the twine, he took the necklace and placed it around her head. A hagstone was a traditional ward, to keep away evil spirits and those with bad intent, and he could think of no better time or place to use it than here. Ceili was surrounded by those who intended evil against her. If the blood bond and bone circle couldn't protect them, perhaps the hagstone would.

Austin took Ceili's wounded hands and held them in his own. She stopped crying then, and wide tearful eyes looked up and met his own.

"I'm sorry, baby," he whispered. "I will make it up to you, I promise."

He looked around them at the bones and closed his eyes a moment. He had to think. It wasn't as easy as simply throwing bones and relics about. You had to invoke something. There needed to be intent, and a calling. Something to bind the relics and the desire.

"I call upon the ghosts of light, the spirits of healing, the angels of protection," he said aloud. "The forces of darkness are gathered around us, preparing to strike. We need your help. Lend us your strength and protection. Make the space between us impenetrable as a wall of stone. Our will is yours, our life is yours. Join with us now to drive the dark away."

Austin had no idea if anything he said was right. There was no previously fashioned 'spell' or calling here to draw from. Regina's journal had suggested that it wasn't the actual words that mattered in a spell, only the intent behind them. The words provided a focus, so the more structured they were, the better off the spell caster was – they could focus on the intent behind the words versus thinking of what to say.

He had needed to think of what to say, but it came easily. In this instance, he knew exactly what he was asking for. Whether any force was in the room that would grant it was another question.

The sound of Regina's voice behind him had been a lulling background the whole time he'd been preparing his 'counterspell' to her ritual. But now, the room was suddenly quiet. As he recognised the change, he felt a cold hand grip his heart. Something was changing. He instinctively knew that couldn't bode well.

He looked up from Ceili's wide-eyed face and met the gaze of

Regina. She stood just a few feet away and had stopped her ritual to stare at what he was doing.

"Do you really dare to presume?" she said when she saw that she had his attention. "Do you think that you can form a circle within a circle? You have no training in the arts. Where did you find those bones? Do you think you can just grab chicken bones from the trash and use them to invoke demons?"

"I'm not calling demons or using garbage," Austin answered.

Regina laughed and shook her head. "You can try to play this game, but you will fail," she said. "You don't know the rules. No matter what you do here tonight, there is one thing that is not going to change. Your circle will not stop it. One of you will die here tonight. The only question is which one."

Austin shook his head. "You will not break this circle," he said.

Father Vernon laughed at the challenge and stepped easily over the bones. He reached down and grabbed Austin by the neck with both hands, yanking him to his feet. Regina stepped forward and lifted Ceili from his grasp.

"You have to believe in the magic to use it," the priest said, and then tossed Austin backward. His feet left the floor for a second and he stumbled and fell back to the ground.

Regina handed Ceili back to the ex-priest, and the baby began to cry again.

"Don't play with what you don't understand," Regina said. "Sisters?"

Suddenly a group of half-naked women surrounded Austin before he could rise from the floor. He looked up and saw black silk and knees. And then he saw Brandy in their midst. His former babysitter held a knitting needle in one hand, and some kind of doll in the other. It looked like a crude clay model, but he could see arms and legs and a head. And he could see the shreds of denim that wrapped its middle, and a scrap of black T-shirt that covered its upper half. He realised that Regina had been holding something similar the night that she had led him to hold a knife to the neck of the bloody 'bride'.

Brandy smiled at him with a grin reminiscent of a shark. He

started to get to his feet, but she pressed the needle down into the leg of the doll.

A white-hot pain erupted in Austin's left thigh, and before he had fully stood up, he found himself crumpled to the ground.

"*This* is the power of magic," Regina said from beyond the circle. "It is a power that takes years to invoke. You must have a relationship with those spirits and the power you call upon. Study and sacrifice and most of all, faith. You have none of these things."

Regina bent over one of her acolytes and smiled sadly at him. "You could have made this so much easier on yourself, you know." Then she pointed at the floor. "Sisters, remove the circle."

The nuns all turned and bent to the floor. When they faced him again, they each held a shard of the bone that he'd laid out on the floor.

"Turn the power of the circle upon him," Regina demanded.

Austin didn't know what she meant, and he was still holding his thigh and moaning at the pain when Brandy held the doll out over his head. One of the sisters held a leg or an arm bone from his circle of protection and pressed it down into the soft clay of the doll.

As the pointed shard of the bone pressed into the forearm of the clay doll, a stabbing pain suddenly knifed through Austin's arm just below the wrist. He screamed and grabbed at the wound, but of course, there was no wound. Only…horrible, horrible pain.

He writhed and twitched on the floor at their feet, and then another sister held out a bone, and stabbed it into the other arm of the doll. Austin shrieked.

And there was more. The nuns stabbed the effigy in the legs and arms and groin, until Austin was curled in a foetal ball on the floor crying hopelessly for the pain to stop.

At last, Regina's voice cut through his screams with a single word. "Enough."

The pain began to drain away, and as Austin looked up, eyes blurred with tears, he saw the sisters removing bone after bone from the abused doll.

Regina held the doll now and caught his eye. She clearly wanted him to see what she was doing. With one finger she moved the arm of the doll until it bent in and touched the doll's chest.

Austin suddenly found his own arm bending, and his palm slapped firm and held at his heart. And then Regina held the doll upright, arranging its legs and arms as if it were a man standing.

Austin's own legs suddenly sprang to independent life and he rose from the floor as if nothing had just happened.

The power of real magic was suddenly clear to him. This was not all bullshit hocus-pocus. This was real. And Regina had him tied somehow to her doll like a puppet.

"All of those nights we spent together were preparation," she said. "I took what I needed."

It was an oblique explanation, but still, explanation enough. To Austin it simply translated as, "You're fucked."

CHAPTER THIRTY-TWO

Regina stood before him, a black veil on her head, a black cape cinched around her throat. She wore nothing else. She leaned forward to kiss him, and as her tongue traced the rim of his lips, he felt static fill his mind. When she touched him, all of his senses dulled. It had been that way for some time now, and he'd chalked it up to the blinding power of love before, but now he knew it was something else. It was dark magic. She had made him her toy. He realised that this was not the first time she had used him. And now she could move his legs and arms however she wished to accomplish the goals of her game.

"I hate you," he whispered when she broke off a kiss.

"No, you don't," she said. "You hate being weak and foolish. But that's not my fault."

She stepped back then with a grin and turned her attention to the throngs of satanic worshippers all around them.

"And now," she said. "We begin at last."

Austin felt the world had become a grey blur. His eyes were open, but everything grew fainter, fuzzier. He struggled to stay alert. His legs moved suddenly of their own accord, as Regina held up the doll and mimicked the motions of walking. He tried to stop his feet, but it was no use. They did not respond to him.

This really was the end. He no longer had any control at all.

He tried to move his hands and was able to make a fist with his left. That was something. She didn't control every muscle. Yet.

He slipped his hand into his pocket and his heart fluttered when he felt the shape inside. He still had the skull of the incinerator infant in his pocket. He hadn't used it as part of the circle on the floor.

He gripped the skull in his hand, closing his eyes to focus on what he needed now to say. Magic was real. And he needed somehow to invoke it.

"I believe," he said, thinking of Father Vernon's critique. *"You have to believe in the magic to use it."*

"I believe in the power of magic," he said softly. "I believe in the power of love."

He paused and gathered his thoughts. He knew that he needed to channel his request in the right way. He needed to frame his invocation.

"I loved you then," he whispered. He teased the centre of his palm with his fourth finger, opening the wound that he'd made to form a circle with Ceili. He could feel the tip of his finger grow damp, and he smiled. He had released blood for this spell. His fingers touched and slipped inside the eye sockets of the infant's tiny skull as he framed his calling. He made sure to smear his blood across the bone of the cranium, linking him to whatever latent power remained in the relic. "My blood to your bone," he said. "Our hearts beat the same time; our minds thought the same thoughts. I would have done anything for you." He forced his voice to be silent, though his lips continued to move.

I needed you then, when we were young and together. But I need you more now that you are not here. I need you to do something for me now. For us. I call upon the ashes of our love. I call upon the memory of our desire. I call upon the strength of our past to save the seed of our future. I need you. But Ceili needs you more. Help us before the Eye of Darkness peers down from the Devil's Equinox and holds us in its deadly sight.

He needed to say more. He needed to call for a specific action… but suddenly his body was not his own.

Austin felt his hands lift, and his lips stilled. He felt paralysed; his body was a block of stone, and yet, with his eyes, he could see parts of himself in motion. One part was his right hand, which reached out toward Regina. She held the clay doll in one hand, moving pieces of it with a finger. But then she reached out to one of her sisters and returned with a silver blade. She held it out to him, and Austin watched as his fingers opened and closed on the haft of the knife.

He had just accepted a knife that he did not want. At least not for the job he knew it was intended for. Unless he could turn it to his own ends.

He tried to move the arm that held the knife, but nothing happened.

Regina controlled his body completely. But she did not control his mind. And in his mind, he continued to call for help, even though his hand no longer touched the skull. He poured the power of his soul into his calling, begging for forgiveness. Begging for help. Not for him, but for Ceili.

Around him, the room began to echo with a single phrase, repeated again and again.

"Unto us, look down."

"Unto us, look down."

"The eye of darkness is opening, sisters. Reveal yourselves to him so that he may see you for what you are. Release all pretense and costume."

Regina pulled off the veil that topped her hair and unclasped the thin cape from around her neck. She stood naked before him, as all around the room the sisters emulated her. Habits and vestments and seductive silk fell to the floor until the circle around Austin and Ceili was a circle of flesh.

Two of the sisters approached Father Vernon and reached up to unclasp the vestment from around his neck. When it fell to the floor, one continued to unbutton his black shirt while the other knelt and released his belt before pulling down his zipper. The old man wore a stained white T-shirt and briefs beneath the uniform of his office, and the sisters removed those as well, leaving him standing bare, wearing only a pair of black socks. The man's gut hung down below his belt line, and the grey curls of pubic hair almost obscured the knob of his sex. Austin wished it was completely hidden but could not avert his eyes. When the sisters had helped him remove his socks, they both kissed the priest on the lips, and then stepped back to the witches' circle.

Father Vernon bent down to pick up Ceili and held her to hoary white hair thatched across his chest.

Regina stepped toward him once more.

"Will you let your daughter be raised by this man?" she asked, pointing to the priest, whose hands were rubbing slowly up and down the baby's legs. More of his penis was now becoming visible.

"Or will you sacrifice her tonight and in doing so save her? Her blood will bring power to our circle, and her soul will go free. I love this child as my own, and I am telling you this is the best thing you can do for her. If you choose otherwise, you are selfish and as useless as your wife used to tell me you were."

At the mention of Angie, Austin's throat constricted. Had she really said things like that to Regina?

"So, which will it be, Austin? Will you give Ceili to a child molester? Or will you give her to us?"

He shook his head. "I will not kill my baby. That takes away all of her chances."

"So, you'd rather sentence her to a childhood of daily abuse? Angie was right about you."

"You just want power," he said.

She lifted the clay doll. "I have power," she said. "And after tonight, I may spend days…weeks perhaps…doing this every hour and watching the result."

She stabbed a long pin in the belly of the doll, and Austin instantly screamed and doubled over. The knife fell from his hand and clattered to the floor.

She smiled. "It took me years to learn how to do that. But now, I can do it whenever I want."

She stabbed the needle into the doll's thigh, and instantly Austin toppled over as a stabbing pain show up his leg.

"I could do this all night," she said. And with that, she stabbed a needle into the eye of the doll.

Austin shrieked, and fell backward on the ground. His feet kicked and his brain felt as if a red-hot poker had gouged itself right through his left eye.

Tears ran down his face, and all he could see was a haze of red.

He realised after a minute that he was still screaming and tried to stop. He couldn't breathe.

When the pain subsided, and he blinked back his vision, Regina stood over him. Even now he admired her body. Her skin was flawless, her thighs lean. The delta of her sex was tightly cropped and dark. Glossy. He remembered the nights she'd drawn him beneath the sheets in his bed. He'd thought she was the answer to all of his prayers. Instead, here she was, standing above him naked with a voodoo doll designed to make him suffer. She was the worst nightmare a man could have. She was beautiful. Seductive.

And utterly evil.

"What do you decide?" she asked. "We are out of time and must begin. We will go forward with or without your consent. But it would be easier if you'd do the right thing for Ceili."

"You'll have to kill me," Austin said, and tensed, waiting for the next horrible bolt of pain.

But it didn't come.

Instead, Regina only shook her head, and raised the doll upright in her hands.

"I have a better idea," she said.

Without deciding to do so, Austin found himself getting to his feet. Regina reached down and retrieved the knife and held it out to him once more. He found his hand extending to accept it.

"The ritual calls for a father or mother to knowingly sacrifice their child beneath the gaze of the Dark Eye. I would think a truly voluntary act would serve us better, but you will knowingly give Ceili's life to us." She shrugged. "It will work. We must begin."

She beckoned Austin forward. His feet answered her call, though in his head, he resisted with all of his might. His will did not slow the movement of his legs at all.

"Sisters, choose your mount," Regina said. "Observe the moon." She pointed at a large television screen that had flickered to life on the wall. It was strangely out of place in this underground chamber of stone and altars and false religious costume. But Austin saw it served a purpose. The moon was captured in its frame, its aura deep and bloody in the night sky.

There was a burst of motion among the nuns; it looked like a round of musical chairs. Each of the women moved quickly to try to put her hand on the shoulder of and claim one of the priests in the inner circle for her own. Austin saw that even the Irreverent Mother had joined the group; she had taken the man who had worn the black bishop's hat. But there were far more women here than men, and some found themselves standing to the side. Meanwhile, the women who had scored a 'mount' were quickly fastening collars and leashes to the men. Once finished, they held the leashes in their hands and stepped behind the men who remained crouched on the floor. They straddled the men's hips from the back and pulled on the leashes to raise the heads of the men to attention.

Regina looked around the circle, nodding at the strange, erotic position of the couples. She beckoned to the women without partners. "You will be my Arrow for this ceremony, the Dark Eye will see through you. Join me now and be my echo and amplifiers."

The single women moved to form two lines in a *V* shape behind Regina. When she raised her arms toward the ceiling, the entire *V* followed her lead and did the same.

"I call upon the Eye of Darkness to look through the clouds of space and the buildings of men to see us here, in our secret space. In the space that we dedicate to your deeds. Observe us now as we celebrate the body."

She brought her arms down and pointed at the sisters of the circle. "Mount your servants now. Let him hear you in your ecstasy."

The circle changed, as the nuns pushed all of the men to lie on their backs on the ground. The men's feet all pointed to the centre of the circle, where Father Vernon and Ceili and Austin remained. The women all faced the centre of the circle as well, as they straddled the hips of the men, and began to move and shift in a slow erotic rhythm. Their flanks glowed in the reflections of the flames from the sconces on the walls, and their breasts and bellies shivered and shook, moving sinuously and with growing fervour.

"Sing to him, my sisters," Regina said, turning to the *V* of women and the altar behind her. "Let him hear the Song of Satan now to pique his interest in our tiny church. Let him hear us and come among us."

She began the song, raising her eyes and hands to the sky once again. Austin could not understand the words, but now and then he picked out a familiar phrase, like 'Satanico'.

*"Auriele des Satanico
Lauder ist vederno Sin
Semen Sordo Sylib Santi
Orgo mastic mondo ne...."*

Regina led the song, which was slow and dirgy, and the women who formed her Arrow all sang along with her. As they sang, they all swayed and followed the lead of Regina, who ran her hands slowly and suggestively across her breasts and waist and thighs. It was like a satanic burlesque show, with sex happening in a circle around the floor and women emphasising their curves and singing no doubt sacrilegious lyrics above them.

Austin tried to move, but remained frozen in place, his muscles locked against his will.

"The Eye is open," Regina called out suddenly. "Can you feel his gaze upon you? Can you feel him in your bones, driving you to darker ecstasy? Open your hearts and legs and let him in!"

The moon on the screen beyond the altar looked blood red now, and the room glowed with its unnatural light. Its edges were now partially obscured in shadow and Austin realised that it truly resembled a blood-red eye.

The sisters on the floor answered Regina's call with moans and guttural growls of passion, increasing their rhythm.

The women of the Arrow continued to writhe and sing the unintelligible syllables of the Song of Satan as screams of orgasm began to erupt from the floor.

"Sisters," she called. "The time is now. The Eye has opened and its gaze is upon us. Show him now that we are serious. Show him the demon in your passion. Show him that we will not stop short of any abomination he asks. Show him the truth in blood."

Almost as one, the rutting women turned their backs to the centre of the circle to face the men. They leaned forward, most of them still connected to the men in copulation. As they ground their backsides into the men's thighs, they reached forward and felt along the collars of their willing slaves.

Austin could see two couples clearly in front of him and watched as the eyes of the men rolled back in pleasure while the women kissed and kept their sex in slow, humping motion. He watched as a brunette with dark eyelashes and a witch's star tattooed across her back pulled a small square piece of silver from a small sleeve attached to the collar.

"Show us your intention," Regina called. Behind her, the Arrow echoed her words. "Show us your intention."

The brunette raised one hand in the air behind her head as she balanced on her other one, still pounding her groin to the man beneath her. One by one, the rest of the circle followed suit, until the entire circle held a silver glimmer in the air while cries of pleasure groaned from the flesh beneath them.

"Show him that you can be his brides," Regina said. "Bathe in the blood until you reach your nadir and know that it is he who moves inside you now. Begin!"

As she said the final word, the hands in the air all descended as one, and the moans of pleasure turned to screams of agony. The floor was suddenly painted in red and a mist of blood rose in the air above the women, who slashed and then struggled to keep the dying men down. Some of the men turned the tables, rolling the women over to their backs, but the women only held tight to their chains, and pulled them close for another slash of the razor. The bleeding out was fast. One by one, the women rose up on their knees as their mounts lay dying or already dead beneath them. Blood dripped from noses and chins and breasts as if they'd been sprayed by a hose of crimson. Some of the sisters had red raked and smeared across the light skin of their backs and the rounds of their asses. Regardless, they kept their hips in motion, still taking the remains of the men inside them. For some reason, whether biology or dark magic, the erections continued after the mounts were expired.

Regina and her Arrow continued to sing, their voices rising ever louder to be heard above the screams and cries of orgasmic passion from the rest of the women.

"There is no other lord than you," she called finally, switching from song to English. "We beseech you come into us and live as our master. See through us with your Dark Eye and grant us your trust to use your dark magic. We will forever be your convent, your Sisters of Satan."

With that, Regina fell to her knees, as did the women behind her.

"The time is now," Regina called. "The Eye has opened but soon will close. Before it does, it must see the blood of the babe. Only in this can we hope to feel the touch of his hand on our breast."

Regina pointed at Father Vernon, who walked across the blood-slicked floor to place Ceili on the altar. The bloody moon looked thinner but its 'eye' was still open on the TV behind. Austin stared hopelessly at Ceili, whose arms shifted and grabbed at the air above her. For some reason she didn't cry, only swatted at the ceiling as if she were playing with balls on a baby mobile. He looked above her hands and stared at the image of the strangely eclipsing moon.

The moon blinked.

For one horrible second, Austin could have sworn there truly was an eyeball in the heart of the moon, looking down at him in a hideous humour.... It grabbed his gaze and did not let go, and he felt the chill of evil suddenly slipping down the back of his neck and into his throat and into his heart. He shook with the cold of winter and at the same time, felt his body break out in sweat. The room suddenly felt electrified. Pregnant with a hideous power.

"Bring him forward," Regina demanded, and the Arrow moved from behind her to behind him. Austin felt the pricks of dozens of fingernails suddenly pressing into his back and arms and thighs as the women urged him step by step to the altar. Regina joined Father Vernon there, and as Austin stepped out of the circle of dead, abandoned men, their chains dropped to the floor near where their throats had been slit, he realised that he and Vernon were the only men left alive in this hidden chapel.

Austin stared at the eye glaring out of the moon from over their bare shoulders and forced himself to look down and away. It was no longer the moon, but truly the Devil's eye staring back at him. Ceili turned her head on the altar and looked at him with a smile.

"It's okay, baby," he whispered. But no words escaped his mouth. Regina had completely locked his body up to her control. She did not control his mind, however. And in his head, he wished again and again for help. For something to stop this train he was trapped on.

Nobody answered his silent cries.

"Now is the moment when the father will give up his daughter to Satan. We are all Satan's daughters and in this symbolic gift, we prove that we serve only the Dark Eye. His vision is ours, our sight is his. He may see the sacrifice of the father as he has seen our sacrifices of the husbands. And in the release of life and blood, we are all married to the dark. We are his forever, and he will live within us as we make our way unknown in the world. He will bring us his power and make our lives complete. No one shall stand in our way and live. Those who stand against us will find their hearts attack, their breasts filled with cancer, their brains haemorrhage with clots. They will lose their place on the corporate ladder and be run down by the senile on the road. Ours will be the power of nature, and we shall wield it with strength and sanguinity."

Regina held the clay doll out so that he could see it, and with one finger, she raised one of its arms. He felt one of his arms rise at the same time. And after a second of not getting it, he realised which arm it was.

His knife arm.

And right now, it was aimed at the altar. Aimed at Ceili.

Silently he called once more for Angie. His attempt at a spell earlier had apparently done nothing. The ghost of his wife had not returned. *I need you more than I ever have now*, his mind cried. *Angie, I invoke you*, he silently called. And then the crushing blanket of defeat covered him. He'd been a fool to think that he could use magic against witches. He had no power. As Father Vernon had taunted him, he didn't have a lifetime of training and belief to call upon.

Regina touched the doll's feet and his body took another step forward. All around him, the women now pressed close, a sea of warm flesh pulsing against him. They wanted to be touching him as he stabbed his daughter, he understood that now. They desperately jockeyed for positions closer to him, stifling him as they pressed and grabbed his flesh.

Austin arrived at the altar regardless. The baleful eye of the Devil himself shivered on the screen ahead.

"Oh Dark Lord, we pledge Ceili's heart to you. Take it and magnify its innocence. Bring our coven into covenant with you, so that we may serve you better in the years ahead."

In his head he was screaming. *No, you will not, will not move my arm again. No, No, No!*

He poured all of his mind and heart and power into denying Regina's control over his limbs, but even as he felt there might be a chink in her armour, that he might have moved his hand just an inch in the opposite direction that she demanded, he suddenly felt a terrible heat overcome him. It was as if his entire body had stepped into a sauna on overload. He looked up to see Regina's smile, and the moon eye behind her, and suddenly everything began to grow blurry. He was losing.

Father Vernon held Ceili out over the centre of the altar, presenting her for his knife. Austin looked down into her trusting blue eyes, and a tear dripped down to run across her cheek. "I would never hurt you," he tried to say, but his mouth did not move, and Ceili's face began to grow hazy.

The twin lights of her eyes were the only things left that he could focus on. The curved tip of the knife came down slowly from the air until he could see his hand clenched around the haft, the blade just two feet away from the baby's tiny chest.

"Tonight, on the Devil's Equinox, we give to the Devil, a daughter," Regina said from someplace far away.

"To save her, you must kill her," Father Vernon insisted.

Austin gripped the skull in his pocket tighter as he silently tried to scream. The knife in his other hand began to move.

A new scream came then, from another mouth. A horrible banshee shriek filled the room. At first Austin thought it came from the TV – that somehow the Dark Eye itself was screaming. But then, through the grey fog that remained of his vision, he saw her. She bulled through the circle of blood-spattered brides of Satan and the room suddenly filled with the stench of the grave. As Austin's arm came down, the corpse of Angie bludgeoned the other women away and reached out with rotting hands to steal the baby away from the false priest. Instead of the blade burying itself in the heart of his child, Austin's blade lodged deep in the grey curled hair of Father Vernon's chest.

The old man's eyes shot wide with surprise. Screams of both fear and anger erupted through the room. Regina dropped the doll and grabbed for him. Suddenly the stranglehold on his body disappeared, and Austin felt his hand burning. He pulled it from his pocket and brought out the skull of the child.

"This is the only baby I will give you," he said, and thrust the skull between the breasts of Regina. "I call upon the Dark Eye to see the false ceremony this is. I call upon the ghost of Carolyn Jones to give back what she got."

In a moment that Austin knew he would never forget, the small infant's skull suddenly appeared clothed in flesh once more. It was dark, rotting flesh, but its eyes were black and bright, and its teeth opened sharp as an alien carnivore.

The baby snapped and tore at the flesh of Regina's breast, leaving a bloody hole in its wake before spitting the chunk to the floor and chomping down for a second bite.

Regina screamed. But she wasn't beaten. She batted the demonic skull to the floor, but it only rolled mouth over head twice and then stopped...and rose again on its own power. It flew through the air to bury itself in the soft flesh of her breast once again and again Regina shrieked.

"Sisters!" she cried. "Don't let her take the child! Stop his calling. The doll!"

Austin felt something strange in his head. Almost a feeling of... pure power. Hunger. And as he watched the skull turning Regina's chest to gore, he knew that the power was shared. He had called... something...that had taken the form of the skull, but that something was connected to him too. And probably the Dark Eye.

He silently urged the creature on, to destroy Regina and stop this ceremony. A group of the women rushed to help Regina. But another group of the sisters retrieved the clay doll from the floor.

They placed it on the altar and began to pound their fists on it. Something smashed Austin's chest and thighs and belly and he was suddenly flat on his back on the floor gasping for breath. He distantly heard Regina's voice, and someone called for the knife.

And then something with the force of a freight train at 60 mph hit him in the face, and the grey fog went instantly black.

CHAPTER THIRTY-THREE

The silence was deafening.

When Austin awoke, he could hear the air buzzing with... emptiness. He almost rolled over to think about going back to sleep when he realised he was lying on a cold floor and the events of last night all came rushing back. He hadn't gone to bed; he'd been used like a puppet and then knocked out by Regina's kewpie doll.

His eyes shot open and he sat up with a start. The motion almost made him sick. His whole body ached as if he'd truly taken the beating that they had given the doll. He almost let himself lie back down, but then stopped himself.

Where were they all?

He looked around and saw that the room was completely empty. The image on the TV screen showed the empty expanse of a dawn sky. The floor was littered with discarded clothes and splattered everywhere with blood, but all of the bodies were gone.

Nearly.

Austin saw feet sticking out from beyond the altar. He forced himself upright, and after teetering a moment, staggered toward the sacrificial table. Father Vernon's corpse lay twisted behind it, a puddle of blood pooled on the floor next to him. His face still looked surprised.

He should have felt remorse, but instead, as he looked at the pale hairy body of the old man, he only felt disdain. Father Vernon had disgraced his order. He had been a smiling liar and a foul paedophile and had tried to manoeuver Austin into killing Ceili. He had no sympathy for the man or guilt for his actions. He had killed a mosquito.

Austin turned away from the altar and saw the white skull of the baby from the furnace. It was back to its original form, no longer a ravening demon head. He bent down and picked it up, gingerly slipping it back into his pocket. Then a thought occurred to him and he looked for the place where he'd put the rest of the bones in a circle. It wasn't good to separate the bones of the dead, he thought. He picked up the ones he could find and put them back into his pocket with the skull. But now what?

From the blue-sky image still being broadcast on the TV, the night was over. The Devil's Equinox was done. He had stopped them from killing his baby. Or had he?

He had seen Angie – or what was left of her – snatch Ceili away from Father Vernon, but then he had no memory after the witches had crushed the doll likeness of him on the altar. Had Regina gotten the baby back and completed the ceremony?

Where had they all gone?

He walked slowly out of the Sacristy and down an empty hallway. The torches were still lit, but as he walked down one hall and through another to reach the front area where the main 'club' was, he did not hear a sound beyond the air in the ventilation ducts.

He poked his head into room after room and all were empty. When he reached the front club, all of the lights were off, but he could see the empty bar and chairs turned upside down and resting on tables so the night crew could go through and wash the floor. Presumably, that had already happened since he could see the light of morning filtering in through the shutters.

Austin turned and walked the back halls of the club once more. He descended to the lowest level and walked through the empty museum space and the abandoned torture room where he'd originally found Father Vernon.

After a half hour of searching, he had to admit that the club was empty. Ceili…and Regina…were gone.

Austin walked out into the crisp morning air and felt empty. Lost. The rays of the sun felt sterile and pale. Everything he had ever loved in his life was gone. There was nothing that he could do but go home. He would come back here tonight when the club was open. In the meantime, he needed to prepare.

He tapped the skull in his pocket and considered the power of blood and magic. One way or the other, Regina would pay for what she had done.

* * *

Austin parked and walked into the empty house through the garage as he always did. He stepped through the shadowed kitchen and resisted the impulse to turn on a light. He was going upstairs to take a shower anyway.

He stopped at the living room and stared at the sofa where he had come home so many times to see Regina sitting with Ceili, often writing in her Book of Shadows. He'd thought it an innocent thing, a woman's journal. He couldn't believe how wrong he had been.

How easy a man is to deceive when a woman is involved.

He shook his head and stepped into the foyer to go up the stairs to his bedroom. He had one foot on the first step before what he was looking at really hit him.

There were footsteps on the white carpet leading up the stairs. Black muddy footprints.

Who had been here? Those had not been here when he'd left last night.

Austin took a hesitant second step. What if the intruder was still upstairs? He didn't see a return path of steps leading down. Though maybe the mud had worn off the shoes by then?

A baby cried upstairs.

Austin didn't hesitate then but dashed up the steps and turned at the landing toward the nursery. The crying stopped before he reached the top step. His heart filled with hope, but even as he ran, he cautioned himself that this couldn't be. Who would have brought his baby home? Was this just another trap from Regina?

He pushed through the nursery door and was greeted with the surprised face of Ceili. She looked across the room at him and smiled, waving a pudgy fist in the air in his direction.

The problem was, she waved at him from the arms of her mother. And well…Angie had seen better days. Her hair was matted, and her eyes were yellow and pale. The flesh of her forehead hung in blackened strips, and the arms that held his infant were grey and yellow with dark sores and purpled bruises. She smiled as he came in, and the inside of her mouth was black against the white of her teeth.

"Welcome home," Angie said. "I've been waiting for you."

Austin thought something crawled along the inside of her lip and over the tips of her teeth. Something with a lot of legs. She stroked the baby's head with one blackened hand and cocked her head.

"Did you miss me?"

AFTERWORD

I've always had a sweet spot for stories of the occult – secret societies, druids, witches. Ancient rituals and secrets. *The Devil's Equinox*, my eleventh novel, plays off of all of those tropes, so this truly was a case of me writing a book that I'd want to read myself! And it's been a long time in coming to fruition.

A lot of writers keep idea journals and are constantly coming up with new ideas for stories and jotting them down. I keep lists of story ideas too. However, 'constantly' isn't really part of my regimen. I'm not spinning out new ideas every other day on the fly and scribbling them all in an ever-growing notebook. Most of my novels have actually come out of just a handful of brainstorming sessions that I've held over the past dozen years. I'll sit down every two or three years and brainstorm a series of plot ideas. I don't spend a lot of time on each one at first…just write down a few sentences and then move on to the next idea. Later, I'll come back to the list and decide what things I want to actually expand on and develop. Some become short stories, and some novels. Some never become anything.

Looking back at the file creation dates on my computer, it appears *The Devil's Equinox* was first brainstormed thirteen years ago! A single paragraph describing the gist of the plot for this novel – along with a couple sentences that were the core idea for *The Family Tree*, which I eventually wrote in 2013 – both are in a Word document that I saved back in 2006. I wrote a full nine-page synopsis for *The Devil's Equinox* two years later, in 2008, which would have been the period when I was trying to decide what book should follow my third novel, *The 13th*. I believe at that time, given that I'd just written another 'occult' horror novel, I decided to go in a different direction, and instead developed *Siren* as my next book.

So, I knew what *The Devil's Equinox* was going to be eleven years ago! What took so long? Time flies and I can only write so much in a year. Looking at the original outline – not much changed in the story between the outline of 2008 and when I sat down a decade later to finally write it. Over the years, the story stuck with me, and last year it finally seemed the right time to dive in.

Those who've read the introductions to my other novels know that I typically write in a variety of places. For many years, I travelled a lot for work, and so I wrote on the road – typically in pubs, because I hate sitting in hotel rooms. I also have a few local haunts that I've spent many hours in working on books after heading home from my day job. Last year, however, I didn't travel much and I put in a lot of long hours at the office, so I didn't go out to my local pubs after work. So aside from a couple nights at Spears Bourbon Burger bar in Wheeling, IL and Bub City in Rosemont, IL after attending two local conventions, I really wrote nearly all of *The Devil's Equinox* at the oak bar I built in my basement, or at the glass bar that sits on my patio, with a steady soundtrack of Elsiane, Delerium, Cocteau Twins and other dreampop artists. For whatever it's worth, this novel was probably written more at home than any other.

I hope you've enjoyed the dark dreams I spun there!

John Everson
Naperville, IL
March 2019

ACKNOWLEDGEMENTS

Thanks, as always, to my longtime editor, Don D'Auria, and Flame Tree publisher Nick Wells, for not only buying my books but helping to make them better with comments and edits. There are some friends and fans who have always encouraged me to keep typing on, when the way seemed dark. It's thanks in part to them that instead of playing a lot more pinball and watching dozens more giallo and *poliziotteschi* movies from the 70s, I wrote this novel instead. My wife, Geri, has encouraged me and given me strength. My writer friends, Bill Gagliani, Dave Benton, Jonathan Maberry, Brian Pinkerton, Tim Waggoner and Mort Castle have graced me with their energy, advice and support. Likewise my non-writer friends and longtime supporters, including Chris Brook, Raymond Brown, Jerry Chandler, Lon Czarnecki, Lynn Frost, Lionel Ray Green, Leah and Joe Guillemette, Sarah Ham, Sheila Mallec, Don May, Jr. John Nardi, Lynn Neering, Peg Phillips, Coral Rose, Mike Sickler, Mickey Thompson, Karen Toonen, Russell Vangilder and many others have all helped drive me forward. I hope you'll enjoy the result!

FLAME TREE PRESS
FICTION WITHOUT FRONTIERS
Award-Winning Authors & Original Voices

Flame Tree Press is the trade fiction imprint of Flame Tree Publishing, focusing on excellent writing in horror and the supernatural, crime and mystery, science fiction and fantasy. Our aim is to explore beyond the boundaries of the everyday, with tales from both award-winning authors and original voices.

.

Also available by John Everson:
The House by the Cemetery

Other horror titles available include:
Thirteen Days by Sunset Beach by Ramsey Campbell
Think Yourself Lucky by Ramsey Campbell
The Hungry Moon by Ramsey Campbell
The Haunting of Henderson Close by Catherine Cavendish
The Toy Thief by D.W. Gillespie
Black Wings by Megan Hart
Stoker's Wilde by Steven Hopstaken & Melissa Prusi
The Playing Card Killer by Russell James
The Siren and the Spectre by Jonathan Janz
Wolf Land by Jonathan Janz
The Sorrows by Jonathan Janz
Savage Species by Jonathan Janz
The Nightmare Girl by Jonathan Janz
The Dark Game by Jonathan Janz
House of Skin by Jonathan Janz
Will Haunt You by Brian Kirk
Creature by Hunter Shea
Ghost Mine by Hunter Shea
The Mouth of the Dark by Tim Waggoner

.

Join our mailing list for free short stories, new release details, news about our authors and special promotions:

flametreepress.com